Stella Nova

Millie's Scar

Text copyright © 2018 Stela Ivanova. All rights reserved

Thank you so much for all you have done for my book. For your support, professionalism, for being patient. Special thanks to Diana and Helen without whom this book wouldn't be the same.

Editor BG: Diana Sirakova
Editor EN : Helen Simpson
Translator: Svetoslav Bogdanov
Cover Design: Hristo Tihov
Cover photo: Lazarina Karaivanova
Cover model : Tanya Ivanova

I dedicate this book to all saviors.

Chapter One

'Will others cry when I die?' Millie asked.

'Is that what this was about?' he bent to sharpen his pencil over the napkin, raising his eyebrows, frowning and inclined his head.

'Probably. Why do you care? Besides, you are still young for such thoughts.'

'I just want to know, it's important to me.'

'Probably some of them will cry, and others won't, it will depend' - he said, continuing to work intently on the already deadly point of the pencil.

'It depends on what?' she asked.

'On a lot of things,' he left the pencil and the knife, leaned back and continued, glancing at her, then letting his gaze drift to the window.

'Whether there is someone to cry for you, whether you are young or old, whether you are beautiful or ugly, whether ....'

'Wait, ugly? What difference does that make?'

'Oh, it does, believe me! People tend to cry more for the beautiful ones.'

Millie was startled, and she opened her eyes, her heart racing. Even with the first ray of light that found her eyes, she felt the crushing weight in her chest. The events of the last few days passed through her mind like flashes of grim paintings, and the tears welled again in her eyes.

She didn't want to see anyone and hear anything, she wanted to fall asleep again and to stop thinking. It would be best if she could simply press a button, turn herself off. Immediately and forever. Her life was a morass of suffering and she did not want to live it anymore. Everything was about Bella, the faces and voices of everyone around her, the conversations and meetings that were taking place, all of which added to her loss. Bella had been the

Millie's scar

closest person to her, who understood her intimately and loved her unconditionally, now she was gone and nothing could change that.

Millie got up, switched the kettle on and began mechanically preparing her coffee. She was currently surviving on caffeine and cigarettes. She went out onto the terrace and lit up. On top of everything else it was raining. It was as if God were mourning too.

Ten minutes later she locked the door and left her apartment. She left herself little time in the morning wishing to sleep as long as possible. On her way to the bus stop, smoking her second cigarette, she looked at the two trees on which she had placed her obituaries. For the first time since Bella's death it was raining. A rain drops had blurred a wide path the length of the first obituary, and the second was completely soaked. This made her feel even more depressed. Thoughts popped into her mind about the fresh wet grave, with Bella in it.

She stood at the bus stop absently looking in the direction from where the bus came, her thoughts always with Bella. They had found this apartment when they had to move out of their old one at short notice. Their former landlord, was presented with an order by the local authority to upgrade the gas installation, so they had to leave for a month. This new apartment became available at just the right time, at a more affordable price, and with more convenient transport links for both of them.

The bus was passing through wet streets, and Millie stared at the gray landscape out of the window while listening to the radio on her phone and thinking it would be better to just stop breathing and for everything to be over. She had given all of Bella's personal belongings to her mother, but she had missed a jacket, buried deep in the wardrobe. When she found it, she moved it to a front hanger so that she could give it back to her mother the next weekend. However, every time she glanced at it, it startled her, inflicting the pain of loss anew. The pain was like lightning, a devastating feeling, killing everything it passed through.

She thought she would someday regret not keeping at least something of Bellas, such as the mirror she always carried in her pocket, but she felt she could not endure it anymore. Everything of Bella's that she saw was killing her. She sensed that if she wanted to survive, she had to cleanse herself of all memories, to leave this apartment and even this city. Not only was she not happy here anymore, but she also knew for sure that for her, happiness had left that place irrevocably and nothing, and no one could return it.

During the day she avoided going out with her colleagues for a cigarette because conversation always turned to Bella, especially if Millie was there. And even if they did not raise the subject, their eyes held such sympathy, Millie couldn't bear it. They would not have known Bella, but for a temporary position in the office that had become available the previous year. The part-time post meant she could attend lectures and earn at the same time, and: "Most importantly, my dear Millie, I will be closer to you!" - Bella said, hugging her hard. Thus, Millie made the introductions and Bella, having charmed everyone at her interview, took the temporary position. The memory brought tears to Millie's eyes, she puffed the cigarette several times more and went inside.

The next day around noon, while Millie was in the office, Bella's brother called.

'Hello Millie how are you? I just wanted to tell you that the court concluded that Bella's death was accidental. The incident was because of a ridiculous set of circumstances following damage to a section of road and no one is to be held responsible.

"Dear God," – thought Millie, - "to die at the age of 22, a young woman, with her whole life ahead of her, because of a bump on the road!"

They spoke briefly, and Millie hung up.

Millie's scar

On the day of the crash, Bella had just missed a bus home, and she had decided to share a taxi with a female colleague. Shortly after they set off, a car blew a tyre, one lane away from them. The seventy-four-year-old woman in the middle lane was startled by the noise and pulled her car to the left. The taxi driver who was driving Bella did the same, in an attempt to avoid the crash but failed. The old woman's car hit him, the taxi turned over, landing on it's side, dragging sideways along the carriageway until it was stopped by a pillar. Not a spectacular accident, but fatal for Bella. Broken collarbone, jaw, brain trauma, induced coma and after four days - death. Death at 22. Millie closed her eyes, grabbed her head and hid behind the monitor as her tears fell again.

6 Months Later

"You don't understand, I don't want to hear this, just stop talking! You have no right to speak at all! You have not given me a fraction of the love she gave me," Millie was shouting to her mother. Her face was red and puffy from tears.
"I am not saying anything wrong, it's just that the girl died, you must get over it, may God rest her soul, and move on," her mother replied.
"I'm telling you to shut up! You talk about her as if she's a stranger, you're disrespecting her - do you understand? She's not just someone who's dead, she's Bella!" - Millie fled the room, trembling with rage.
She washed her face, cooling her hot, red eyes and stared at herself in the mirror, trying to regain her calm. Her mother had trivialised Bella's death several times, saying, "Well, she died, what is there to do?" This was making Millie very mad. Her mother had no right to speak like that, she was insulting Bella's memory and what she had meant to Millie. But her mother persisted, even though she saw it was hurting Millie.

Millie's scar

The evening went by silently, and soon both of them went to bed, but Millie's mind was racing. For the past six months, hectic midnight thoughts did not give her peace. Her mind was churning until the morning hours, and it was exhausting her, her head started hurting her, and she could no longer remember the last time she didn't have a headache. This was Millie's most difficult year so far. Two months after Bella's death, she found a small loft on Mill Street. Once it was a two-storey house, later converted into two flats and a loft for rent. Millie did not care what it was, she just wanted to get out of the apartment - it was unbearable for her to stay there. Though she knew that Bella would not return, she was expecting her at any moment. They had lived together only for a little over a year, and they were already making plans to live together for at least another 5 years. Both were single, and neither in a hurry to be in a relationship. They were young, Millie was four years older than Bella, and life was just beginning for them. They enjoyed partying, clubbing, socialising with their friends, and flirting with random boys. They shared their experiences and played make-believe for their future, whether as friends, or why not as relatives? They fantasized about meeting brothers, and marrying them so they would be sisters, or that whoever married first would invite the other to be her maid of honor. Sometimes they even fell asleep together on the sofa in the living room or in Millie's bedroom. Bella could sleep through anything, and often when they were watching a movie, Millie would find Bella sleeping beside her. For the two months after her death, Bella was an everpresent ghost in the apartment. Millie felt a desperate need to see her, and so she constantly imagined her. She even missed the things about Bella that irritated her, her habitual tardiness and ability to mess up the whole apartment in under three minutes, It got so bad that one day Millie just packed her belongings and took them to the office. She didn't have much - a suitcase, a backpack and two shopping bags from M&S. She had decided that if she did not find a place to sleep by the end of the day, she would return to the apartment, but without the stuff. The mere act of removing her belongings brought a sense of relief. Even if she was sleeping there, she felt this chapter of her life was closed, she had physically removed herself, and it was only a matter of time before a new one began.

By the end of the day she had found the loft, but the earliest she could move in was a weeks time, so she went to sleep at Daniel's place for a few days. He lived in a large student house where there was almost always a free room, because of the frequent comings and goings. In this case, it was Daniel himself, as he was doing an internship in Northampton. Daniel had been Bella's last boyfriend and was also grieving for her. Had the two of them brought their suffering together it would have been too much for them to bear. But this scenario was perfect for Millie, and she moved into Daniel's room without fuss.

Within a week, Millie moved to the new apartment, which was even closer to her work. She slowly accepted the new place as her home. The Connelly family lived on the ground floor, a husband and wife in their mid 40's, their daughter was studying at Cambridge. The one-room apartment beneath the loft was available and there was Hampton's To Let sign in front of the house. Millie would hear potential tenants coming in to look around now and then. Finally, a guy called Erik rented it. He was young, about Millie's age, and athletic. He had a very expensive bicycle, which he did not appear to ride. As soon as he moved in, he parked the bike in the small space in front of the door, and sometimes Millie had difficulty getting to her room if she was carrying more than one bag. Since childhood, she had developed her own understanding regarding neighbours. They were like relatives. You cannot choose them, but at least you can ignore them.

At school, they were brainwashed from very young with an idealistic vision of a united society, diligently keeping the peace.

Millie would have believed in these values, if not for the dreadful signs stuck to the lamp posts of every self-respecting English street. They used to say: "Neighbourhood Watch," and above the sign were depicted several people who were laughing ominously, worthy of film from Steven King. She was left in no doubt as to the trouble that could befall someone as a result of observant neighbours. That's why she had become cynical at a very young age about the friendliness of neighbours and with a broad, friendly smile, and without waiting for conversation, she would continue on her way. So it appeared she lived at peace in her new apartment, but her sadness refused to leave her.

  She very gradually began to lose herself, failing to control angry outbursts and being plagued by deeply depressive thoughts. Several times she went out with her old friends, but they had already begun to break apart as a group. No Bella, no group. The lack of female company was isolating her and at the last two meetings she drank too much and became unhinged, screaming and crying and inadvertently insulting those who tried to comfort her. They in turn began avoiding her.

  There were also changes in Millie's work. The company she worked for, "Excel Package Services" or "EPS", with a staff of 160 people, was bought out by a company called "Fly", and much of the management team was replaced. Working methods, clients, and work patterns all changed, as did Millie's manager. In her place was appointed an odious, lazy, middle-aged, relic who expected his staff to carry him. This was another serious blow to Millie. Her job was fairly monotonous and dull, but the office was friendly, and it was a convenient place to make money. Millie could think about whatever she wanted. About men, about parties, about fun, and lately about her grief at losing Bella. She had never had any issue with her hours, working 8am until 4pm left her plenty of free time to enjoy living in a metropolis like

Millie's scar

London. Her new manager, Bob Mason, created a two shift pattern. Each staff member was required to work from 6.30am to 3.30pm and from 1.30pm to 10.30pm. Both shifts had a half-hour break and two 10-minute breaks. He also made it clear that he would watch closely to see whether they were being adhered to. He also hinted that redundancies might happen in the future and everyone needed to be on their best behaviour.

Millie felt as if everything was going against her, if it wasn't one thing going wrong it was another. It was as if life had decided to give her a wake-up call "You've been living in a dream, from now on, real life begins"

She felt so alone, with no friends, no relatives, no desire to continue living. It felt a very long time since she had anything to smile about. She had insomnia which meant she suffered from a headache all day long. When she felt things couldn't get any worse, her mother appeared. After suffering from severe abdominal pain for a while, her GP had referred her to a Consultant Gastroenterologist at Charing Cross Hospital. At first it was just for one consultation, but then it turned into a second and a third. After which followed several laparoscopies to try and identify why she was experiencing so much pain. Her visits were much more frequent than Millie wanted them to be. She said she wanted to stay with Millie to spend more time with her, but the truth was that her second husband was not giving her money again. She would take the money from her salary, set aside some for food and bills, and she would drink away the rest. She couldn't forget her childhood and how cruel and unjust her parents had been to her, and how she couldn't wait to leave them when she turned 18. Loyalty meant she had to offer her mother a place to stay while she was in London. Millie kept quiet, hoping that soon the examinations and operations would be over, and her mother would go home to her failed marriage in Bath. But she couldn't stay silent when her mother spoke so disparagingly about her Bella. Her mother didn't understand her daughter's relationship with Bella. She had never felt such a strong love for anyone, much less for a friend.

In the morning her mother prepared breakfast and waited for Millie to wake up. It was a Saturday, and Millie had warned her that because of her shift, she needed to sleep. By the time Millie awoke at 11.00am, her mother had packed her bags and left them by the door. She waited quietly while Millie ate her breakfast, then asked her: "Will you come with me to the station, Millie? You don't have to, I can go by myself. You may not want to come after last night's conversation, it's clear you have little respect for me."

Millie looked at her, took a deep breath, rolled her eyes in annoyance, and decided that all this was too much for her.

"Listen, mother"- she said. "I don't understand why you're so insulted. Can you remember the last time you hugged me? When was the last time you asked me how I am? Do you remember?!" Millie was gaining momentum.

"You don't remember, do you? Because it's never happened, mother!" The daughter pointed out and went on. "And Bella? Bella hugged me every day. Every day she told me that she loved me and treated me like a sister!"

Millie grew silent, got up, took her cigarettes and lit one. She took a long drag on the cigarette and continued: "You know what, just go. You don't need me anymore. The operations are over, I am of no use to you anymore, am I?" She looked at her mother, who was calmly putting on her shoes.

"Say it, mum, say it, at least once, just be honest!"

Her mother turned to her:

"Yes, Millie, you're right, I was not a good mother, but you don't know how hard it was for me to raise you...".

"Oh, please, here we go again" – Millie said, and waved her hand, as a sign for her mother to leave.

Millie's scar

"But you know what, Millie," her mother tried to justify herself, "you were always a burden. With your bad temper, your dark moods, I never felt like I had a daughter. More exactly, I felt like..". She paused, then bent down, took her bags and left.

Chapter Two

A week later, Millie met Daniel on her way home. Recently, they often met by chance. Her new appartment was only a 10-minute walk from his, and he was often out and about in the neighbourhood. Every time he said he was involved with something at the university, but in reality he was just idling away his time, drinking beer, and wondering which drunken gathering he would go to next.

"Hey, Millie, whereto, are you going home?" He asked her.

"Hi Daniel, yes, I've just finished work and I'm going home, I'm tired."

"You don't look so good, are you doing ok? It's maybe time to start going out? To meet friends again?" he said casually, standing with his hands in the pockets of his faded jeans, then went on. "Next Friday we're having a party. It's Chris's birthday, do you remember him?" Millie nodded and stepped forward nervously. She didn't care about Daniel's parties and she didn't know any Chris, she had other things on her mind.

"I don't know Daniel, my mother has some health problems and I'm looking after her just now" Millie lied, hoping to finish the conversation quickly and escape.

"OK, but if you change your mind give me a shout" - Daniel said. He tapped her gently on the shoulder as a kind of friendly goodbye, and said, "I'd better go, this course has completely taken over my life!". He winked at her and continued on his way.

Millie returned to her dark loft with a single skylight through which the sun entered for an hour in the morning. She sat down on the couch. Her room, though dark, was warm and snug, the winter was barely felt. The small radiator under the skylight was enough to warm the 18-square-foot loft. She was feeling good

Millie's scar

here. It was big enough for a single girl and she had everything she needed. At the back of the room there was a single bed with a bedside table and a small TV on the chest on the opposite side. At the other end of the room, opposite the bed, a small alcove on which they had hung two doors and installed a rail. The agent who showed her the apartment called this "a nice wardrobe". For Millie it was not a wardrobe. It did not have a back, and when she opened the doors, she could see an old dirty wall behind that they hadn't bothered to paint with the rest of the room. There were no shelves and drawers. She had improvised a couple of shelves, which often fell. They were not cut to size, and they were barely held in by the nails Millie had hammered in at odd angles. To the left of the wardrobe was the kitchen. Again, it had enjoyed an exaggerated presentation by the agent. The kitchen was in fact a single kitchen cabinet with three doors, below which was a washing machine and a small built-in refrigerator, as well as a sink. There was a small space beneath the sink where Millie had a small supply of Cif and Ariel . On the very left side, built into the worktop there was a small hob with two ceramic rings. Next to this stool the kettle that Millie had bought so that she could make herself coffee, a jar of Nescafe, an old jam jar with a Hartleys label contained brown sugar, and a plastic tray with a few blueberries. Above this box there was a small cabinet with two doors attached to the wall. There, Millie kept her modest set of tableware, three deep-dishes, a bowl, a small and large pot, a grater, and six cups of varying sizes. In the middle of the loft, between the bed and the wardrobe there was a small two-seater sofa bed on which her mother slept. A door led to the tiny bathroom, barely two metres square, in which Millie had turned bathing without injury became an art form. There were several pipes sticking out at odd angles, the purpose of which Millie had never understood. She often hit her elbows on them and cried out as her funny bone spread the pain throughout her arm.

Millie's scar

The furniture was well worn, but not so much as to create a sense of shabby and old, more precisely, they created the feeling of being used and a little dirty. The shades were muted, brown and beige, the walls, magnolia giving it a fresh feel. Millie got up and opened the fridge. There were two eggs, a little bit of chopped salami flavored with honey, a long forgotten mozzarella, and a few shriveled spring onions.

"Damn it", Millie cursed and slammed the fridge door. She put on her shoes and walked down to the street. There was no fresh milk, and she hated drinking her coffee without milk and knew that in the morning it would ruin her mood. As she headed to the corner shop for milk, bread and beer, her phone rang. It was Nicole, an old colleague from the time she had worked briefly at McDonalds. Nicole was cool, positive and always had a lot to say. Millie had never seen her dispirited, even though she had heard rumours that she had reason to be. But no, Nicole was one of the most positive people Millie had ever met.

"Hey, Nicole, I'm so glad to hear from you! How are you?" - Millie asked, a smile lighting her face for the first time in ages. "Hello, Millie, I've been meaning to ring you for so long, I've missed you so much. It's ages since we spoke, but you know how it is. Work, lectures, and a few months ago, there was this guy, and, well, I completely lost the plot. Tell me, how are you? How are things? Let's have coffee?" she heard Nicole's excited voice.

"Oh yes please, that sounds great, you have no idea how much I need to get out. A lot has happened since we last met, I'll explain when I see you. When are you free? Millie asked, looking at the shop door.

"Oh, I'm free, I've been jobless for two weeks, and to be honest with you – I'm in no hurry to get another. My boyfriend is visiting his cousin in Southampton and I'm at a loose end right now. If you're up for it we could meet now? Maybe somewhere in Kingston? Fancy it?" Nicole asked.

Millie's scar

"Sounds great Nicole" Millie replied as she paid for her purchases, took the bag and left the shop. "I just need to pop home, then I'll meet you by the phone boxes in about 15 minutes. Is that OK?" Millie finished.

"Perfect, I'll see you then shortly". Nicole said, and hung up.

Suddenly, Millie felt energised, smiling to herself she picked up her pace. The girls hugged and walked towards Starbucks chatting loudly while smoking. They sat in Starbucks, watching the busses turn at the corner of Edan Street away from the pedestrian shopping area.

It was already after five, the daylight was long gone, but the streets were bright and lively. Christmas lights twinkled and above their heads there were multicoloured crowns gently swaying in the breeze. Street lamps became glowing lotuses and along the entire length of the street on both sides was built a Christmas market consisting of wooden houses with artificial snow on the roofs and a lot of decoration at their entrances. Large numbers of people moved in a complicated ballet, carrying bags full of gifts for Christmas. Millie felt that life inside of her was returning. Nicole returned from the toilet, sat down and spoke excitedly.

"Let us first discuss an urgent matter" - she smiled as she stirred her coffee, "Who has a birthday soon, eh?" Her face shone, staring at Millie, as if she did not know the answer.

Millie smiled, she felt warm inside. This colleague of hers, with whom she had worked for only a few months and whom she rarely saw, had remembered her birthday. Someone had thought about her and for a nice reason.

"Yes, me" Millie answered shyly.

"Do you have any plans, because if you don't, we can think of something? So, your birthday is next Thursday, if you want, we could go out on Friday?" Nicole suggested.

"Yes, that would be lovely. I've been really down of late, and I realize I definitely need to relax a little. A friend invited me to a party next Friday. His mate has a birthday too, we could go together maybe?"

"That's great, it's going to be more fun at a party instead of the two of us in some bar. Although, you know, two cool girls in a bar is an invitaton in itself! - Nicole started giggling, and then said, "Actually, I've changed a lot since I met Ollie. Other men ceased to exist for me. Have you met anyone special?

The two young women talked for a long time. Nicole about her new love, of how she was let go from work because she was always late. In the end, they asked her to leave but offered to give her a reference. Millie told her about Bella's death and how miserable it had made her. She spoke about the problems with her mother and the changes at work and the new boss, Bob Mason. When they left, they exchanged several kisses and confirmed once again the plan for Millie's birthday.

"The week passed quickly. On her birthday, her colleagues gave her a gift card for TK Maxx. She took in chocolates, drinks and a large lemon cheesecake, and spent the evening, lying in bed with a beer, a bag of chips and four episodes of her favorite TV show. In the morning she woke up in a mood for fun and had decided she would not let anyone spoil it.

After work, she got back, bathed, and lit a cigarette. The worst part about this apartment was that there was no terrace for her to smoke on, or even window to lean out of. In her contract it was forbidden to smoke inside, and at first she complied. She used to go down to the front of the house every time she wanted a cigarette, but then it got cold and she decided she would smoke inside. The cigarette smoke made everything in the loft stink, despite the fragrant candles that Millie lit. It was cold and she closed the skylight, and resigned herself to the smell.

Millie did not like when she was born, and more precisely the month of December. It was always too cold to wear a strappy dress. She loved strappy dresses, but they looked inappropriate in

Millie's scar

winter. She decided to put on a short sleeved olive green mini dress. She put it on while her hair was still wet and regarded herself in the mirror. She liked her reflection, she looked beautiful, the dress showing off her slim figure. She had ample, firm breasts and protruding nipples that she liked to accentuate by wearing figure hugging clothes. She considered it seductive, her efforts being rewarded by the considerable attention she got from strangers.

At 167 cm she was neither too short or too tall. Rarely were men shorter than her, and often they were only up to 10 cm taller. The difference diminished when she was wearing heels. Her legs were also flawless with soft, gentle curves. She weighed only 50kg, making every dress she tried on look as good, if not better on her, than on the skeletal models in the magazines. A flat belly, a small, tight bum, delicate hands reaching towards slender shoulders, highlighting her beautiful neck and collarbone. All this wrapped in velvety soft skin. But Millie did not have the same opinion of her face. She liked it but she constantly found imperfections on it. For example, she did not like the tiny mole on her chin or that her upper lip was slightly larger than the lower one. She did not know that it was precisely this quirk which made her lips so tempting for her many admirers.

Millie dried her thick, glossy, brown hair that fell to just below her shoulders, teasing it into soft waves with a round brush.Tonight, she tied it softy back, leaving tendrils to frame her face and finishing with earrings, a little make-up and a dab of perfume. As she left the flat to meet Nicole she felt excited, walking quickly. She wanted to drink, dance, forget, at least for a short time, about Bella and have some fun. She deserved it. The last six months had been hard, and she definitely needed to try and enjoy herself again. To that end, she bought herself a bottle of Bacardi, apple juice, lemons, and a little fresh peppermint. For Nicole, she bought a bottle of whiskey and soda, she knew that this was her drink of choice, she had also bought some nuts and

Millie's scar

crisps. The girls giggled together as they walked towards the birthday boy's apartment.

"Millie, I'm very excited, I know I shouldn't say anything yet, but I need to share this with someone." Nicole said.

"Tell me quickly, what is it?"

"I'm pregnant, Millie!" Nicole said, and when Millie looked at her, she was glowing with happiness.

"Oh, Nicole, good for you, this is great news! I see you're happy. Does the future dad know already?" Millie asked, jumping over a puddle, still holding Nicole's hand.

"Oh, yes, I told him, I couldn't help myself! I wanted to tell him in person, but he will be back in a week, so I called him and told him." Nicole said in an excited voice, and before letting Millie ask directly, she started talking.

"He paused at first, but for no more than 10 seconds, then he asked: - You're not joking, right? - and when I told him I was totally serious, he said, "Oh, God, that's great, we'll become parents, Nicole! Do you hear me, we have created life, me and you! God, that's great!" -Nicole paused for a moment and saw Millie's excited face, and continued "Honestly, I did not expect him to be so happy. I think he was even happier than me."

As they boarded the bus, Nicole kept telling her about Ollie's reaction and how he had started making plans for their future. How they will get to know each other's parents and so on. She then turned to Millie and said, "At last, Millie, at last I can say I'm truly happy!"

Millie smiled, she was sincerely happy for Nicole, but she felt a little sad as well. She thought of herself and her miserable state. She also thought of the fact that Bella would never be able to tell her she was pregnant. She felt the sadness in her heart again, but she quickly recalled that she was going to her own birthday party and turned back to Nicole.

Millie's scar

"Ah, girl, you're going to give up on me now, aren't you?!" her eyes glowed and she laughed. Nicole looked at her blankly and Millie continued:

"You're pregnant, you won't be drinking, who did I buy this whisky for? Who am I going to have fun with now?" The two of them laughed, and Nicole promised her that she might not drink, but she would not stop dancing, and that was perfect for Millie. She wanted exactly that – just to dance.

The party was at the birthday boy's flat. A nineteen-year-old kid who had just discovered that life is for living, and not to be spent on a screen with Fortnite. There were a couple of his friends, Daniel, two couples kissing on the sofas and two girls. The evening went on, Millie drank three quick cocktails, the music became louder and everyone started dancing. She was pleasantly dizzy from the alcohol and dancing up a storm, when a girl came in. Daniel leapt up to greet her, kissed her on the neck, said something to her, and led her over to Millie and Nicole.

"This is Monica" he said and started pouring her a drink.

Millie looked at the girl more closely. She was young, perhaps no more than 18, and still looked silly and naive. But what caught her eye was that something about her reminded her of Bella. They did not look alike, but there was a familiarity. When the song was over, Millie went out onto the terrace and lit a cigarette. She looked at the sky, black, cloudy, starless. She drew the last of the smoke into her lungs and tried to force herself to go back inside and have fun, to ignore the girl and just enjoy herself. Daniel joined her on the terrace, put a hand on her waist and stood beside her.

"Hey, Millie, I have to tell you about Monica", he started to explain himself. "Life goes on, Millie, I'm a man, I cannot stop living because Bella died." These words struck Millie and it became clear that the party was over for her. She looked at him and said:

"You do not have to explain yourself, Danny, it's your life."

Millie's scar

"I know! I just wanted to tell you that life goes on. It's time for you to move on too" he said to her, then changed the tone and tried more lightly. "Let's go back insde, you'll freeze to death out here."

"Just give me a moment," said Millie, looking back to see him going in. As the door closed, she again looked towards the sky and said aloud:

"What a fool, to replace her with a pale imitation after only six months, claiming to have forgotten her and that he needs sex. Idiot!" She threw the cigarette end away and went inside, made herself another cocktail, put the bottles in her bag and told Nicole that when she was done with the cocktail she would like to leave. One of the girls standing near them, watching the drunken couples terrible dancing, began to laugh. She looked at Millie and said:

"Dumb party, isn't it? Let's continue somewhere else girls?

"I'll be going home, girls, I'm tired" Nicole said, looking intently at Millie, knowing that she would understand her fatigue.

Millie liked the idea, she wanted to continue her birthday, and didn't want that idiot Daniel to ruin everything. It occurred to her that the Connelly's were away for the Christmas holidays and her new neighbour hadn't moved in just yet, so out of spite, and so as not to go back by herself to the dark loft, she said, "I even know where the party will continue!" Millie smiled. "Come to mine." She finished her drink in one gulp, the girl approached the other girl standing near Daniel, who was too preoccupied with the breasts of his new fling. She whispered something in her ear, she then turned towards her boyfriend and two more guys. They all looked at Millie, gathered their things, and left with her.

They said good night to Nicole, who went to catch another bus, and within the hour they were all in Millie's loft. They played music, poured drinks, and everyone settled where they found fit. About an hour later, Millie was enjoying being drunk and was

Millie's scar

dancing in front of the mirror. She had drunk more than half a bottle of Bacardi, but she didn't feel sick, she was having fun. She felt happy, she knew it was only temporary, that it was the result of the alcohol, but that was fine right now. She wanted to dance, smile, to feel excited, and to laugh as she had not done in over six months. The others also enjoyed themselves. Miguel – a French student of applied arts, was so drunk that it was difficult for him to stand, so he was lying on the floor in front of the cabinet. Isabella and Kate had been discussing something intently all night, Millie's guess was love dramas which they did not want to share with the rest. At least they did not stop drinking and occasionally danced. Dariya - the girl who suggested they leave the previous party, smoked weed on the way and was the most entertaining of them all. She danced, told jokes which everyone laughed at and constantly topped up their empty cups. She made toasts, hitting her glass a few times on the table so that people would look at her shouting: Cheers! Looking at her, Millie thought that someday in the future, she might be able to grow fond of another woman and call her a friend. She was glad the party was at her apartment, it made her feel significant amongst these friends she didn't know. She continued to dance, staring at the mirror, admiring her beautiful body and how seductively she moved when drunk. Often, when she was dancing, she would be looking in a mirror at a night club or just her silhouette reflected in glass.

A song by the Red Hot Chili Peppers had just started when there was a loud crash as the outer door fell to the floor centimeters behind Millie. She spun around to see a tall, large man with a mass of curly hair, standing where her door had stood. He made two big steps, stepping on the door and found himself next to Millie. He grabbed her by the hair, yanking her head backwards and shouted:

"I heard there were whores here!"

Everyone froze. Millie saw another man entering who was just as big and tall, and stood beside his friend and said, peering inside:

"Yes, there are!"

Who were these guys and what the hell did they want? - Millie thought horrified, wondering how to free herself of this huge and terrible man. She needed urgently to pee.

Someone stopped the music. The big-haired man let go of Millie, pushing her head forward so that she stumbled and fell. Trying to get up, she saw two of the girls slip out, and heard the sound of breaking glass and falling objects coming from her room. Miguel regained the ability to walk and also left as fast as he could. Millie, Dariya and those two had remained. Millie heard Dariya say:

"Damn it, how did they find me?"

"Do you know them, Dariya?" - Millie turned to her scared and angry. Dariya did not even look at her, as if she did not hear her, as if she was not there anymore, but had sunk deep into a dreadful nightmare. Her face was pale and she was trembling, looking at the door. Millie's heart was beating very fast, her thoughts were racing like crazy and she couldn't make her limbs work. She was totally numb. Sounds of breaking could still be heard from outside, and the screams of the two girls, as well as running down the stairs, were heard. The sound of a slap. Millie was shivering. She didn't understand who these men were and what they wanted. Why were they smashing everything up? God, what would she say to her neighbors, and what did they have to do with Dariya? These two men were destroying the house and everything in it. She was lost. Everything belonging to the Connelly family and Eric was being broken. For a moment she thought of running, then she remembered that she was actually at home and that she should try to preserve her home as mush as possible.

Millie's scar

One of the men went in and started jumping on the door until he broke through it. Millie came to her senses and screamed at them:

"Who are you and what do you want? Why are you breaking my house?"

The guy opposite her swung his hand and hit Millie across the face, although the blow was meant for Dariya. She was standing behind Millie, trying to call the police. The man took the phone out of her hand and hit her a second time with the back of his hand. Dariya fell.

"How many times do I have to tell you that you're not allowed to talk on the phone in my presence, whore?!" The man screamed like a beast. His eyes were glazed, and saliva showered from his mouth as he screamed.

He pushed Millie aside with his elbow and started kicking Dariya in the stomach. Millie screamed in fright. He was going to kill her. She did not know Dariya, but it didn't matter, he was going to kill her, right there, in her loft, right before her eyes. Then he was going to kill Millie as well because she was a witness. Dariya started coughing up blood, and the guy kept kicking her. Millie threw herself on him, trying to get him off Dariya, but it was impossible for her to move this huge man. He turned to one side, flicking Millie off his back and fell to the floor. Dazed, she decided to run for help. It had been no more than three minutes, everything was going so fast. Millie felt she was peeing herself and could not control it. She was trembling all over her body. She looked towards the door and the second guy was nowhere to be seen, it was her moment, she got up and ran towards it, there was no sign left of the alcohol, she was feeling completely sober now.

"Where are you going, little girl!" - Said the other man, and stood before her at the door, blocking her way.

"Please leave us, we have not done anything to you, I will give you all the money I have."

The man smiled, and pushed her back into the room with one hand and said:

"Nobody's going anywhere until we say so, is it clear?!"

It seemed to Millie that he was more normal than the brute attacking Dariya, she had the feeling that she could negotiate with him. He was cruelly handsome with beautiful cold, blue eyes, a sculpted, smoothly shaven face, and clean cut. The big-haired guy had stopped kicking Dariya. Millie turned and saw that she was lying on the ground, lifeless. When Millie looked at the big-haired man, her heart stopped, she screamed and she finally realized the situation she was in. The big-haired man had unbuttoned his fly and was masturbating above Dariya's still body.

Chapter Three

Millie was slumped on the bed shivering, her tear blurred eyes watching Dariya's lifeless body and the blood that was dripping from her mouth across the light gray carpet. She thought she would have to leave the loft immediately. Her neatly dressed and ordered room was destroyed. The door was no longer lying on the floor, they had lifted it and leaned it on its hinges, but it was full of holes, as if it had been attacked with an axe.

The big-haired guy put out his second cigarette on the sofa. He spat on Dariya and said:

"This is my whore, you are Greg's, do you understand?"

Millie was in shock, her mind racing. What would they do to her? Rape was uppermost in her mind, but she also feared for her life.

"Did you hear me, bitch? he shouted again. Millie looked towards him, her eyes full of tears and shuddered. "Yes", she murmured.

"She's pissed herself, she stinks, I don't want her," - said the other, aiming a sharp kick at Millie's right ankle. Millie moaned with pain and grabbed her foot.

"Well, throw her in the bath you idiot, do I have to tell you everything! - the big-haired guy sniped.

Millie began to sob. Her tears dripped, she could not calm down, but she had to. She had to figure out how to escape. But her mind was empty, the horror paralysing her.

"Please, please just leave us alone, we won't tell anybody, I swear to you. She tried to be convincing, the tears streaming from her eyes. Greg grabbed her and pulled her roughly.

"Get in the bath, whore!"

Millie grew rigid, fear stopped her limbs working. She didn't want to move because that would mean they would hurt her. She stumbled, blinded by her tears, as Greg dragged her towards the bathroom.

"I told you to move, you'll save yourself a beating if you do what I say!" he growled and shoved her into the bathroom. He followed her in, undoing his fly. Millie stared at him and trembled. She pleaded with him again.

"Please, I can see you're not as cruel than your friend. You've not done anything yet, you can get away with this if you just leave now." Even before the words left her mouth, Greg slapped her so hard that she found herself on the ground in the narrow bathroom. Her head hit the pipes, and she wet herself again. He turned the cold shower on her. Millie began crying loudly, screaming as loud as she could. Greg grabbed her by the hair and pulled her to her feet, as she shook from terror and cold.

"Don't you care about your life, whore? You're saying that I'm softer than Cloudy?" he laughed, pushing his face close to hers. It was only then she saw the tiny tattooed tear at the side of his right eye. She had read somewhere that murderers in prison tattooed tears on their faces. A tear drop for every victim. Millie knew that if she wanted to stay alive, it was better to just do what he wanted. Greg removed her dress in one swoop and raped her under the cold shower. He then wiped himself with her robe, threw it over her, and said:

"Clean up and get in here! he paused for a second, then added "Naked!"

He closed the door and Millie saw her reflection in the bathroom mirror. Her face was puffy with tears, her eyes were red, there was blood and semen on her groin. She didn't know that rape hurt so much. The tears wouldn't stop falling, she washed herself thoroughly, trembling with cold and pain. All she could think of was her own death, she actually desired it. What

Millie's scar

more could they do to her if not to kill her? Her tears continued as she wiped her legs, delaying as long as possible the moment she had to return to them. They could not do anything else but kill her. How could she continue living? She didn't want this life anymore. Absolutely alone in this world, without a mother and a father, without her favourite Bella, and now she no longer with had any dignity. But how did she get here, what had she done that God was punishing her so harshly? Why did she have to experience this and what did she do to cause it? Questions with no answers. And after everything, she felt only despair. Despair. She was startled by the shout of the big-haired guy. She tossed the towel to the ground and entered the room. The scene of carnage hit her again - the room was in the same condition, and the holes in the couch had increased. There was no point in counting them anymore. Both men were naked. Greg was lying on the bed, smoking. Cloudy, this perverse freak, had ripped Dariya's clothes off and was peeing on her while screaming insults at her. The smell of urine hit her and made her feel sick, she blocked her mouth so as not to vomit. She stumbled back into the bathroom while the men laughed at her. Millie vomited into the sink. Anger hit her then. As she had decided it was better to die, she began to seriously think that she would rather kill them both. In that moment she knew she was capable of murder, but she didn't think she could reach any of the knives in the kitchen quickly enough. She decided to run, but she was completely naked, and it was -2 degrees outside. If she could escape from the house, where was she supposed to go? The street behind the house led to the neighbouring houses, but it was about 1.30 at night, everyone was asleep and no one would hear her screams. Opposite the house was Firefild Park, which resembled a gigantic football field, with an avenue of trees through the middle. It was too open and deserted, they would find her easily. On the right there was a small intersection which was empty at this time, and on the left, after about 3 minutes of running, she would reach the intersection of Surbiton Road. This was where she would run, even at night there was traffic, and the police station was a little further up. She took a deep breath, opened the door to the bathroom quietly, and at once saw the front door standing on its hinges. She quickly decided she would just push it down behind her as she ran. The two men would immediately find out, but she would have a head start, and maybe they would decide to put their pants on at least. She pushed the door with all of her strength and ran down the stairs. She was jumping down several steps at a time, holding on to the railing. Her flight reflex had kicked in and her adrenaline was at its peak. She knew if they caught her, they would kill her. She heard heavy footsteps behind her, they caught up with her very quickly, and just as she reached the front door and half opened it, everything went dark.

She did not know how long she was unconscious.

When she awoke Dariya and Cloudy were gone. She was lying in bed naked, and Greg was on the couch in his underpants and was drinking from the whisky bottle that Millie had bought for Nicole. She desperately wanted to call Nicole and ask her to call the police. Her mind whirred to her phone's dead battery she was doomed, she couldn't escape, she couldn't make a call. The neighbours wouldn't return for at least a week, and no one from work would come round if her phone was dead. Even if they wanted to call her, it would not be until Monday. After her attempted escape, they wouldn't trust her anymore. They would just kill her, her life becoming just another tear under a murderer's eye.

Greg looked at her and said:

"Well, look who woke up, the running whore!" - He got up and moved to her side of the bed. Millie felt a terrible pain in her head as she tried to move her naked body away from Greg's.

"Tell you what, little girl" he said "you're probably confused. I'm not some 20 year old brat who'll fuck you and then boast in

Millie's scar

front of his friends. I'm the one who will make you wish you'd never been born. You are all whores and me and Cloudy will exploit you as much and for as long as we want."

"Where is Dariya?" Millie interrupted him, assessing her chances of getting out of this alive.

"Don't think about that dumb bitch, she always thinks she can escape, but there's no way a whore can escape us. Get that through your thick head right now, if you don't want to receive the beating she got today. And get this idea out of your head that I'm softer than Cloudy. Now you're my whore, do you understand?" He said, and Millie thought " Oh dear God, this isn't going to end tonight! They will go after me and they will rape me and torture me whenever they want to."

He continued, sliding his hand over the inside of her thigh.

Get up now, I want you to keep me company. His hand touched her vulva, and she pulled back abruptly. He grinned and sat down on the couch, pulling out some bags.

"Get me a spoon bitch" - he said, opening the bags.

Millie pulled out a spoon and handed it to him. Then she saw what he was about to do. He put some sort of small lump in the spoon and started heating it from below with a lighter.

"How did I not figure this out, these guys are miserable drug addicts, they're capable of killing their own mother" Millie thought. He signalled her to sit next to him. When the lump melted, he handed her the lighter and pulled out a small cone and told her to hold the lighter underneath the spoon.

Millie did what he was telling her. A thin stream of smoke appeared, which he inhaled through the funnel, he did it several times. He handed her the funnel and said:

"Now it's your turn."

"I don't want to" - she replied, but from his gaze she knew he was not asking her.

She took the funnel and started doing what he was doing. Either way, everything seemed hopeless, maybe an overdose would get rid of her troubles. He smoked several times, then she did, until the liquid disappeared from the spoon. Greg constantly spat directly on the carpet. At first everything seemed normal, but then Millie realized she could not move, she could not even speak. She felt very tired. He switched off the lamp and lit a cigarette. She also wanted to light up, but she could neither ask for, nor take one. It was as if time had somehow changed, the room too, her sensation was as if everything was happening in slow-motion. Each of her actions took an eternity. And then - nothing. A white spot. Some sort of memory of cum everywhere. She is all sticky, something is leaking down her face. She is suffocating and she vomits several times. A phone pointed at her. Cloudy is here. In fact, she's alone now. There is no one. It's dark. She can hear planes overhead.

Millie opens her eyes and immediately vomits. The room is spinning. She vomits again. It is afternoon, she hears the postman ringing, he usually comes around five o'clock. She pukes once more, it's dark and she's shivering, it's very cold. There is no blanket, no water, she is thirsty and terribly hungry. Again she heaves. Her legs are trembling, blood is leaking on them. She reaches the wardrobe and pulls out a blanket. She pushes back from the wardrobe and reaches the bed. She covers herself.

"What is hope, Hugh?" Millie asked. He looks up in surprise, as if not expecting her.

"It's nothing " he said, leaning back down again. He was making a key.

"Tell me, please, I have to know, I need to know."

"You do not need hope, child" he said without looking up.

"I need it" she said.

"Hope is a lack of faith. Faith is what you need!"

"Millie, Oh God, Millie, wake up. Millie heard Nicole's voice as if coming from the afterlife. It took her a moment to realise that Nicole was shaking her and shouting, leaning over her.

Millie's scar

"Millie, wake up, please, what happened, what happened to you, who did all this? Millie, wake up!" Nicole repeated in a trembling voice.

Millie opened her eyes with difficulty and tried to keep her eyes focused.

"My God, Millie, what happened? I thought you were dead! What happened that night or did this happen last night, who was it, and why did he do all this?"

Millie started coming to her senses and to remember what had happened. Nicole continued:

"That girl from the party, Dariya, was waiting for me at home this morning, she remembered that I live next to the cinema and she was waiting for me. She looked like hell. She said I had to come and tell you to run. She also said she was sorry, and that she feels very guilty to have involved you in all this. What should you be running away from, Millie? What happened? Get up and tell me, please!" Nicole didn't stop.

"She mentioned some kind of video" she continued. "She said they had uploaded it to a group? I didn't remember the name, she sounded so frightened and she was in a hurry, she only said: "Tell her to run away and never go to any familiar places ever again. Not to work or to meet with acquaintances. She said they would find you and constantly repeated for you to run. She said they already knew everything about you and you should not trust anyone. Millie, who are these people, what happened, get up, please, and tell me!"

Millie opened her eyes again, and the tears ran down her cheeks.

"Oh, oh my dear, what have you been through?" - Nicole leaned over and kissed her forehead, then looked at the room, and Millie saw the horror written on her face.

Dariya was right - she must run, she must gather strength and get out of here as soon as possible before those freaks came back for her again. Before the neighbours saw the broken house and reported her to the landlord. Probably she would have to work half a year to cover the damages.

She rose slightly and leaned against the bed frame. Nicole was sitting on the bed beside her, worry etched into her features, waiting. She waited for what seemed like an eternity for Millie to speak.

Millie's eyes filled with tears, and she lost sight of Nicole. She cried, she cried a lot. Nicole also cried as she surveyed the horror of Millie's flat. She could see the blood on her legs, and she could see scales of something dry, she could see the bed and floor covered in vomit. The burned couch, the broken furniture, she saw that she had already lost her friend. Millie was gone. These were pieces of Millie, this was her defiled body and her soul covered in vomit.

After they calmed down, Millie took a bath, dressed herself, gathered her most needed clothes and belongings in a bag, and they left. Eric's expensive bike was gone, and that only reinforced Millie's belief that she had to leave. The bike was worth at least 2,000 pounds. The Police were going to want to question her about the damage and missing items, but she couldn't think of dealing with that right now. Outside it was colder and more deserted than she had expected. The Christmas holiday had begun and Londoners had left the city or were cosied up at home, celebrating with too much food and drink. Millie was terrified

and kept peering everywhere. They didn't see anybody, but she felt as if from every window people were staring at her. She felt danger lurked everywhere. They decided to go to the St John the Evangelist Church, which was just a few roads from them, but it was always empty. Millie had walked past it a thousand times, but she had not entered it, nor had she ever seen anyone come out. The doors of the church were almost constantly open. They arrived quickly and walked in. There was no one and they sat down on a bench that was further away from the door, and Millie

Millie's scar

told Nicole everything, or at least what she remembered. She did not know anything about the video Dariya had spoken of to Nicole. But she had a memory of seeing a phone pointed at her. She assumed the bastards had videoed her being abused and uploaded it to some sort of group. Her abuse and humiliation would now be available for all to see. Millie buried her head in her palms and leaned against Nicole's shoulder. Nicole was looking at the chapel and was thinking of what kind of low life's would do something like that to her friend. She felt she was beginning to suffer for Millie, and she felt very scared. She began to worry for herself and her baby and thought she should try to distance herself from the danger and the sorrow. She even imagined how Olly would react if he knew that she had involved herself in all this. She was exposing their future to danger. She immediately felt ashamed of her selfishness and turned to Millie, grabbing her shoulders, and said quickly:

"Millie, what are we still doing here? We should go to the police."

"Nicole, I'm just too scared to do that right now, Greg threatened to kill me if I went to the police, he said a friend of his works in CID and if I report it, he will know and they will kill me. I can't take that risk."

"Then we have to get you out, you have to go somewhere far away. Think of a relative living in some far away village towards Wales or Scotland?" Nicole looked at Millie in anticipation. Millie looked up and shook her head in despair:

"I'm alone, Nicole, I don't even rely on my parents, I'm alone in this, and the worse thing is that I only have 180 pounds to my name. They took everything from me, my purse with all my personal documents and my bank card, I've just been paid and I expect they've emptied my account, them made me tell them my pin. I had hidden £180 for a rainy day. With this money, I will at best manage for a couple of weeks, let alone the cost of travel.

Nicole pulled out her wallet and said:

Millie's scar

- I only have this - 34 pounds, take it, we'll find an ATM, and I'll give you another 50. I'm sorry, I'm unemployed, I'm expecting a child and ... I just don't have very much." Nicole looked at her regretfully. "I know Nicole. Thank you for this, I would not take it, but I have no choice now. Someday I'll pay you back when we see each other again."

Nicole hugged her, thinking she might be seeing her for the last time.

"Just take care of yourself." She stood up, glanced at her and grabbed her nose and slightly shook her face:

"Hey, Girl! You're the strongest girl I've ever met, you must survive, you have to! I know you don't see it now, but I know, one day you will be happy!" - She said and hugged her again. Then she got up:

"Let's go now and don't tell anyone where you're going, even I don't want to know."

They left the church and walked in the direction of Kingston College and they split up at the first ATM they found.

Chapter Four

Millie bought a ticket at Victoria Coach Station, waited for her bus and got on. Her ticket was not as expensive as she expected - only 11 pounds. She chose to travel by bus as it was cheaper and less busy at this time of year. It was now 4.30pm and it was getting dark. In a little over 3 hours she would be in Bath. Arriving in her home town after dark ensured fewer people would notice her. She had lived there for 18 years. Bath was a small town, people knew each other, someone would recognize her, and the next day her mother and her father would know she was there. And, of course, they would know where to look for her. There was nowhere else for her to go except to Francesca. Francesca was her best friend from childhood, a child of an English woman and an Italian man. A very handsome Italian man. Her mother had met him when she was in Florence on holiday and it was love at first sight, firstly the city and then him. But Philippe wasn't an easy man to pin down, he was in the hearts of many women, and some of them were very rich. In order to win him over, Fran's mother, Anne, decided to go to extremes. She sent him a letter from Queen Elizabeth II. The letter said that Philippe would be honoured by the royal family if he were to marry Anne. He assumed the letter to be a fake, but nonetheless Philippe was touched by the gesture, and he came to see Anne in England and in turn fell in love with Bath. He loved the medieval feel of the town, and he would joke all the time that he was expecting Robin Hood to put an arrow through their door. Everybody, however, claims that the handwriting was just like that of the queen, and that her personal stamp, which she only used for letters to her very trusted people, was placed on the bottom of the letter.

Millie's scar

Just like this story, the friendship between Millie and Francesca was magical. At first, they just matched in games, then in their general interests. For some reason, despite Francesca's Italian features, when they were together, they were often mistaken for sisters. Francesca secretly pitied Millie for the life she had as a child, so she spent her time trying to cheer her up. She dreamed of becoming a dancer, and for Millie to be a singer so they could go on tour together. When they grew up, Millie went to London to work, and Fran married Alan – a young surgical registrar at the local hospital. Millie was a bridesmaid at their wedding. She also took photos of Alan carrying Fran across the threshold into their newly bought house for the first time. She listened to their plans for furnishing it, seeing the love and joy in their eyes. It was then that she realized they were no longer children, and she was glad that Fran was so happy.

Fran's greatest legacy, however, was giving Millie her name. Fran was the first to call her Millie. In fact, Millie's given name was Milla, but ever since Fran started calling her Millie when they were children, it had stuck, and she never used her given name. Ever since she turned 18 and moved to London, she just started to introduce herself as Millie, and everyone called her so.

The bus was almost empty. Millie sat in a backseat over which the lights did not work. She sank into the darkness looking out the window. She felt secure and at last calm. She would have three hours to think about what to do. About what had happened to her. The bus swept through a London dressed for Christmas, everything was shining. It was beautiful and people looked happy. She would miss London. She loved London. Her best years had been here. Bella was here. All this now in the past tense. She loved the anonymity that London had given her. And at the same time, London gave unlimited opportunities to anyone who wanted to make a name for themselves, to be 'somebody', for their words to be heard. But Millie wasn't like that. For the six

Millie's scar

years she had worked at PackageService she had more than one chance to climb the corporate ladder. Not that she hadn't thought about it, of course, she had several offers of promotion, but she would decline them quickly every time. The higher position carried greater responsibility, more stress, less leisure time, more commitments. And she wanted her mind to be free. Free for Bella. Her life began at 4:00 in the afternoon at the end of her working day. She was in a hurry to go home and start her day with her beloved Bella. To do whatever they wanted unencumbered by work commitments. Millie soon realized she was not ambitious and was not ashamed to admit it. She worried her bosses would think her lazy. She was not lazy. She had plans to someday enrol to study psychology. She was interested in helping people with emotional problems. She imagined she would be a particularly good analytical psychologist. Now everything had changed. Now she could be no one. She wanted to go unnoticed to everyone who did not know her. The small town knew everything about everyone, there was no personal life, it all sooner or later became public. It was hard to hide in it. Milla swallowed the bitterness that threatened to choke her, and continued to watch the swiftly passing landscapes. Half an hour later they joined the motorway and the landscape changed from the bright lights of a festive London to dark trees, fields, roadside barriers, and passing headlights.

  Millie was going to the small and loathsome Bath. Everything in this city reminded her of her unhappy childhood. Bath looked like a ghost town. She thought that all the suffering ghosts from the Middle Ages had settled there. The city was on high ground and the road to it was enchanting. Winding turns passing through green forests and endless green meadows. Magnificent views were visible from the top, but the city was grey, built of limestone that had lost its golden hue. It looked like an ancient castle with outbuildings for the peasants around it. It was not colorful or diverse like London. Millie liked London's houses of red, white,

Millie's scar

grey and brown bricks. She also liked the blend of modern and traditional, whereas Bath displayed a single tone palate. If she had had a happy childhood, she would surely have loved and cherished the city. But no, she hated it. Just as the hatred between her mother and her father transferred to her and they both forgot about her. Maybe they were too busy thinking about themselves - she thought. The only thing that had prevented Millie from never returning to Bath, was Fran. Her guardian angel, her fairy godmother. She always helped her, always giving her the best advice. Fran was the one who suggested Millie should go to London and build a life to be proud of. She was selfless and happy for Millie to go, knowing that her relationship with her parents was so bad, but also knowing how much she would miss her. And now. What had happened to her life? It was a complete failure. She wondered about how she would tell Fran. She imagined her sad face. Yes, Millie had no doubt that Fran would suffer for her. She did not want to bother her with her own problems, and the last thing she wanted was for her to be exposed to the danger of Greg and Cloudy, but she had no choice, only Fran could provide a safe haven. Millie felt so terribly lonely, the thing she wanted most in the world was a hug from someone who she knew loved her. Someone to calm her, and offer her hope that her life would soon be back on track.

Millie's thoughts raced through her mind with the speed of the moving bus. She remembered that she had to notify her bank, the DVLC and the Passport Office about her stolen documents. It was important. Firstly, because someone could take advantage of them, and because only then would she be able get new ones. Nowadays it was difficult to live without any form of ID. And without money and ID, it was untenable. It was also important to notify the authorities, especially as the police would be looking for her because of the damage to the house. She should tell them the truth about Greg and Cloudy, she would tell them how they stole

Millie's scar

Eric's bike, her identity documents, and her money. How they destroyed the house, raped her several times and videoed it, forced her to take drugs and threatened her life. She would explain that she ran away to save herself. And if they asked her why she had not reported the assault to the police before, she would say she had been too afraid after being threatened. We live in a modern world, there are so many organizations to help women protect themselves from violence. Maybe it was her chance, Millie thought. These are people who know their work. They would help her. She would go to Fran and together they would decide to whom to turn. Millie leaned back and felt better, feeling optimistic. She felt that she had escaped and that she would just forget everything and start her life again, from the beginning. London was not the only city she could live in, there were still many opportunities. Manchester, for example. Suddenly she thought that it would be a good idea to call work, because Greg and Cloudy had her pass. Who knows what they could do? She suddenly felt very sad that she had lost her good job. She felt secure there. It's nothing - she said to herself. I'm only 27 years old, who knows how many jobs I will have, and there will be other good ones for me.

When she arrived at Fran's house, the place was in darkness and she realized with disappointment that there was nobody there. Damnit - she thought - they must have gone out somewhere. What now?

She sat down on a bench at the rear of their house and began thinking. She was such a fool, she should have called in advance. It may have been a wasted journey. And now what, where would she sleep?

The streets were empty and quiet, it was ten past eight. She decided to wait a few hours, maybe they had gone to a restaurant and would come back. At twelve there was still no one. Millie was freezing, her feet as cold as ice. She decided she had to move, look for something to eat. There was a hostel at the other end of town

Millie's scar

and she began walking towards it. In the morning she would come back.

She bought a cold sandwich at a garage and although she wanted a can of Coke, she remembered she needed to save her money. Thank God, she did not see familiar faces on the way to the hostel.

There was no one at reception, but as she entered a loud buzzer sounded and she waited for someone to come. A scruffy, large man shuffled in with a wet spot on his sweater and wet lips, smelling of beer. The sound of a football match could be heard through the door he'd just opened and he was clearly agitated at being disturbed. He asked Millie for ID, she told him how it had been stolen from her, and she would go to the police to report it first thing in the morning, but she had no place to spend the night, and it was so cold outside. He wanted to watch the match, so he said:

"£12, on the second floor, the second door on the right, a room with 6 beds, yours is next to the window. Do not make any noise, everyone is sleeping. He put the money in the cash-desk and went back through the door.

Two of the beds were taken. Millie took her clothes off quickly, put on a T-shirt, laid down and fell asleep instantly.

In the morning she went back to Fran's house but there was no one there. She was already certain they had gone away for Christmas. Oh, Fran, I can't believe my luck, I really need you right now!

She went to the police station to report the stolen documents, using only back roads. It turned out not to be a simple task. She had to describe in detail the theft and the story had to match the things she would say if she had to go to court for the bike's theft and the damage to the property. Panicking, she lied that she had learned of the break-in when she was already on the bus to Bath.

Millie's scar

"Standard or express, miss?" The woman in the post office asked her after she filled in her details and was photographed.

"What's the difference in price, please?" asked Millie.

"Standard is £85 and you will receive your passport at the address you specify within 20 business days. Express costs £142 and you'll receive it within 5 business days.

"Can I have it sent here please? - Millie asked

The woman raised her eyebrows suspiciously and asked:

"Can I ask why you don't want secure delivery to your home address?"

Millie leaned over the desk and whispered:

"My mum's not well, I don't want to worry her, so I haven't told her about the theft." Millie hoped the woman might have children of her own. But she just looked down at her keyboard and began typing something quickly. Millie felt anxious, her cheeks becoming pink with fear.

"So which service do you want?"

"Quick!" Millie said, deciding that she had to finish as quickly as possible and get out of here. And what would she do for a month in Bath, she needed to get this resolved as quickly as possible.

Millie then went to a branch of Barclays Bank to report her stolen bank card. After a tortuous interview where she struggled to prove her identity without any documents, the bank finally told her that all her money had been withdrawn from her account. In tears, Millie asked if the bank would refund it. But when she couldn't provide a crime number, the bank refused to help her. She would receive her new card within a week. Millie gave Fran's address just to be sure. She headed towards the hostel, upset and despondent.

The cost of the Passport had taken a large chunk of her money. What would she do? She had to pay for five more nights at the hostel and eat, that meant another 100 pounds by then at least. She returned to the hostel, paid for another night, and went into her room. She didn't want to be seen on the streets during the day. Frustration overwhelmed her and she shouted to herself,

"Damn it, get a grip Millie! Then she became silent and began to walk nervously across the small path between the two rows of beds working things out. Because of all the days off around the holidays and the weekends, she wouldn't get her passport before January 2nd. It was the fifth working day. Her mind whirred, if she paid to stay at the hostel that would take all her money and she would most likely starve.

"Fran, where are you?" Millie groaned and fell onto one of the beds with her head in her hands.

She thought long and hard and decided that she would have to swallow her pride and go to her mother. She would make up a story about how she felt sorry they had quarrelled. She had decided to come and visit her for Christmas so that they could fix things between them. She did not want to see John, the drunkard, but the alternative was too hard. Meanwhile, Fran must return. Yes, she was sure she'd be back, perhaps even before New Year. She remembered the words Nicole had shared from Dariya, that they knew everything about her and to run away. She doubted that they travel around the country looking for her. Still, they could find some other poor girl for their perverse enjoyment. It was unlikely that they would pursue her for her entire life. Let's not forget that they are drug addicts, drug addicts are lazy Millie thought. She that's what she would do, she would stay with her mother. Tomorrow. Either way, she had paid for tonight. Nobody slept in her room tonight. She was alone. She charged her phone, there were no messages. She turned it off. She kept the battery charged just in case she had to flee. The next morning, she was walking to her mother's house contemplating what she would say to her. She'll be at work, she thought, John will be there. I'll just wait for mother to get home.

Millie's scar

Millie walked quickly with her head down and a heavy heart. She did not want to do this, but it was the best she could do in these circumstances. And Fran would return. As she turned into her mother's street she saw him. He was walking forward clumsily and turned on the small path toward her house. He opened the small gate and entered. There was no doubt, it was Cloudy. Her heart started beating wildly. She wanted to flee, but she also wanted to see what was going to happen, but the trees in the neighbouring house's garden were blocking her view. She ran across to the other side and crouched next to a red Renault Xenic.

John was at the door, they talked about something. John was shaking his head. Cloudy reached into his back pocket and handed him something. John scratched his right ear, then turned around and walked back into the house. Cloudy also turned and headed towards where Millie was hiding. She crawled around the car, staying out of sight. Cloudy passed by her and then turned into the street from which she had come.

Millie sat on the ground with her legs curled up, leaning against the car and holding her head. She stared blankly at the garage door in front of her. Was this real or a nightmare? She pinched herself, even though she knew she would not wake up. Then she started crying, big silent tears rolled down her face. Her heart was empty, her hopes had died, she herself would not be alive for much longer. Cloudy was here, probably Greg too. They knew where her mother lived. Now they would probably go to her father's house. Perhaps Greg was talking to him at this moment.

She was doomed. Why did they come here? Dariya was right, they knew everything about her and will pursue her for as long as they want. She remembered Greg's words: "No whore can escape us!" and she imagined that they would actually catch her. They assumed she would run home and they were right. And Greg was a jailbird, he has killed a person, and God knows what else. He's a criminal, he's trained for this. And she is not. Millie did not know anything about how to run away from criminals. And there is no one she can rely on for help or money. They probably choose their victims, it is unlikely that they could do to any girl what they did with her and Dariya. What if the girl has a solid family behind her, or even someone rich or corrupt enough to stop them?

Millie's scar

Chapter Five

Millie decided to check if Fran had returned, the chance was small, but if she had come back, she would save her. There was no way for them to know about Fran, so they would not look for her there. She lowered her hood and picked up her pace. There was a lot of movement on the streets today. It was a working day. On the opposite pavement, she saw her mother's neighbour Mrs. Dawson, who seemed to have aged. She turned her head in the other direction, and they passed each other without recognition. Millie thought it would be good to change her appearance a bit, maybe cut and dye her hair. She remembered that when her colleague Maria dyed her hair blond, she barely recognized her. Fran was going to colour her hair, Millie thought optimistically.

There was no one at Fran's house. Millie headed back to the hostel, there was nowhere else to go except there. She prayed they were not staying there too. If they were, there were people there, the situation was radically different. They would not allow themselves to break things, to beat and rape her. There they would be heard, and the police would arrive in two minutes, Millie calmed herself.

It started to rain heavily and Millie went into a small café, and ordered a latte to go. She went outside and lit her last cigarette under a lean-to roof. She had to quit them. A pack of cigarettes cost eight pounds, an impossible price in this situation. Even when she was working it was quite an expensive pleasure. I will quit them - she said - life is more important.

She smoked the cigarette, drank her coffee and decided to head to a small Boots on the way to the hostel. She headed to the hair section and grabbed the cheapest and brightest dye she saw. Her hair was dark brown hair, she had never dyed it, so she trusted the packaging. She added a cheap pair of scissors, paid and left. It

Millie's scar

was still raining, but Millie kept moving. She thought the rain gave her an advantage, everyone was hiding.

She reached the hostel, paid for another night, ate the 2 sausage rolls which she bought from Greggs and began reading the instructions for the hair dye. In an hour, she was more red than blond. When she saw her hair she couldn't believe her eyes and began swearing. It wasn't even, there were two dark spots the size of an orange on either side near her ears. And her roots seemed more honey blonde.

"Damn it!" she threw the comb in the sink in the common bathroom, and looked hard at her reflection as tears, again, rolled down her face. Everything she touched failed. She wasn't especially lucky, but the things that happened to her in the past 6 months crossed all limits. Millie decided it would be better to cut all her hair off. She began cutting it. It got shorter and shorter, she even though people might think of her as a boy. She surprised herself by liking the new cut she left the fringe long to cover her face, but the cut was really quite good.

She stepped out of the bathroom, wearing a towel, and spread her damp, freshly washed underwear on one of the boards on her bed and lay down with her phone in her hand. There were two voice messages:

"Milla, where are you?" she heard her mother's voice. "Today a man came looking for you at home. Are you in Bath, Milla? What's happening? Who is this man? He scared John quite a bit. What are you up to? He says you owe him money, Milla? Please call me. He said he would come again tomorrow. Please find the money you owe him and pay him back. I don't want him to bother us. He's been to your Father's too. You are a grown woman now, we can't pay your debts for you!" Then her mother paused for a moment, and John's angry voice was heard. "Call us, Milla, if you're in Bath we want to see you. The man said you were in Bath. Call us"

45

Millie's scar

"Was this woman really her mother?" Millie asked herself. At no point did she ask Millie if she was OK. It was better she did not go to her, she would believe anyone rather than her own daughter, and would hand her right over. Her face turned red with anger. She couldn't count on anyone, even her mother and father, Millie repeated to herself. She sat up in the bed and turned on the second message. Her heart stopped, she couldn't breathe. It was Greg.

"If you turn around, whore, I'll be there. Run, whore, run, it just makes the game more exciting. Then you'll see how hard you've made me, whore." His laughter ended the message.

Millie couldn't stop trembling. The tears appeared by themselves. She got up, left the phone and went to the bathroom, wiping at her tears.

It was 9 o'clock in the evening, and she she couldn't sleep, her heart was beating like crazy, her hands were trembling. It kept raining outside and there was a chilly wind blowing. She heard footsteps on the stairs. She hid from the door, turned her head and listened. The door opened. Someone placed a bag, opened it, something was making noise. Removal of shoes, creaking of the bed.

"Hi, dad, I've arrived in Bath, I have a meeting tomorrow with Mr. Morrison and Mrs. Disher. I'll call you after that to tell you what we've decided." He paused, then went on. "Yes, of course, you have nothing to worry about." He paused again, "No, don't worry, I have enough money. You don't have to send me more. I'll close now because I'm tired. Speak soon. Good night and kiss Mikey from me."

Millie pulled back the covers from her head and relaxed. She thought that Greg and Cloudy could be staying at the same hostel, but she was trying not to think about it because there was nowhere for her to go with so little money. But after his message, one thing was for sure, Millie had to leave Bath as soon as possible. She could not go back to London, but where? She racked her mind for people who might help her. She thought of Timothy, who had been in love with her for years when they were kids, but she had never returned his feelings. She liked being courted, but the truth was that he lacked the confidence or dynamism to make a go of it. She also thought him small minded. Years passed, and he didn't seem to move on or change, he stayed in the same place doing the same thing, living a mile from his parents, never pushing any boundaries. Two or three years ago she learned from Fran that he had become a priest and had moved to Liverpool. She was sure he would help her, he was a priest after all, and she had no doubt that when he saw her, his eyes would light up. Despite her new reduced circumstances and the crazy maniacs pursuing her. The only difficulty was finding him. Millie decided that she had no choice, she must leave for Liverpool. She would go around the churches and find him. There was no way for Greg to know where she had gone after Bath for him to follow her. And she would come back in January to get her passport. The temporary documents she had received from the police were valid until January 20th. Greg and Cloudy would surely give up after a month and then Fran would be back.

Millie sighed with relief and closed her eyes, trying to find sleep. She really thought that she would get away this time. It was logical for Greg and Cloudy to follow her to Bath, her parents lived here, it gave them a reason to do so. But there was no way he could find out about Liverpool. If only she could get away from here. Now there was another reason to hate this city. The city of the suffering souls - she repeated softly, then fell asleep.

She awoke well after midnight and got up and walked to the toilet, sleepy and barely looking.

As she left the toilet, she heard part of a conversation.

"Just the one night, gentlemen?" The receptionist asked.

"Yes, old man." Cloudy answered.

Millie's scar

Millie put her hand over her mouth to avoid screaming, and immediately slipped into her room. She ran to her bed, covered herself and turned her back to the rest of the room. The good thing was that her bed was furthest from the door, they would only see her back. And the way she was covered, with her short red hair, she looked like a boy. Her heart was pounding and she was struggling to control her breathing. Millie, calm down - she repeated – nothing bad can happen to you in here. They will fall asleep and you'll escape, calm down. Heavy approaching steps were heard. The door opened, the light from the corridor illuminated the room. They came in and closed the door. Then she heard a whisper.

"Where did that bastard say we could sleep?" Cloudy asked.

"What do you care, wherever you want." Greg replied.

When she heard his voice, Millie grabbed her crotch instinctively. As if to protect it. Then she thought he would find this a turn-on and she let go. She was still sore there. Everything was still hurting her, but she did not have time to think about her wounds. Her head, her groin, her calves were scratched. Millie thought that as they dragged her up the stairs, her calves were hit and dragged on the stairs. Her hips were also hurt, there were bruises on them, probably from Greg's grip while she was being raped. They laid down on two beds opposite the door, because the boy who had come in earlier was lying on the first bed behind the door.

"I'll catch this whore tomorrow, and I'll rip apart her ass. The other day I spared it, but tomorrow, she will regret that she was born."- said Greg to Cloudy.

"You're a dumb bastard, what were you saving her for, you have to fuck her until you wear her out, then toss her aside." he laughed, and turned to one side, then went on "Come on, let's sleep because tomorrow I'll have fun with another whore. That Francesca, she seems like a top notch whore." Millie couldn't believe her ears. Fran, oh dear God, Fran, she thought, where did he find her, she must have come back in the evening.

"Dude, I have 600 likes and 28 shares of the video." Greg said excitedly, playing the clip on his phone, lowering the sound so that Millie could only hear, "Swallow!"

A tear ran down her right cheek and her throat filled with bitterness. 28 shares, she thought, this made the audience endless, because sharing would grow in waves. No one had ever hurt, humiliated and insulted Millie more than Greg. She hated him with all of her being. She hated him for everything he had done to her. For the pain, the shame, her torn apart life after Bella's death. She hated him from the bottom of her soul and swore she might die, but neither he nor Cloudy would touch Fran. She had only her and no one else in the world. Undoubtedly, if Fran suffered, she would have lost her forever as a friend and a person she could trust. After Bella, Fran was Millie's most cherished friend, and she would not stand by, regardless of her fear, while they hurt her. Better to be Greg's slave for the end of her days than for Fran to suffer. The thought of slavery shook her. The room grew silent. Millie turned slightly, just so much as to look.

They seemed to be asleep, but it wasn't so, as Greg watched the video again. The boy next to Millie rolled over in his sleep and she quickly turned back to face the window. There was a strong storm outside. The trees were being battered by the strong north easterly, the driving rain hitting the window. It was freezing and nothing else would have made Millie go outside except to save hers and Fran's lives. She waited close to an hour, though it seemed like 5. Cloudy was snoring loudly, the boy beside her grunted something a few times, obviously dreaming, and Greg wasn't moving. At this hour Millie though of a plan of action. She decided to ditch her bag, it was too uncomfortable and heavy to carry, let alone trying to run with it. She moved as quietly as possible, opened the leather bag's zipper slowly and pulled out the

Millie's scar

charger, the phone, a thin long-sleeved blouse, a thick sweater, a wedge, her jeans, two pairs of socks, and two pairs of knickers. She put everything on, one on top of another. She put the phone and the charger in the jacket's inside pocket and checked whether the money and the temporary passport were in the other pocket. She took her shoes and jacket in hand and began walking on tiptoe towards the door. She stopped in front of Cloudy's bed, saw that he had left the keys to the car on the floor beside him. She hesitated, thinking that they did not know she was here, and even if they woke up, they wouldn't run after her. Then she remembered that in the morning they would go to Fran, and she had to slow them down and make it as hard as possible for them. So she took two steps, reached out and took the keys. The noise filled the room. Millie froze, but no one moved. She began walking backwards, turned and reached the door. The light from the corridor slipped through the door's slits. As she opened the door, this light would shine directly onto Cloudy's face. She lifted the hand with which she held her jacket, gently pressed the handle and opened slightly. She estimated how to place her hand so that the jacket would cast a shadow on Cloudy. But she didn't have to, she managed to sneak through the small slit and close the door. She walked down the stairs carefully but felt as if everyone could hear her. She put on her boots at the alley in front of the door, put on her jacket, pulled her hood up, and ran into the storm as fast as she could.

Chapter Six

She knocked on the door as hard as she could. Her hands were cold and she was soaked. Even the hood could not save her, it was too wide and the wind was constantly pulling it down, and the rain drenched her face. Water was dripping from her hair, her trousers were dragging with the weight of the water. Her boots were soaked. No one opened. She had been knocking for five minutes now. She began thinking that Cloudy had spoken of another Francesca. Someone finally got up on the top floor and she heard footsteps coming towards the door. Alan opened sleepily. At first he did not recognize her, then Millie started talking:

"I'm so sorry to wake you, Alan, it's Millie, don't you recognize me?" He nodded, but still did not move, she continued. "I have to talk to Fran, I know it's 3 in the morning, but it's urgent. I'm in trouble."

He took a step back and said:

"Come in Millie, even at 3 o'clock, she'll be very glad to see you. She constantly talks about you." He closed the door behind her and began climbing up the stairs while talking:

"I'll wake her up now and get you a towel and some dry things."

Millie couldn't believe she was in a safe place. She stood in front of a large grey 5-seater sofa. In front of it was a square oak table with a candlestick and a newspaper on it. Behind the couch there were dark grey curtains reaching to the back of the couch drawn across the window. The roughhewn stone walls gave way to a stone fireplace which still radiated heat, and in the centre of the ceiling was a brass chandelier. Over the fireplace a massive frame held happy family photographs. To the left of the fireplace was

Millie's scar

an alcove which led to the dining room , and to the right was a large TV.

Within a minute, Fran ran down the stairs, wrapping her dressing gown around her:

"My God, Millie, I'm so glad to see you." she took one look at Millie and shouted "Allen, bring one of my dressing gowns, a towel and warm slippers for Millie, please."

Then she hugged her with a little caution so as not to get herself wet too, then gripped her tightly in her arms, speaking softly to her ear.

"My God, are you OK? You don't look like yourself."

Millie again swallowed the bitterness in her throat and said:

"I've been here for three days waiting for you, I'm in a lot of trouble, Fran." - she wiped her tears and heard that Alan was coming down, so she went silent. Alan brought everything that Fran had told him to and went back upstairs, saying "Call me if you need me, and disappeared back to bed.

Millie wiped her face and her hair with the towel, took off her jacket and boots while making a puddle. She looked at Fran, she waved her hand and said:

"Leave it, we'll take care of it later, take off these wet clothes and tell me." While Millie was changing her clothes, Fran made coffee. They went to the back of the house, where there was a cosy and warm conservatory overlooking the back garden. Fran sat on one of the armchairs, left the coffee, pulled out a cigarette, lit it, exhaled, and said:

"I was able to convince Alan to use the conservatory for smoking in winter time. Of course, this convinced him that I will never quit" she laughed and then asked, "Are you warmer, do you want me to put a blanket over you?" Millie shook her head, sat down and tucked her feet up under her. Then she started her story.

She told Fran everything, even the smallest detail. About Bella's death, about her sadness, about the change of apartment, about the operations and the quarrel with her mother. About that unfortunate night, about the escape and about the fact that they were now not only looking for her, but are planning on going after Fran too. Fran was silent and listened, with every minute she was getting more and more lost in thought and worry lines were etching themselves on her face. Fran she got up, walked to the living room, pulled the curtains tightly, wrote something on a sheet of paper, and stuck it on the front door. She put on her shoes and a jacket, took the keys to the car and drove it into the garage, and locked the door. She returned to Millie and smiled at her puzzled face.

"There's nothing to be afraid of, dear, now we'll go to bed and get some sleep, and tomorrow we'll decide what to do."

Millie tried to object:

"You don't understand, they will be here tomorrow, and Allen will not be able to do anything to stop them. They're monsters, Fran!" Fran smiled calmly and said:

"I'm absolutely sure about that, Millie, but they will not find us here tomorrow. Stay calm, let me show you where you'll sleep and tomorrow we'll figure something out."

Millie went to bed in the bedroom next to theirs, but couldn't fall sleep for at least an hour. She knew Fran would think of something. She is so smart and so calm, so knowledgeable and balanced. She did not hesitate when she found out about the threat I brought with me, Millie thought. At last someone in my life who is not ashamed of me, who loves me and who will protect me. Millie's thoughts continued. Snuggled up in the warm and soft bed and feeling at home, she drifted off and fell asleep.

"Why did God not save me, Hugh?"

"God does not create your sufferings for you so you can ask him to save you."

Millie paused, she didn't know what to ask him, but he knew what she wanted to know, so he went on:

Millie's scar

"God is trust, Millie, trust him and he will lead you."

Millie woke up and jumped out of bed, looking straight at the sheets.

"Oh" she moaned. Her period had begun while she was asleep and she had made a small Armageddon beneath her. She began to feverishly remove the sheets. She threw them on the floor and went to the toilet to clean herself up. At the door was Fran, smiling and cheerful. Her face was puffy. She glanced at the sheets on the floor, waved her hand, and with a smile on her face she said:

"Oh, don't worry, the mattress has a protector, and the sheets are already worn out anyway." Then she turned around and took some clothes folded in a pile from the bamboo stool, placed in the right corner of the bathroom door, and continued:

"You can take a bath and put on these clothes. Yours are washed and are currently getting dry. Alan made pancakes, we're waiting for you downstairs, dear." she stroked Millie's cheek, kissed her, then took the sheets and walked down the stairs.

Millie entered the bathroom and sighed. Everything in the house was so comfortable and smelled so lovely, Fran certainly had taste. The bathroom was huge, perhaps 20 metres square. The biggest bathroom Millie had ever seen in a house. And it was so stylish. It had floor to ceiling mirrors, behind which stood a single cubicle with two showers and an exit on either side. To the right there was a large round bathtub. Against the bathtub on the left side there was a massive oak table of at least 2 meters in size. It looked like a whole piece of wood, with the bark on the outside, it was rough on top and had slits just like trees have. It had a slight glow. There were two round glass sinks embedded in it, and behind them there were elegant mixer taps. Under the table there was an equally elegant cabinet with 4 doors, and over it a large mirror along its length, reaching to the ceiling. Millie inhaled lily-of-the-valley and dreaming of such a bath in her future house, slipped into the shower. She let the water pour over her, and she

Millie's scar

closed her eyes and hugged herself. The warm water was caressing her skin and was washing all the dirt that had been gathered in the last days.

For a second, she remembered the icy shower and the raping, then shook her head to drive away the thought, and promised herself that someday she would remember nothing of that night.

She turned back and saw the shampoo, conditioner and shower gel in the embedded hole next to the other shower. Apparently, the other shower was preferred by her. She reached out, took the shampoo and rubbed her little red head. For a moment she had forgotten that she cut her hair. She showered and examined with interest Alan and Fran's choice of toiletries, smelling each one. Everything looked and smelled so good, there was harmony, exquisiteness, originality and taste. Millie felt like a child who had found itself in the house of successful and wealthy people. She imagined that all this was accomplished with a lot of hard work and perseverance and blamed herself of a lack of ambition and the pursuit of a good life. From a child she dreamed of a beautiful house like this. Her mother was definitely not a good housekeeper. Torn between work and trying to satisfy her alcoholic husband, she never kept their home in good order. There was never any money for new furniture or nice things. Her salary was spent on food and bills, the essentials. John didn't work, he just drank his way through his war veteran's pension. He had been involved in the war in Afghanistan and had returned after only two weeks, wounded with shrapnel in his leg. He had had a limp ever since. Her mother was able to cook decent meals, but their house has always been an embarrassment for Millie. That's why she never had friends to visit. She used to clean her own room as well as the whole house growing up. No matter how hard she tried, everything seemed old and broken. Then, when she moved to London, she lived for several years in a house share. She had a small room with a bed, a wardrobe and a desk. It was so small she could not even move the furniture around. The wardrobe was always too big, and she couldn't open it as it hit against the bed. Then she met Bella and a few months later they rented the small two-bedroom apartment. The bedrooms were also very narrow, and the living room looked packed with furniture. An ordinary square room had to accommodate a dining room and a living room. The cost of the flat was extortionate, being as it was in central London, and with their small income, they could afford few of the niceties.

Millie got dressed and went downstairs. Alan had already had breakfast and was watching TV. He looked at Millie and said:

"Good morning, Millie, I hope you managed to get some rest."

"I slept very well, thanks for the hospitality, Alan."

He smiled and getting up from the sofa, poured her a cup of coffee:

"I'll call Fran, she's smoking in the conservatory."

"It's OK Alan, I'll join her" she said to him, took her coffee cup and headed to the back of the house. Alan muttered.

"Ah, these cigarettes, when are you going to stop smoking? You don't know what you're doing to yourselves and this smell, how can you tolerate it?" Millie smiled and opened the door of the conservatory. Fran was sitting on one of the armchairs and staring thoughtfully at the garden. The cigarette smoke moved in a thin stream upward. When she heard the door open, she turned and smiled, saying:

"Come on, sit down, I was wondering if you found some Tampax in the cabinet under the sink?"

"Yes, I found them, thank you." – Millie said, feeling so comfortable and good here as if she were part of their family. Millie felt a pleasant easiness, from the warm shower, from the fragrant clothes which Fran was wearing, from their attitude. From the attempts of the sun to tear up the clouds and enter the conservatory as if it were doing it to warm Millie's soul.

Millie's scar

Millie put the coffee cup on the little table and knelt at Fran's feet, putting her hands on her lap.

"Fran, I don't know how to thank you. I feel like an orphan that found itself in a sacred monastery. Bathed, fed and loved. Thank you so much for everything."

Fran's eyes got teary and she said:

"I haven't done anything, Millie. I'm so sorry for everything you've been through, it's so hard. I thank God that you're alive. Everything's going to turn out fine, you will see, I believe everything will be okay. Now you're in a safe place. Nothing bad is going to happen to you here." she caressed Millie's head and said: "Come on, sit down and have a cigarette."

Millie took a deep breath and lit one, and Fran said:

"Don't be mad, but I told Allen about what you've been through. And it's good that I did. He knows what to do, we need him, I had to tell him. Two women cannot deal with two criminals alone."

Millie nodded in agreement. It was hard for her that Alan knew she was raped, but now she felt even safer.

"You're right, I'm not mad at you, how could I ever get mad with you for anything. What are we going to do? They will come looking for us today, Greg will look for me, and Cloudy for you."

"Try not to worry, calm down. Alan has already taken care that these two don't come close to our house." she said with a satisfying smile, tossed her cigarette into the ashtray and went on "A year ago Allen saved the life of the daughter of a policeman in town. No one held out any hope, but Alan refused to give up on her." she took a puff of her cigarette, then she put it out and went on. Millie watched her, listening impatiently in order to hear the happy ending.

"The man feels hugely indebted to Alan and is constantly reminding of how much he owes him. He is so grateful. Alan called him at dawn, told him about them, and that they had

Millie's scar

threatened the safety of a close friend and his wife. The policeman went to the hostel and saw Cloudy just as he was walking around his car, wondering how to open it." Fran smiled with satisfaction. "He introduced himself and offered to call a locksmith. The locksmith came and opened the car. And Alan's friend said he had to search the car. Cloudy objected, but didn't want to get arrested, the policeman found heroin in the glove compartment. He told him that he was going to arrest him. Cloudy began to bargain and assured him that he was leaving the city and never come back to Bath. He agreed to let him go. He left Bath, and the policeman entered the car's registration into the system and said they would not be able to get into town anymore without the cameras locating him and alerting the authorities. It's over, dear. Calm down now and let's get you some breakfast because there's a lot of work waiting for us. You can't spend Christmas with this insane haircut." Fran said as she stood up and walked to the dining room with a happy smile.

"We'll go to my hairdresser." she said with authority and stepped out of the room.

Millie's eyes filled with tears, this time with joy. I knew it - she said to herself - I knew Fran was my guardian angel. She got up and went to the dining room, stood before Allen and said:

"Allen, you're the best person in the world, I can't thank you enough for your protection."

Alan smiled and said:

"It's nothing, I'm sorry for everything you've been through, Millie." He said, stood up and hugged her, then went on. And before I leave you by yourselves at the shops and hairdressers, we'll stop at the hospital, I've made an appointment to get you checked over. It's important we get you tested and treated for any nasties as soon as possible."

"I told you we needed him" Fran said smiling at Millie "Don't worry, I'll come with you." Millie nodded her head in agreement.

"Thank you Alan", a tear rolling down her face as she felt so cared for. "But what time is it, when did you manage to do all this?" Millie asked, looking around for a clock on the walls.

"11" Fran answered, and Alan continued:

"We got up early, apparently Fran had not slept and woke me up at 6:30 to tell me."

Millie felt bad that she had slept so late while Fran and Alan were busy saving her, but Fran read her thoughts and said:

"You've been through a lot, probably in your place I'd have slept until 5 in the afternoon." Fran is exceptionally kind as always Millie thought.

Millie ate a large breakfast, she was hungry, and the pancakes were delicious.

Meanwhile, Fran gave her a spirited summary of the talk they had gone to on Sunday night. The briefing's subject was: "The Technological Dimension of Neurosurgery", in which Alan was a speaker. She was telling Millie with pride in her voice about how respected her husband was, how everyone wanted to talk to him, how his speech showed his high level of knowledge and depth on the subject. How the applause afterwards was the loudest and longest. How she got teary and how they all treated her as if she was the First Lady. Alan listened to her with gentle protestations but a smile on his face, the words gently stroking his ego. Fran finished with the words:

"From now on, I will come to all your talks and conferences every time, honey. I thought them a little dull, but it was actually so interesting and fun. I felt so proud of you my dear."

She approached him on the couch, kissed him on the lips, he grabbed her face with his palms, and returned her kiss. He said he would be sure to take her with him, a little light in his eyes.

After her breakfast, she and Fran went upstairs to her bedroom and started choosing what to wear out of Fran's wardrobe for their walk. Fran and Allen's bedroom was impressive. In the

Millie's scar

middle of the room there was a huge bed with several large pillows scattered across it. It looked soft and comfortable. The wall behind it drew your attention immediately. The entire wall was clad in finest mahogany with decorative carvings, back lit for effect. This made the room look very grand. Beyond the bed there were large fitted wardrobes with a mirrored front, bouncing light around the room. The floor was of oak parquet with a large, thick, white run taking up most of the room. Elegant fine white curtains hid picture windows opening onto panoramic views of Bath. Millie gasped in her mind.

She and Fran had almost identical figures, but Fran had slightly wider hips and a bigger bust. The difference in height was minimal, maybe 2 cm in favour of Fran. Millie waited for Fran to decide what to wear. Then she grabbed a pair of jeans and a dark blue sweater with a white band at the neckline and sleeves and put them on. She loved blue, in fact most of her clothes were different shades of blue. She looked at herself in the bathroom mirror and agreed with Fran that her haircut and colour were ludicrous. She went back to her room and sat on the bed putting on a little makeup in front of the mirror.

Fran exuded grace, she was one of those women whose movements enchanted men and made women envious. Yes, Millie imagined that angels would look like Fran. Her long dark brown hair reached down her back, the glossy waves ending in gentle curls where her hair touched her waist. Her perfect pear, Latin-American-like, according to Millie, emphasized her naturally small waist and ample breasts. Fran turned to look at Millie, feeling her gaze on her, and said:

"I'm almost ready."

She always used makeup to emphasize her big, almost black eyes, and add glow to her perfect skin and sensual big lips. Millie always considered Fran to be more beautiful than herself. She always felt that she was trying to live up to her, but she never quite got there. Fran was the queen of the accessory, she loved them, unlike Millie, who would put on earrings at best. Her nails were always well-kept and with at least one ring on both hands. Even years ago, Fran had a lot of scarves which she collected from boutique shops, so Millie had never seen similar ones before. These scarves always adorned her neck. The colours and their combination, as well as the texture, accentuated and enhanced her beauty. It was no coincidence that Fran received four marriage proposals before marrying Alan.

They went downstairs, put on their shoes, Millie's still wet from last night she borrowed a pair of Fran's which were a little big, she put on one of Fran's jackets and they all got in Fran's car.

Fran drove her Nissan Qashqai with a huge panoramic window in the roof. On the way, she told Millie about her new job, her colleagues, that although she likes it and is well paid, she is thinking of looking for a job that gives her greater opportunities for promotion to senior associate. She had graduated from Law school, but after graduating and trying to work as a lawyer, she had decided that this job was not right for her. So she started working for a well-established notary office.

Millie slunk against the backrest, she was still hiding. She couldn't shake the feeling that Greg and Cloudy were around every corner. She also had no desire to see her mother, John or her father and his evil wife.

The consultation at the hospital made Millie feel like she was being invaded all over again. Although, with Alan's influence, she jumped the queue and it was, at least, concluded fast. Having a swab taken to test for any sexually transmitted diseases felt awful. She also gave a sample of blood to test for HIV and pregnancy although the gynecologist she saw told her that it was really too early to check for either, and he made her an appointment for a weeks' time. She would need a follow up test for HIV in 4 weeks too. Fran stayed with Millie the whole time and helped her on

Millie's scar

with her coat after it was all done. They left Alan at the hospital and headed for the hairdresser.

Two hours later Millie had a dark brown pixie cut. She thought she looked like Madonna in her early years before she became a blond bombshell. She felt good. They walked around a few shops, drank coffee at Costa, and talked. They talked a lot. They had a lot to talk about. With every minute and with every story told between the two, London was becoming more remote. Bella, Greg, Cloudy, and the last 7 years of her life. She was starting to relax and remember her life before that.

They gossiped about old friends in Bath, she learned spicy stories about them and laughed out loud at one of them. She wished to see some classmates and walking down the street to the parking lot she was looking for familiar faces. But there were none. It was as if she had been out of town for an eternity, not just 7 years.

They walked arm in arm and happy, with a bag of gifts each. Fran was adamant that Millie would buy a Christmas sweater. Ridiculous sweaters with deer, Santa, snowmen and snowflakes, but she couldn't refuse her. Also, pyjamas, underwear, socks and light grey sweatshirt. Green woollen trousers with low waist and side pockets at the thighs in which Millie really liked herself. Fran bought herself a sweater, and some pretty lingerie, but Millie thought she was buying them to make Millie relax from the pressure of spending her money. She simply said to her - it's time to pamper ourselves, upon entering the shopping centre.

They got home at 5:30 and after they changed clothes, the two of them prepared dinner. Veal steak with asparagus spears, boiled potatoes and tomato and basil salad with mozzarella.

Alan stayed discretely in his office and made several calls. He avoided bothering the women, understanding their need to talk and Millie's need to heal.

Later they had dinner, sharing what they had done during the day, and laughing at the memory of the hairdresser's desperate face when she saw Millie's hair.

Alan then watched the news and a comedy show, and Fran and Millie did not leave the conservatory for at least 2 hours, talking all the time.

The next day was Christmas Eve. They spent the whole day at home, preparing everything for Christmas dinner. Millie helped Fran to clean the house, discovering more and more things she loved about it. She felt good here in Fran's company, but her thoughts were elsewhere. The previous night before falling asleep she had listened to the six messages Greg had left. Again, there were insults and threats of life-long sex slavery. Again screaming. This scared her and shook her sense of security. No matter how well she felt here in Fran's company, and in her lovely house, she realized that she could not always stay in this shelter under Fran's wing. She had to decide what she would do in the future. She had to decide where to go next. Her heart was aching from the feeling of loneliness that awaited her. Wherever she went, she had to start everything from scratch, all alone.

She also could not get over the question of what had happened in her old apartment. Whether the Connelly family had returned and finding the devastated house, what had they done? In the afternoon after they had lunch, Millie shared her concerns with Fran as they drank coffee and smoked at the conservatory.

I think you have no choice, Millie." said Fran "It's best to stay in Bath. Here you will be safe. If those thugs come back to look for you, we'll find out first before they get into the city."

Millie understood Fran.

"But what am I going to do here? I don't like the city, you know, everything here reminds me of my childhood." she said to her.

Millie's scar

"Millie, you have to grow up." Fran said to her bluntly "you're going to build your life here from scratch, you'll see the city from a different perspective and you'll gather new and better memories. Gradually you will get used to and love the city. Besides, you don't have to visit your mother and father, they will hardly insist.

"Yes, they were only eager to see me if it meant avoiding trouble for them" Millie said sarcastically.

"Look, you're going to get your passport on January 2nd, and you'll stay here until you get back on your feet. Alan will ask if there is any work in the hospital for you, for starters. There are two cafes there, you can start by making sandwiches and coffees, waiting tables. It's a good start."

"Yes, it sounds good" Millie felt that she was relaxing and seeing the future which Fran was painting for her.

"If Alan can't find a job for you in the hospital, I will help you write your CV and send it to all the recruitment agencies. Something will turn up" she took a sip of her coffee and continued "I will not leave you on the street, hungry and wet, as you came to us on that night, Millie. I'll take care of you, it's no problem, you'll stay here for as long as you need until you find your own place."

Millie smiled, but it was hard for her, she felt she was a burden, though Fran would never admit it. As if reading her thoughts:

"Don't worry about the expenses. Alan earns more than we need, in 5 years we've paid off the mortgage on the house, we only have four more payments. I also earn good money. And the room you sleep in is empty anyway. I have missed you very much, Millie, and I don't want you to disappear once more and for me to lose you again." she said this with such emotion in her voice that Millie believed her without question. Again, she heaved a sigh of relief. Fran made her worries disappear.

"I don't know how I will ever be able to repay your kindness? She said, and hugged her. "You're my guardian angel" then went on:

"One more thing bothers me."

"What?" - Fran asked.

"What is happening in the house I lived in, and whether they're going to declare me a thief? I wonder if I should go to the police and give an explanation on what happened?"

"Yes, of course, I will ask Allan to call his friend to advise us on what to do, on what would be best."

Later she and Fran decorated the Christmas tree.

Dinner was delicious and relaxed in the secure, cosy setting. The fireplace burned all night, and the glare of the fire on the windows made Millie sit on the couch and stare outside. There was snow falling.

A real Christmas Eve, she thought. The chimneys of all the houses outside smoked, the windows glowed, and there were happy celebrating families visible through them. The splendid decorations of the houses, the glowing lights, and the smell of woodsmoke brought Millie into a fairy tale world. If only all of her Christmases had been like this one, but, alas this was her first real Christmas Eve.

Chapter Seven

The next morning, they went to meet Alan's friend at the Police station. The Police worked every day, it did not matter that it was a bank holiday, on the contrary, it was a busy time for them.

Officer Porter met her in his office and listened quietly to the whole story, including the threat that they would kill Millie if she went to the Police. He then said:

"The forensic doctor will examine you, but I'm pretty sure that after so many days there will not be any evidence of the rape, which makes it very hard to bring rape charges. Even if we do, it's your word against his and that is the hardest case in which to get a conviction." He continued sympathetically. "You say that he forced you to take drugs, but you have no proof or witness to the coercion itself. When we test your blood, we will find drugs and my guess is he will show the video in court, in which you do not resist. Everyone in the court will see that video, and if the case gets popular, you could end up with some or all of that video in the public domain. You have to think really carefully about what you will need to go through to bring this case to court let alone the prosecution itself." he turned the page, looked at it, then brought it back and continued. "We can bring charges for vandalism and willful destruction of property. Our colleagues in London will find evidence that the perpetrators were in your flat, unless of course, they set the house on fire." He went on. "But there is one major problem above all else so far," he looked at her from under his eyebrows, looked back at the sheets and continued. "You don't know anything about them. Except for one name, Greg, and one nickname, Cloudy. I checked the car's registration that was in front of the hostel. It turned out to be a fake plate, it was from a car which hasn't been on the road in a long time. They probably took it from a breakers yard. If I'd known the whole story, I would have arrested them then and there. Alan should have told me at the beginning." he sighed and continued. "We can try and create an E-Fit of the men, do you think you can accurately describe their faces? But this is usually only helpful if they are in our system. Even if their fingerprints are found, if they are not present in the system, we can only wait for them to screw up again for us to catch them. Even if some camera has taken a snap of them, again we can't find them if they're not in the system. Do you want to press charges of vandalism and try to do an E-Fit?"

Millie paused with her eyes locked on the desk. She felt foolish. Everything that had happened to her had been trivialised and thrown into the rubbish bin as though it was nothing more than a childish misdemeanour. She felt helpless, insulted and angry at the fact that Greg wouldn't receive any punishment for the rape, the great pain and humiliation he had caused and for the hole in her soul that he had carved. She thought she didn't want to go trough the ordeal of pressing charges, she didn't have the money for one thing. But she was determined not to be thought a thief and pursued for vandalism. When she tried to recreate their faces in her mind, and though she could see them clearly, so she decided she had to try.

"Yes, I want to try to do the E-Fit. Will I have to meet them in court?" She asked a shiver making it's way down her spine.

"Not necessarily, they will probably reach a settlement and just pay damages. The probability of delaying the case is small, if there is obvious evidence of guilt, any lawyer would advise them to settle out of court."

"Alright then at least let them pay for the damages. God will obviously judge them for the rest." Millie said sarcastically and swallowed the bitterness.

"Let's get to work then."

Millie's scar

Millie endured the next few hours in a blur. There was filing of declarations, description of the prosecution, an examination by a physician. As officer Porter said, he could not find any evidence of rape, except for slight abrasions that could be as a result of consensual intercourse. Her period had not left any trace of Greg's semen. Then, for about 40 minutes, she described their faces to the E-Fit officer. It turned out to be easier than she had expected. She couldn't stop worrying that they could enter the city at any time using another license plate. They could even be in Fran's house at this very moment. Millie shuddered.

Just after 6 o'clock Fran took her from the Police station, and they went home.

She wouldn't forget this Christmas. The Christmas she spent at the Police station. She would not forget the humiliation she experienced while recounting the rape to the Policeman and his calm and logical but devestating conclusion. The physician's guarded face and the questions he had asked her. The lack of evidence for her words made her feel like a fool. It was even possible that they wouldn't find them. They seemed to manage to outwit even a Policeman. Nobody told her that she was a liar, but the fact that she could not prove her words made her look like that in the eyes of others. They probably don't believe anyone - she thought - that's their job. They only believe the facts. They don't trust tearful stories and the words of stupid young girls. The sorrow caused a few tears to roll down her face. The only thing left for her was to wait and hope that they would find them.

Fran drove silently, gazing at Millie from time to time who was looking out the window. She knew she was crying, she knew she was suffering, and she did not know how to calm her. She had the perfect reason to cry. Fran parked in front of her garage and put her hand on Millie's knee. Millie wiped her tears with her hand and looked at Fran with red eyes.

"I feel like a complete fool."

"It will pass, you will see. I have a friend who is a psychologist, she is very good. You will meet her after New Year. I'm sure she'll help you overcome the trauma. Together we will overcome it, do you hear? I'm with you and won't leave you." She put her arms around her and held her briefly in her embrace. Millie went back to her room and lay on the bed. She stared at the ceiling for a long time, thinking of what to do. She had to leave, after all that Fran and Alan had done for her, she could not risk their safety, it was unthinkable. She had to go away but without telling them, because they wouldn't let her leave, and she would not forgive herself if something bad happened to Fran. The memory of the abuse of the bleeding Dariya came into her head. Her eyes were again filled with tears. She just couldn't stay here. Fran was not aware of the danger, she didn't understand the brutality of these guys who were targeting Millie. If they looked for her again at Fran's house and found out that she was gone, Fran would not get hurt, she thought. Perhaps she had to figure out how to make them look for her in another city, not Bath. There was nothing in this world that would make her expose this tender and gentle woman to experience that she and Dariya had endured. She decided firmly that after getting her passport and bank card she would go to Liverpool and look for Tim, who would help her. She only prayed for one thing, that Cloudy and Greg would not come before that.

She turned on her phone and dialed Officer Porter's phone number.

"I'm sorry to bother you again, it's Millie."

"Hello, Millie, how can I help?"

"Is there a possibility for the charges that I filed to appear to have been issued from another city, like Brighton?"

"I'm afraid not, the charges have already been filed on behalf of the investigator. Why do you ask?"

Millie's scar

"Given that you can no longer detect them when they enter the city, they could be here right now and looking for me. I want to make them look for me elsewhere, far from here. Is that possible? I don't feel safe Officer Porter, and I don't want to put Fran and Alan in danger."

"I understand Millie, I will think about what can be done and call you if I find a solution."

"Thank you, Officer Porter and Merry Christmas."

"Merry Christmas to you too, good bye."

Millie hung up, put on her Christmas sweater and went downstairs.

Alan and Fran were laying the table. Christmas Carols played softly in the background as they both moved their bodies in tune with the song.

"What can I help with?" Millie asked, gazing at the table, but everything was done, all carefully and stylishly arranged. Beautiful green and gold china, crystal wine glasses, porceline tableware, decorations, nuts, sliced ham and several types of cheeses. She remembered her miserable and modest tableware in London.

"Everything is ready, we can sit down." Fran said, her arms wide-spread and her face shining. Alan kissed her and sat down, and Millie followed.

Fran is doing all she can to cheer me up, Millie was sure, and she thought it was the only explanation for Fran's upbeat mood. Except, of course, for Christmas itself.

They drank wine and talked. About Alan, his career, his persistent efforts, the recognition he had received, his dedication at work, and how many happy patients he has.

"At first, I was cross with him, he didn't spend any time with me. We had become a boring couple in the first year after the marriage. All work and no play." Fran talked in a visibly joyful state, "I don't know how he put up with me, I wouldn't stop bothering him, and he kept telling me, 'Fran, we must be serious, we have a mortgage to pay, we need to make good money'"

Reshaping her voice and face into a serious Fran. "But my darling turned out to be right. He has worked so hard and he has achieved so much. We have almost paid the house in such a short period. He's my hero." she caressed him, and he was shaking his head gently now trying to imitate her. "I'm proud of you, sweetie." She said, stood behind him and kissed him several times on the neck.

"As always you are lucky, Fran," Millie noted "do you know how many times she passed between the raindrops while everyone else got into trouble? Always!" she told Alan. "Her luck is notorious. Do you remember Mr. O'Neill and the flat tyre?" They both laughed sharply and loudly. "Fran punctured Mr. O'Neill's tyre because he called her a little good-for-nothing, and do you know who he found next to the tyre? Me! I was even trying to fix it to save Fran's skin, but how could he believe me when he saw me with an icepick in my hand, squatting next to his flat tyre. I was using the icepick to plug the hole with glue." They both continued laughing.

"Do you remember that fool, Derek, who used to kill pigeons and then would scare us with them?" Fran said, "this idiot became the principal of Royal High School!" and they both burst out laughing again. "Thank God it was for a very short time, he caused some kind of trouble on the first month and quit with a statement of being in poor health."

"And what happened to Sumer?" Millie asked, "I liked her very much, she was different from all our friends. I thought one day she would become a film star, she had talent, do you remember how she got all the good roles?"

"Yes, I'm not sure, I think she got pregnant very young, maybe at 18, and went to Edinburgh with her husband, then I heard they separated, but I don't know the details." Fran replied.

"And my eternal admirer, Tim?" Millie directed the conversation in order to find out as much as possible about him.

Millie's scar

"Don't you know, he became a clergyman, I'm not sure what rank he got to, but he left for some church in Liverpool about 5 years ago. I heard he was very devoted, and that he had been involved in various charity campaigns. His mother was very proud, she was always talking about him. I think she started him down this path, I remember that as a child she would take him to church every day."

"Millie" Alan said, "I remember now that Ms. Hughes is looking for a saleswoman in her French café. The best café in the area. They make incredible croissants and coffee, as well as all types of bread. She will soon open her French restaurant as well, right next to the store and I'm sure she'll need staff."

"That sounds good" Millie said.

Fran sensed that the subject returned Millie to a dark place and gently pushed Alan, saying – "It's Christmas, darling, let's have fun."

"You're right" he replied, picking up his glass for a toast. "Let's have a toast for Millie. Because she returned to Bath and brought my Fran's smile back. Now she will finally stop complaining that she has no friends." Alan laughed, and after him both women did too. Then Fran said:

"I think it's time to tell her, Alan," she grabbed his hand, glancing at him, and then turned to Millie. "Alan and I decided it was time to grow the family and try for another Alan or Francesca!" she lit up.

"Oh-h-h, that's wonderful news!" Millie rejoiced, and everyone gave cheers for their health.

"Now it's time for presents. We were not expecting Santa during the night, and if I have to be honest, Millie, I bought your present today, while you were in the Police station." Fran got up and brought the presents, saying, "And so that you do not feel embarrassed that you have no presents for us I bought for us those surprise gifts that are packaged and you don't know what's inside." She gave Millie her present and said "I love you" quietly, and then she handed Alan his gift, kissed him, and then shouted "Merry Christmas!"

"My dear Fran, considerate as always." Millie said, and went around the table to hug and kiss her.

They opened the presents and laughed at the surprise gifts. Fran's gift turned out to be a yoga ball, and Alan's was a Shellac set.

Fran had bought Millie an incredible sweater in dusky pink with a big cowl neck. An adventure novel and a photo frame in which she had put a picture of the two of them from the day of their graduation. Alan's present was a luxurious set of leather gloves, belt and a pocket wallet.

During dinner, they talked again about the comical situations of Millie and Fran's past. Both knew it was safe ground to keep them distracted from recent events. What Fran did not know was that Millie wanted to talk about the past because she did not want the dinner to be over quickly and for her to have to plot her departure to Liverpool. And what neither of them knew was that Fran was talking about the past, not to cheer up Millie but herself. When she went to collect Millie from the Police station, Fran had seen Cloudy, she knew him because he had come to the house the night before Millie arrived to look for her. She saw him for only a couple of seconds as their cars passed by each other. He also saw her, and as they passed, he stopped suddenly at the side of the road. Fran stared at him in her side mirror, and saw that he was also looking in his mirror. On the way back she went a completely different route home. But as soon as they go home, she pulled the curtains again. She didn't say anything to anyone, because it was Christmas and because she hoped desperately to be mistaken. It was only after this had happened that Fran began to realize that the danger was not over, on the contrary, it could beat down the door at any moment.

73

Millie's scar

After they had dinner, Alan went to watch TV saying he was stuffed and wanted to doze in front of the box. Fran and Millie went to the conservatory. They talked briefly about the evening, the weather outside, then smoked silently, while looking at the dark garden in front of them, as both pretended to be relaxing. They were both lost in their own thoughts. Fran decided not to question Millie tonight about what happened at the Police station. Although she wanted to calm herself that the Police had the power to stop those two. Millie was worried that Fran would get suspicious if she asked too many questions related to Tim, and when Millie ran away, she would remember and guess right away where she had gone. And she wasn't supposed to know. She had to stay away from this affair. No matter how much she wanted to help Millie, and as much as Millie wanted for that to happen, it was unfortunately not in her power. Millie had to get out of this by herself. She had to wait for her passport and find some money to be able to get away. A few more days and she would protect Fran from the danger. God help them until then, Millie thought and said she was going to bed.

"Show me the future, Hugh."

"You don't want to know it," he replied. He was fixing a clock. He was wearing a black hat with a hood on his head.

"On the contrary, I desperately need to know it." Millie said.

"Go and look behind the mirror then."

A huge mirror appeared at the bottom of the room. Millie passed through it.

She was in a cul-de-sac, but walking away from it, towards an intersection in a strange town.

Chapter Eight

Millie woke up contemplating her dream with Hugh. Ever since childhood, Hugh was her dream companion whenever she was nervous. At first she decided he was her guardian angel, and as she grew, she decided that he was a subconscious construction, answering her questions. Everything was repeated, the room in which he welcomed her was the same, with a desk and two chairs, he was sitting on one of them, and the other one was placed for her. She always stood by the door and did not go inside. There was a large window to her left. He was a middle aged Asian man, short, thin and with darkened, slightly wrinkled skin, always working on some small thing with his hands, She would ask questions, he would answer, somewhat reluctantly, and then the dream would end. Her questions came from deep inside her soul - she thought.

A dead-end road in a strange city - this must be Liverpool, she surmised. The crossroads probably meant she would have to make some choices there.

She got up, dressed and went downstairs. Alan was at work, and Fran was working on the computer in their office. She told Millie she'd be working for 3-4 hours, but it actually took longer. Millie watched TV, took a bath and had some food. She found an ad on the internet for a part-time job in a packing warehouse during the holidays. She called and they said she could start that same night. The work was the night shift and was until January 3rd. She would earn £260. It's something, she thought. She needed this money for her trip to Liverpool. She managed to convince Fran that she would feel better if she was busy, and that she should take this job. She felt bad, having a secret plan, and tried to avoid talking about the future with Fran. She knew Fran would be

Millie's scar

offended when she ran away and tried to act as natural and casual as possible. She printed a list of the addresses of all the churches in Liverpool and put it away. The evening passed calmly. The next few days up to New Year passed quickly. At night time Millie went to work at the warehouse and slept during the day. The work was monotonous, she packaged different products in boxes, depending on what the order was. Shampoos, household goods, gardening supplies, lighting fixtures and other stuff. Then she sealed them, recorded what batch they were supposed to go to and then brought them to the relevant place with a cart. The weather was cold, it snowed and she spent most of the time in the house, watching TV or talking to Fran. The day before New Year Millie checked if the documents had arrived, but they hadn't. There was no information about the charges she had filed with the Police. Officer Porter was on holiday for a few days, and detective Carter was not very talkative. He said nothing more than that they hadn't found them, and he wouldn't give any other information. It even seemed that he was avoiding her. The fact that they hadn't found them reinforced her belief that she had to get out of Bath as quickly as possible. For now, she didn't see any suspicious cars stopping in front of the house, nor anyone following her when she went out. Everything seemed normal. Greg and Cloudy were obviously in London, or they were captured, she thought hopefully. She was afraid, but the tranquility of the small town around the holidays made her think that maybe everything was over. The Police had found evidence in the destroyed house and had arrested them.

Fran managed to add another seat to the table at the Italian restaurant she had reserved for New Year's Eve and Millie joined her and Alan for dinner. The evening was fun and lively. The proprietors of the restaurant had invited singers and comedians to take turns entertaining their diners. The songs of Queen, Michael Jackson and George Michael rang out and the whole place was jumping. The comedians told funny stories about family life and the whole place laughed and clapped. Millie also had fun. She drank a little too much wine but was only tipsy. They arrived home at 4 am.

A new year and a new and better life - she thought before falling asleep.

On January 2nd she her bank card arrived and she collected her express passport from the post office. It was the last time she went to work in the warehouse. In the morning when she returned, there was no one. Fran and Alan were at work. Millie packed her luggage in an old backpack that she found in the closet which she thought wouldn't be missed. She took a bath and wrote a note to Fran.

"My Dearest Fran,

Thank you both so very much for all your help. You have always been my guardian angel and the dearest person to my heart. Please don't worry about me, I'm going somewhere a long way away where I'll be safe. All the time I'm here, Greg and Cloudy are a threat to you, your baby and to Alan. I would never forgive myself if something bad happened to you because of me, so I have decided I must leave. Forgive me for not telling you, but I know you would not allow it. As soon as I arrive and am settled I'll ring you so you won't worry about me. I love you so much and we'll speak to each other soon.

Millie".

Millie read the letter, put it on the table in the living room with the keys to the house on it, put on her coat and left.

Millie had been going around Liverpool's churches for four days searching for Tim, but there was no sign of him. It seemed he had disappeared into thin air, which made her despair, and she sat on a bench with hot tea in her hands so as to think. She rolled a cigarette, from the tobacco she had bought the day before and lit it. He was nowhere, no one knew anything about him, as if he had never even been to Liverpool. Didn't these clerics have any

Millie's scar

meetings or councils? She asked herself. How come no one knew anything about Tim? There were a few small churches left outside the city, after which her search would be exhausted. Despair began to take over. Millie doubted she would find him, and dark thoughts began popping up in her head. If he wasn't there, it was all lost. She had almost no money left. She had arrived with £200 pounds and £70 was already gone. She began running out of ideas. If she did not find a job, she would be lost. There was no way back to either Bath or London. She couldn't call Fran to ask for money, given that she had only left her four days ago. She did not want to involve Fran anymore. She had some dignity, though this was not the time to demonstrate it. Fran had achieved so much, her life was happy and settled and full of stability and care and Millie was nothing, a big nothing, bringing nothing but trouble. No, she absolutely did not want to ask Fran for more help, she thought and shook her head firmly. Her life was left in the hands of God, or in the worst case in Greg's hands. While she was looking for Tim, she decided to look at shop windows and restaurants for job vacancies. There were some, mostly Kebab shops, which recruited men only. She also found two local cafes which offered English breakfast and sandwiches. They said they would hand over the cv to their manager and call her. But nobody called. She had bought a new sim card. She also gave her new number to Fran so she would not worry about her and be able to call her, but she did not say in which city she would be. For both our safety, Fran, she told her, you have to understand me, I don't want to put you at any risk, you don't realize how dangerous these two guys are. Now that they can enter Bath whenever they want to, this means I am putting you in danger. You must stay safe, I'll never forgive myself if something happened to you, Millie told her. To her surprise Fran did not argue with her, perhaps she had realized the danger.

She also registered with two recruitment agencies and asked several chains of shops for any job, but everywhere they shrugged their heads and said they would call if they got a vacant position. It seemed to her many times that her phone was ringing and she hurriedly pulled it out of her pocket, but no one rang. She found overnight stays at a hostel for £12 a night. She had never been in a more miserable place before now. The toilets filled the whole building with a foul smell, there were cockroaches in the bedrooms, the blankets were eaten by moths, and hot water was almost never available. The guests of the hostel were even more pathetic than the place itself. But for now there was nothing she could do, it was the cheapest she could find. She looked at the phone again, it was ten minutes to five, already dark, but she had no business in the hostel anyway. So she decided she would go to another address on the list of churches. She chose a small village outside Liverpool called Prescot. She looked at the map. The good thing about Liverpool was that almost any point could be reached with a single bus or train, saving her precious money. This church was no exception and after boarding the number 10, Millie sat, tapping her feet to keep warm, huddled into the seat, gazing out the window with her face tucked inside her collar. Liverpool disappointed her. She had seen pictures where it looked like Las Vegas. On the shores of the Irish Sea were reflected the lights of Liverpool at night, looking majestic and full of life. In fact, the city was more like a ghetto. A dirty, gray and poor city. People were down-trodden and there were a lot of beggars in the streets. The main pedestrian street was very wide with tall gray buildings. It looked more like a cycle-racing track than a central pedestrian street. Millie knew that in a poor city it was hard to find a job and it was even harder to find one with good pay. She was convinced of this after her very first day. Payment started at the minimum wage and there was nothing more than 20% higher. And no one mentioned any increase after a trial period. The only good thing was that rental prices were more than decent. A whole house could be rented for about £400, and a

Millie's scar

small place for perhaps £200 she thought. This would help her as long as she found a job soon. She remained the only passenger on the bus. Half an hour later she arrived. The church was in complete darkness. She walked all around it, it was locked, and looked absolutely deserted. She was just going to the bus stop in order to go back when she saw a light underneath a small window down low. She walked towards it, crossing the grass, and banged several times. A woman approached, peering into the darkness from inside, looked with half-closed eyes. She opened the window, and called:

"Who's there?"

"Good evening, madam. I'm looking for Tim Clark, do you know him? I know that he's a priest." Millie said, holding her breath in hope.

"What do you want with that Judas?"

Millie, baffled by the woman's words, but also overjoyed that someone knew him, continued:

"I'd like to talk to him, can you tell me where to find him?"

"Try the derelict house on Tinling Close, old Elza's place, I last heard that he was there." she said coldly, turning around to finish her job, folding clothes, and placing them in an old dresser, then went on without turning around:

"I don't advise you to go there though, that's the home of the devil herself, and looking at you I can tell that you are a good kid. You'd better go on your way, I have stuff to do right now, I have to finish quickly and leave. It's already 6 o'clock." she said and began closing the window.

"Please wait, how can I get there?"

"Use your feet, this isn't Liverpool, you youngsters have become lazy." The woman snapped and closed the window.

Millie stood up and pulled out the map, she couldn't see anything, she moved under a street lamp, and began looking for the street. It was nearby, no more than 10-15 minutes away on foot. She turned right on Ecleston Street, then left on Warrington

Millie's scar

Road and after 5 minutes she was on Tinling Close. She walked down the street, looking at the houses on both sides. Relatively new houses, no more than 40-50 years old. Almost all of them were either dark or had their curtains firmly drawn. She reached the end of the street then turned back, and saw the house at once. A curtain hanging off it's rail, filthy windows, a flickering candle. She approached and heard shouts from behind the window. She felt the excitement rise in her stomach, she was about to see Tim, but she was also cautious after hearing the words of the woman in the church. After the incident with Greg, she would take her time and not put herself in danger. People change, she said to herself, Tim was a good guy, even boring, but who knew what had happened to him to end up here. What was the shouting about? She felt afraid as she stood in the front garden trying to make out the silhouettes she saw through the window. There were three figures, a large woman or a long-haired man and two more men, one of whom could be Tim. She found her courage and decided she had to knock on the door and ask for him. If he wasn't there, she would just leave. The gate was old and hanging on one hinge, Millie side stepped it and slowly approached the front door. It had no lock and stood slightly opened. Millie knocked and waited. No one heard her, she knocked harder.

"I am not getting up to open it for you, who do you think you are?" A woman's voice, deeply accented, came from inside.

Millie pushed the door slightly and, without crossing the threshold, shouted:

"Excuse me for troubling you, I'm looking for Tim Clark."

The voices inside fell silent, a bed creaked or perhaps a chair and someone walked into the hallway. Millie stepped back, ready to run if necessary.

It was Tim, she barely recognized him, hair filthy and reaching below his chin which had a threadbear beard from which

Millie's scar

something was dripping. He wiped himself with the back of his sleeve and said:

"Who are you? What do you want?"

He was staggering, wearing old worn trousers and a sweater with a big hole on the right of his chest.

"Hello Tim, It's Milla, do you remember me?"

He frowned his brows, focused his gaze, and shouted:

"Oh-oh, my Milla has returned, of course I remember you, baby," he grinned. "I knew that one day we'd meet again."

Millie hesitated, he was very drunk, walking toward her, leaning against the wall with one hand. There was a terrible stench coming from the house. Millie looked behind him, it was very dark, only a glimmering light could be seen coming from the room Tim had come out of. The woman in the church was right, she should not have come here, but it was too late. He stood at the door and asked her:

"What brings you here, Milla?" He went to grab her hand, but she pulled it away and said:

"I was visiting, actually, and I accidentally found out you were here, so I decided to come and see you, but I see this isn't the right moment. I'm going, they're waiting for me for dinner." she lied, taking another step back.

"It's okay, I won't eat you, calm down. Come in, we'll have one drink then you can go, you're already here anyway." He slurred.

"No, I'll go now. If you want, we can meet somewhere tomorrow at noon, in front of the church, maybe? To talk."

"Oh, yes, just not at the church. Make it in front of Tesco on the high street." he said.

"Okay, at 12?"

"Come on, close that door, we're freezing to death in here." a man from inside shouted.

"Yeah, I'm coming." he shouted and turned back towards Millie "I'm there at 12" he winked, and as she was going out through the gate, he went in and bolted the door from inside.

Millie's scar

It's clear, Millie thought while walking back to the bus stop, Tim cannot be counted on for help. He himself is in a worse state than me. But what happened to him? How is it possible for a priest to become an alcoholic? Damnit, he was her only hope, now what would she do? If she did not start work very soon she would be in the same position, even worse. The bus came after 20 minutes, there were only two passengers. Millie got on and sat on one of the back seats. Her teeth chattered from the cold. She coughed but no longer had handkerchiefs, and she had a runny nose. She needed to see a doctor, but there was nowhere to go except A&E, as she didn't have a GP in Liverpool. As she wiped her nose on her sleeve, she was debating whether to go meet Tim the next day. He could hardly help her with anything, but on the other hand he was the only person she knew here. Maybe she would need him at some point. She was so cold that her thoughts wouldn't flow. She hid her face in the collar of her jacket and found herself looking forward to the luke warm water of the shower in the hostel and the moth-eaten blankets. At least the thought warmed her.

An hour and a half later she was already in bed, her coughing was getting worse. She struggled to sleep because of it. She was feverish. She couldn't take a bath, the water was icy, she did not even want to wash her hands it was so cold. She lay down and trembled for twenty minutes until she finally got warm and fell asleep, tired from her adventures in the city. The night was difficult, she had a high temperature, one moment she was sweating, the next shivering from being cold. She could feel a thirst in her throat, but she had no strength to get up, nor to pour herself water, nor to ask for another moth-eaten blanket from the reception. She dreamed of Bella, her beautiful face covered with boils, and she was speaking gibberish. Millie woke up sweating all over, she had not dreamed of Bella for a long time. After falling asleep once more, she dreamed of Greg, huge as a giant, walking

Millie's scar

heavily toward her and holding a burning newspaper, saying, "Heat it with the lighter, whore!" She woke up again, her heart was beating fast. She was burning up. She fell asleep, dreaming that she was drinking water. Several times.

In the morning she woke up early, staggered to the bathroom and poured herself water. Her joints ached, her head throbbed. She lay down again and fell asleep. At 11:30, she decided that she had no strength to get to the meeting with Tim. At 4pm she managed to convince herself that she had to go to the nearest store. She bought paracetamol and went back to bed and fell sleep. By 8pm she felt a little better, she got up and spread butter on a slice of bread, she put salami on top of it. She ate the sandwich and lay down for a little while, and then she fell asleep again. She had the feeling that her head had become at least twice as big.

The next day, Millie felt better, at least she felt well enough to get up. But she was still exhausted and sick. She had a leaky nose, and the cough suffocated her and tore her throat. She took the last of the paracetamol and went down to buy another pack. She smoked a cigarette and paid for two nights, one for the previous night and one for this one. She bought a tea from the vending machine next to the reception desk and took a free local newspaper back to her room. She lay down all day, read the newspaper and looked out the window. She though about how good it was that she had managed to negotiate with the elderly woman at the reception desk when she arrived on her first night. The hostel was made up of three floors of dorms, with rows of beds in each, but there was one small room with only one bed, no more than a cupboard really, but it had a window and Millie has privacy. The door touched the bed when it opened, but she was completely alone. She did not have to worry that she would wake up in the same room as Greg and Cloudy. And now, feeling so poorly, it was good that she was alone in the room. So, although dirty, stinking and without hot water, the hostel gave her what she needed the most, a sense of calm. She doubted that Greg and Cloudy would be staying here, they might have been drug addicts and criminals, but they obviously had no problem with money if they could get around the country looking for her. They probably did not work to be able to afford such long excursions. But they were not the only scary ones here. Almost all the guests at the hostel were outcasts from society. Millie saw two other women, they were certainly prostitutes. Nobody chooses to wear long boots with red fishnets and a short skirt in this weather. They wore heavy make-up, but it did not hide how broken they actually were. One of the woman was well into her middle years but that did not stop her from leading a drunkard up the stairs and rub her hands all over him. She also saw some young guys who looked like drug dealers.

Dressed in tracksuits, with large watches and gold chains around their necks. They did not sleep here, but Millie saw them three times in six days. They were up to something. Millie assumed they were the prostitutes' pimps or dealers or both. They scared her and reminded her of Greg and Cloudy, perhaps they knew them and would tell them where she was. The paranoia grew in her, day by day. By 4.30pm it was dark and Millie fell asleep again. She awoke during the night, feeling rested, and much better than the day before. Just in case, she swallowed another two paracetamol. Then she decided to wait for the sun to come up and then visit several more employment agencies. She prepared two sandwiches with bread, butter and salami, poured tap water into a bottle, and sat down waiting for the sun to come up. A new day, maybe with more luck than the previous ones, she hoped. She would turn on the charm at the agencies and adopt the attitude of a person very keen but not desperate to work. She decided she would look for a job in the many warehouses. Liverpool was a port, ships arrived with shipments, these shipments had to stay somewhere and be processed for delivery.

Millie's scar

Surely there would be a lot of work in warehouses. She quickly invented a CV with 6 years experience working in warehouses. At Heathrow Airport, in a printing press warehouse, in an Iceland frozen food warehouse and Gap and H&M clothes storage. She wasn't certain about what she would do about the references that the agencies usually requested. Then she remembered that she could give her old number and, when she received a message, she would call and pretend to be her referee. She also had to think of something regarding her address. She needed an address that wasn't a hostel. It was unthinkable to apply for anything from here. She remembered Tim's house, it was number 7, she saw it on the broken door. She decided to give the address there, 7, Tinling Close, and after visiting the agencies, she would go and meet him. She would apologize to him and say that she was sick and could not go to their meeting. He would help her, even if he simply handed her any letters. She only needed to find a job, nothing else.

Morning came, Millie got dressed, took coffee from the machine, rolled a cigarette and quickly left the hostel. It was warmer, at least 5-6 degrees and the wind had dropped, the roads were dry and small clouds hung in the otherwise pale blue sky. She could even hear birds singing. Millie smoked the cigarette and set off. The city was coming alive, it was 7.45am, not much would be open yet, but she would go and look around in peace before the clamour of the city took over.

She walked down the streets, looking in shop windows, many of them having given up the battle to stay open, the detritus of their last efforts still strewn across many of the floors. The city was definitely in a bad spot, the people were poor and the shops were closing down. She only hoped that she would be lucky and find some type of work.

At 9.00 she was at the first agency, talking to one of the employees, smiling, empathising about her job, engratiating herself in the hope she would remember the friendly girl with the warm smile and ring her when a job came up. She filled in the applications and went to the next agency. There she repeated the exact same trick, but the agent was a distracted, middle aged man who did not pay her any attention at all. She quickly finished up with the documents and went to the next agency as she had planned. An hour later she was smoking at the number 10 bus stop. She had gone to three other agencies, the only thing she found was a pub looking for a cleaning woman, every night after 12.00 for three hours, she left her phone number. Again, she tried to get the bartender to like her, perhaps here it was possible, she thought, after seeing his big smile. But it was just cleaning for 3 hours and 21 pounds a night.

Forty minutes later, she negotiated the hanging gate at 7, Tinling Close and knocked on the door. She heard shuffling footsteps behind the door and it opened a crack.

"Are you the woman who was after Tim? Well he's not here!" She barked at her in an accent Millie couldn't place. She was startled by the coldness of the woman and stuttered,

"I just wanted to talk to him... "

"Do you want to come in or stay outside?" she asked Millie.

"Do you know when he'll be back?"

"I don't know, everyone's at work, if you're gonna get in, get in! My legs hurt, I can't be standing here all day! He better come back with food, he hasn't brought in anything for three days, he only eats."

Perfect, Millie thought, she was alone and the others were obviously working. And that thing about the food, she didn't like the sound of it.

"Well, if it's convenient..."

The woman turned, leaving the door open and continued:

"You may as well leave it open, it's warmer outside."

Millie stepped forward slowly, the muscles in her neck tightening and her hands clammy, scared about what she might

Millie's scar

find inside. She followed the woman to the first door on the right, where Tim had emerged from the previous night. The woman sat down on the bed, then rolled to one side. She put one of her hands under her head, and with the other she quickly pulled up the blanket and covered herself.

"So, you're Milla, Tim has been babbling on about you since the other night. Well, I'm Elza, and you'd do best not to mess with me or my Tim."

Millie was shocked but spoke to reassure Elza.

"Oh, no, we're just old friends, we grew up together."

"Don't give me that crap, he told me that he was in love with you for years. You have turned the head of my Tim, but I'll tell you one thing, if you plan on making a fool out of him, you'll have me to deal with." she said, pointing to herself and lifting her eyebrows menacingly. "And the whole neighborhood knows Elza, no one wants to have anything to do with me, so be careful!" Elza spoke with all the seriousness she was capable of, and Millie did not doubt her words even for a moment. Although she wondered what this giant of a woman, who could not stand upright for more than three minutes at a time, could do to her? But then she decided she did not want to know what Elza was capable of, even when lying down.

The room was relatively clean. The old lino had certainly not seen a mop for a long time, but it was definitely swept. Elza's bed had a dining table next to it, with a piece of lino on top. An old, halved beer can provided a makeshift ashtray, and an old gas lamp was at the bottom next to the window. On the other side of the table, three different wooden chairs were arranged, leaning on the wall. By the door where Millie was still standing, there was another chair and a fireplace next to it. It was genuinely colder inside than it was out. The house was damp and dark, there was almost no light. Millie sat in the chair beside the fireplace and said:

"Don't worry about Tim, I haven't come here with bad intentions." She took the backpack off her back, left it on the ground beside the chair, and went on – "What does he do for work?"

Elza grinned:

"Well, what do you think?"

"I don't know. I knew he was a priest, I was looking for him in different churches ..."

Elza interrupted her:

"He was a priest, and it's been a long time since then. My Tim did not like to be made a fool. He turned out to be a smart boy and left them" she said. "To be a priest nowadays means to be a hypocrite first, and a man of God after that. What do you think, do the priests live a sacred life in this world right now, huh?"

"Well..." Millie didn't know how to answer, "probably some of them..."

Elza interrupted her again:

"Probably someone in Tibet!" She laughed loudly at her own joke, coughed, then went on. "Don't you read the newspapers? The Pope abdicated, and the priests, only sex with young boys is in their heads. Boys!" She emphasized. "And do you know how much money goes into these churches? Where does it go do you think, to the poor?" she laughed again and reached for the table, took her glasses and put them on, she fixed Millie with a glare, and said "For debauchery, my girl, for debauchery. I can tell you from personal experience, but I don't want to because then they'll gossip about me. Not that I care, but I'm tired of opening their eyes to the truth, and for them to call me senile Elza!" She took a breath and asked:

"Tell me, why are you here and what do you want with Tim?"

Millie had decided that she would not tell anyone anymore about Greg and Cloudy, she had made up a story to tell Tim as well, but she did not expect to have to tell it to Elza first.

Millie's scar

"Well, I want to introduce myself first, my name is Millie, although Tim knows me as Milla."

"I know, Tim told me! I am Elza, known as "Old Elza"." Tell me now and don't take me for a fool" she scolded her.

"I was living in London. The company I was working for was taken over and a large number of people got made redundant, including myself. I've been looking for a job for two months, but I haven't found one. My savings have begun to dwindle, and I decided to try somewhere new, somewhere cheaper than London. That's how I ended up with a job offer in Liverpool. I was due to start on 2nd January but I had a burglary at my flat in London and had to wait for my passport and bank cards to come through. Although I advised my new firm that I was going to be delayed, they gave my job away, so I'm a bit stuck. I'm almost out of money, and there's no work to be found. I'm sleeping at a hostel, but I can't do that forever without work. I thought of Tim, a priest and I thought that he might ..."

So, another mouth to feed!" - Elza said grumpily, shaking her head, then went on. "Listen, girl, I don't care what your problems are, mine are not small either, but keep in mind one thing. If you stay here, in this house, you have to bring food every day, you have to clean and bring water. I may be anything, but I'm not wretched and I don't want the rats to eat me."

"Yes, I see that..."

"Quiet! Let me speak, you will learn to listen. In my house, I speak first" Elza snapped.

"Of course, sorry, I did not mean to interrupt you."

"Before the men come back, let me explain the rules of the house to you."

"But I will not stay here."- Millie tried to interrupt her again. Elza looked at her over the top of her glasses and said:

"They all say that, and then they hang over my head for years, that's why I want food and water to be brought and for cleaning to be done. I can barely walk now anyway, but you are young, you'll clean, cook and wash."

"Of course," Millie agreed, wondering what this woman thought, that Millie would be spending the winter here?

"You bring as much food as you can, and nothing else. What I hate the most is people that bring an entire junkyard home, I already got rid of two people like that. I pity them as they have nowhere to sleep, but they are insolent, bringing all sorts of junk into my house, as if they were at home. Go to the second floor and bring me another blanket because I'm cold." Elza ordered her.

Millie stood up and walked up the stairs, stunned by the fat woman's repertoire. On the second floor there were three bedrooms, one very small. In it there were several mattresses, light shades, blankets, books, an old TV, and other small things piled on the ground. Everything was folded. Millie took a blanket and cast a quick look at the other two rooms. Both of them had two mattresses on the ground with pillows and blankets. Someone was sleeping there. Probably Tim and the other man she saw that night.

Millie got downstairs, went to Elza's bed and covered her, then went back to her chair and, before sitting down, asked her:

"May I use the toilet?"

"At the bottom of the corridor and be careful with the water. You will see a bucket with a jug inside, if you pee – use two glasses of water, if you poop – use the jug until the shit sinks, but be careful not to use up the whole bucket because then you'll have to refill it!" she told her and snuggled into her blanket. Millie went into the toilet, there was a bath with a shower over it, a sink and a toilet, all very old and worn out, but relatively clean. It was apparent they had not worked for a long time. So, as well as no electricity, there was no water in the house. But how did they bathe, she wondered. She didn't need to use the toilet, she said it

Millie's scar

out of curiosity so as to look at the lower floor of the house. She began wondering where the stench she smelt that night had come from, the house did not smell now. She poured a glass of water from the bucket into the toilet bowl and went back to Elza's room, sitting again in the chair.

"You didn't tell me what Tim does for a living?" Millie asked.

Elza grinned, and Millie saw that a lot of teeth in her mouth were missing, she was older than Millie had at first thought.

"He mows the grass and tidies the gardens of a few old ladies hereabouts," she smirked again. "Otherwise, he wanders around with Pete, looking for anything that's been dumped, and they sell it at the Monday market or at the Sunday Car boot sale. They do clearances as well, people who've died, old garages or storage units that need cleared. Most often, they will take away rubbish and move it elsewhere. They are hard-working, not at all lazy, that's why I keep them here." She pulled out a wrapped cigarette from the cigarette case on the table, lit it up and went on. "There was one fool, who I took home, he talked a big game, but he was good for nothing. Since then, I can smell those vagabonds from a mile away. I don't like them at all but there are a lot of them. You must have seen them, beggars and homeless people, as many as you want in this damn city. They like living like that."

Millie raised her eyebrows as she wondered what was the difference between them and the rest. Old Elza understood the question from her look, and immediately answered.

"You think we are like them, don't you? We are not, I keep them on a short leash, men have to be held on a rope, or they start thinking they can do what they want. There are rules in my house. First of all - all my boys are working, I do not need good-for-nothings or thieves, and then - only Liam begs, but he's a very good guy. He is a sad case, he is young and needs help. There was no way I could not shelter him, he's not like those idlers on the streets who drink from morning till night. I told them, if someone gets drunk before five o'clock in the afternoon, do not come back here. They all clean, bring water and food. And they listen to me! They will listen!" Elza spoke in a monologue. "Where would they go, if they want to become good-for-nothings, alcoholics, and thieves, they better get out of my sight."

"When I was looking for Tim, a woman at the church directed me here, she said the house was derelict."

"Derelict?! In another time! They only talk nonsense! It is mine, but I couldn't pay my bills so they cut off my electricity and water. They tried to take my house to pay my debts, but I played them. I won't give them my house so easily. I may have to put up without water and electricity, but the house is mine. They gave up, they're waiting for me to die, and then they will take it. I have no heirs, and even if I had - they would have wanted them to pay my debts."

Millie hears sounds outside, and after a few moments two men, one of them Tim, came in visibly amused. Tim shouted:

"Hey, Elza, get ready for a feast!" then he saw Millie and lit up. "Oh, look, my Milla!"

He walked past her, put two bags on the table and turned to Elza:

"Today was our day. First thing this morning, Pete found five pounds next to the station, then the woman whoes garage we cleared last week saw us and gave us a £20 coupon for Tesco. Finally, we hit the jackpot." he grinned, "We were offered jobs at the car wash, washing the big trucks! He pays a fiver a truck and wants us three days a week. We start a week on Thursday when two of his staff are leaving".

Pete stood at the door, with the biggest smile, and said:

"We worked it out, he said that up to 20 trucks come in every day, that's 300 pounds a week. What do you have to say, Elza?"

Elza looked visibly overwhelmed and bewildered by the news.

"Here, these are my boys!" She glanced at Millie, nodding her head and looking at her from behind her glasses, "I told you,

Millie's scar

hardworking and able to bargain. Good for you, boys, that's what I like to hear!"

Tim turned to Millie and said:

"And you, beautiful, why did you not come to our meeting, I'm no longer 18 to be wrapped around your little finger? I waited for you for an entire hour."

"I'm so sorry Tim, I was ill. I'd been looking for you at every church in the city for four days, and I caught a fever that night. I could not get out of bed for two days. I came as soon as I felt better, I've been here for two hours, waiting for you." said Millie, ashamed that she has to justify herself in front of everyone.

"It's nothing!" he waved his hand. "Come on, Elza, we bought wine and there's a roast chicken, and your favorite feta cheese, set the table, I'll be back in a minute! He walked past Millie, grabbed her by the hand and led her outside, shouting from the doorway, "and there's dessert, a real dessert!" even more joyful.

Everyone looked very happy and excited. Millie was also delighted, even though she did not know exactly what about. She was just infected by their happiness. She shared their joy.

They left Tinling Close and sat down on the curb outside one of the houses.

"Now tell me what's bothering you, you're looking for me for the second time, something serious must be wrong?"

"Oh, I don't know where to start," Millie was trying to gather her thoughts. "I came to Liverpool to work in a company, I got fired in London and I spent all my money. So, I came here, but when I arrived, it turned out the job was a scam. And so I've been going around looking for a job for a week now and I can't find anything. I have money left for five or six stays in a hostel and then I don't know what will happen to me. You were the only person I knew here, and I was hoping you could help me find a job. Also, I hope you don't mind, I gave your address for correspondence, in case they send a letter for me.

Millie's scar

"You chose a bad time," said Tim. "January, in the middle of winter and after Christmas. Everything is very closed down just now, this city comes into it's own in Spring, it comes alive, but just now the last thing anyone wants is new workers. It's okay, don't worry about it, now come and let's drink some wine and eat, you can sleep at our place, and tomorrow you'll come with us, maybe we can find something for you too."

"I'm not sure, Elza said…"

"The old girl got you scared, didn't she?" he interrupted her. "I promise there's nothing to be afraid of, she is a very conscientious old lady. She's helped all of us, she's petulant, yes, but you'll get used to that" he said, as he grabbed her hand and pulled her up.

Millie was not sure she could get used to Elza.

"Come on, I'm starving, we'll talk tomorrow in peace."

Millie got up and they went back to the house. Upon entering Tim told Elza:

"Elza, do you mind if Milla stays for a while?" Millie saw the old woman smirking at herself. She was setting the table and had her back to them, she turned and said:

"We have already come to an understanding, to bring food and water, and to clean."

"I know, I know, we all know the rules, granny." Tim said, walking toward her, he kissed her on the forehead, pulled one of the chairs out and sat down to tackle the chicken. He poured himself a glass of wine and gave Millie a sign to sit next to him.

"Come on, Milla, come next me, sit down and let's eat."

"Millie felt oddly relieved, she did not know these people, she only knew Tim from years ago, but somehow she felt at home. Only Elza frightened her.

"Pete and Elza began to eat. Everyone seemed very hungry, pushing food into their mouths. It was as if they had not eaten for at least a day. Millie didn't feel hungry, and even if she had, it didn't seem right to take food from these people who clearly

95

Millie's scar

struggled to feed themselves. Then there was heard a squeaking of the door and some knocking. Pete shouted:

"Hey, Liam, hurry up, man!"

A young man with crutches stood at the door, he was about 30 years old. When he saw them, his face beamed into a big smile. He had beautiful white teeth and lovely deep gray eyes and dark blond hair. He stepped forward with the crutches, and Millie saw he had only one leg. She stood and offered him her chair, and he looked at her and said, still smiling:

"You must be Milla?"

Millie blushed, Tim really had talked about her.

"Yes, but I prefer to be called Millie."

Tim lifted his eyes, eating more slowly, and said:

"Millie! Fran used to call you that, I did not know you liked it."

"I'm Liam, as you have already heard!" he slapped Pete on the neck jokingly and sat on the chair Millie had offered him. He let the crutches lie on Elza's bed and said:

"Leave some for me!!" looking at the half-eaten chicken.

Millie's phone rang and everyone looked at her. It was Fran, Millie got up and said:

"Excuse me, I'll be back in a minute." and she walked away, while answering the phone.

"Hello, Fran!"

"Hello, Millie, how are you?"

"I'm fine, everything's fine with me, how are you?" Millie asked, worried. Fran had not called her in the evening before, and that made her think that there was a problem with Cloudy and Greg.

"I've just spoken to Officer Porter, and I couldn't wait to tell you the good news." She took a breath and went on. "They've found Greg and Cloudy. Cloudy was captured on CCTV cameras in Bath. Charges have been made against them for the destruction of your flat. Damages against them are estimated at £16,000, £7,000 for your neighbours and £9,000 for your landlord. No charges are to be brought against you at all. Their

Millie's scar

lawyer has already asked for a settlement and so it won't go to court if the plaintiffs agree."

"That's great news, but what happens now?" Millie was delighted, wondering what was going to happen now.

"What does it matter to you, they found them and arrested them, didn't they?"

"I don't know, Fran, I'm afraid, what if now it get's worse? They could get even angrier and start looking for me again?" Millie said as she felt, not relief, as expected, but fear. They may have been accused, but they were free to do whatever they wanted - she thought.

"According to Officer Porter, at least in the near future, there is no such danger. According to him, if there's a second offence within 6 months, they can go to jail."

"That's good, let's hope they take notice of that - 6 whole months of peace would be good!" Millie thought, and she risked a small smile.

"Why don't you come back to Bath?" They won't come here anymore.

"Don't, Fran, I told you, I don't want to put you at risk. I'll be okay here, where I am. Soon I will find a job, I have sent many applications and I'm very hopeful."

"Won't you at least tell me where you are? I worry about you, put yourself in my place. I haven't slept well since you left, I'm always thinking about where you are? Where do you sleep? Are you in danger? Do you have money?"

"Calm down, I'm fine, really. Everything's fine, if I need to, I'll call you, I promise." Millie tried to be convincing, but she knew she would no longer involve Fran in her troubles.

"Okay, call me more often so that I don't worry and if you need something, do not hesitate at all. Just call me, I'll help you with whatever I can."

Millie's scar

"All right, I promise." Millie said. "Good night and say hello to Alan from me."

"Thanks, good night to you too."

Millie hung up, smiled, and walked back into the cold house. Tonight she would sleep peacefully.

Chapter Nine

Tim poured her a glass of wine and urged her to eat again, but she said that she had a sandwich left, and when she was hungry she would eat it. Pete was piling up twigs in the fireplace and was trying to light them. Elza was explaining to Liam that she was very cold during the day, and that they should light the fire in the morning. She would keep it going during the day, just so much as not to tremble from being cold, promising that she would not waste much wood. Tim looked at Milla and said:

"Are you tired, do you want me to show you where you are going to sleep?"

"No, I'm not tired, it's only six, but if you want, you can show me where I'm going to sleep." Millie said, worried if she would be able to sleep calmly in a room with strange men.

They got upstairs and Tim started:

"You'll sleep with Liam, he sleeps in this room." He showed her the bedroom with two mattresses on the ground and a view of the street. Millie looked around the room in full, there used to be a leak in the ceiling once, she noticed, because it had an old damp spot. The window frames were old and wooden, the paint was cracked and there were traces of it on the floor. The walls were gray, perhaps once white, with fragments of tape on them from posters that had once adorned the walls. Liam had established one part of the room for himself by leaving his belongings around the mattress.

Tim went on:

"I'm sleeping with Pete, we're still worried about him not doing anything stupid", he explained, entering the bedroom which was opposite Millie's and Liam's. She looked at him curiously, wanting to know what he meant, and he leaned in close to her ear and

Millie's scar

whispered. "I found him about 6 months ago, he was about to throw himself from the Silver Jubilee Bridge, I talked him down and he's been with us ever since. His wife robbed him, he was left without a home or savings, then his mother died, and he couldn't take it all so he decided to throw himself off the bridge. Since then, he has not made any other attempts, but he is a quite person, we're never shure what he's thinking. That's why I sleep with him. My sleeping is light, I can wake up easily, and I'll hear him if he decides to do anything." He pulled himself back and entered the single room that was next to theirs overlooking the courtyard. He pointed out the blankets, accumulated on the mattresses.

"Choose whatever blankets you want. Liam has a heart of gold, he's a very good boy and he's always laughing. Tim smiled, as if he remembered something, and added. "Do not worry about him, he's very considerate, he won't bother you. When you are tired, just come up and go to bed, do not feel obliged to stay with us if you don't want to.

"Yes, well, but now I'm not sleepy." Millie said, looking at him, thinking that there was hardly any trace of the old lethargic Tim. As if he was a different person. He seemed more mature than his 30 years, and his long hair and beard made him look much older. Millie was thinking about how much he'd changed and admitted to herself that she thought he would always be sloth-like. He would barely unlock the door, slowly move the chair and put on his jacket as if wondering whether to go out or stay at home. But no, he looked and behaved quite differently now. He was lively and even temperamental, he talked with verve, and above all, he was being kind to her. The latter had never changed - she admitted to herself with a smile. This change surprised her pleasantly, she would not have to spend her time with a person so different from her. She would not be annoyed by someone's behavior. She sighed with relief, and her smile remained on her face. Today was a good day, as she had predicted in the morning before she left the hostel.

After she took a liking to two blankets and a pillow, she spread them on the empty mattress in her room, and said:

"Let's go down, I want to drink wine and smoke a cigarette." still smiling, as she walked down the stairs, but still looking at Tim, she said to him. "Fran called me, I was glad to hear from her."

"So you two keep in touch? Great, it's nice to have friends."

They entered the room with the others. Liam was telling some story. Elza had a red face with tears in her eyes from laughter, sitting with her legs raised on the bed. Pete was also laughing. Elza, seeing Tim, told him in a scowling voice and teary eyes:

"Tim, come here to laugh with our Liam, oh, this boy's gonna kill me!" she took off her glasses and wiped the tears from her eyes.

"Tell it to him too, Liam, tell him!" she insisted.

Millie looked at Liam, he had not taken his smile off his face since he had come back. So radiant and infectious. His smile made everyone open their mouths and shine like him. Millie felt she was making such a face as well, expecting Liam to begin the story.

"Okay, I was standing next to McDonald's today and you know, I was waiting for someone to give me money. And at one moment two cool chicks came in and stood in front of me. But they did not look at me at all, and I was looking at them from below - you know?" Liam pointed, turning his head to the ceiling, and opening his mouth. "Both were wearing boots, stockings and coats over the buttocks, purses, sequins, in a word - tootsies. They were talking about something and one of them started farting, she was farting really hard, she almost shat herself." Everyone giggled nervously. "I was trying not to laugh and moved myself to the side. One or two minutes passed and again I heard one long fart.

Millie's scar

I couldn't stop myself and started laughing out loud.. And at that moment she turned around, looked at me and said all flustered:

"Hey, you, why are you farting?"

I was already laughing my ass off and said:

"Oh, excuse me, even you heard it?"

And her girlfriend started waving her hand in front of her nose and shouted:

"It smells, man!"

Everyone burst into laughter. Elza could no longer take a breath, and had put her hand in front of her mouth, staring at the ceiling. Pete had folded into two in the chair and was slapping his hand on his knee. Liam could tell a story in such a captivating way that even if he did not say anything, everyone laughed. Millie looked again at Pete. A tall, thin man, indeterminate age, with slightly grayish black hair, brown eyes and a sharp, hooked nose. With a slightly hollow-cheeked face and shadows under the eyes. Ever since Tim told her of his suicide attempt, she looked at him and felt sorry for his suffering. Silent and secretive, Millie thought, he probably does not like to share his problems. She wished to embrace him and tell him not to feel bad about such a betrayal, but she knew that she herself would have been broken. He felt her gaze, and she pretended that she was simply looking at one face after the other.

Liam began telling a story about a man who everyone else knew. Millie moved to the fire, squatting, and reached her hands forward to get them warm. She listened to them talking while looking into the fire. She didn't know what to talk about, she didn't know them and felt awkward. The evening engendered a feeling of closeness between them tonight, but she decided not to ask any questions. It was her first night here, there would be time to get to know them when she was alone with them. She felt Elza's gaze on her several times during the evening, a testing and harsh look. Millie smiled at her, but she sensed that Elza didn't care for those smiles. So she decided it was better not to draw attention to herself. Tim and Liam were her people, and she intended to keep a connection with them. Pete's story made her sympathize with him, and she would be gentle with him and hope an opportunity for friendship presented itself. Of the group, only Elza did not like Millie, and there was no need to tell her. She had time, six months, to put her life together in the new place without fear of Greg and Cloudy. This in itself was something she would have celebrated if she could. And she would, as soon as she found a job, and got out of here into a placed of her own. Of course, no one had said anything bad, but she did not imagine living here long term. She was not a princess who cared for luxury. No. But life here was too harsh. She wanted to be happy again. To find a job, fall in love, to study psychology one day and have children. A family would be her happiness.

Lost in her thoughts, Millie wished to be alone, to lie in bed and to think in the silence of the darkened room, warmly snuggled. She stood up, and approached Tim, they did not stop talking, they stared intently, as if they were playing poker and watching their opponents. Millie put a hand on Tim's shoulder, he looked at her and she said quietly:

"I'd like to go to bed, please excuse me." She looked at all the faces around the table. "Tomorrow, Tim, please wake me up when you get up so I can come with you." she said, looking back at him. He smiled at her:

"Go, go and get some sleep, because tomorrow a lot of work is waiting for us."

"Good night then," she went to walk out of the room. Liam and Pete wished her good night, but not Elza.

Millie lay down on the mattress and covered herself, thinking about Elza and how she could get on her good side. If not friends, at least Elza had to consider Millie as an asset to the household. So she decided that tomorrow after she came back, she would

Millie's scar

clean the house well. Elza would like that and would, perhaps, accept her more easily. Then she fell asleep.

In the morning when they got up, Pete had lit the fire as Elza had asked him, they had some hot coffee with a cigarette, and left the house. Millie could see that all three men were doing Elza's bidding. Liam walked pretty quickly with his crutches and again had a smile on his face. He had lost his leg from below the knee. He wore trousers with one leg rolled up and held in place with big, ugly stitches. He seemed fresh and happy that the day had begun. His smile, really captivating, Millie thought. One just cannot stop looking at him. He was definitely an interesting man, and she, without hiding it, watched and listened to him with interest.

Pete was almost always silent, responding with a phrase or two. Then, when they reached the station next to the church, they parted. Liam got on a bus to Liverpool's city centre, and Tim, Pete and Millie headed for the graveyard. Millie did not expect to go to a cemetery. But later on, she realized that Tim's friend worked there and helped them out. One of the garages for employees that was never used, he let Tim and Pete use to store various objects, furniture, and junk that they found. The plan for the day was to choose what they would take to the Sunday Car Boot and clean it up for sale. They would then load it on a shopping cart they kept in the garage and take it to the car boot. They had a secret hiding place in a ditch among a number of trees. They left the goods there overnight, put a camouflage tarpaulin on top and the next morning, at eight, their street stall was opened

They opened the garage and began looking around. There were all kinds of things inside. Most of the stuff was kitchen utensils, several cupboards and small antique souvenirs. Millie looked around with interest while Pete and Tim argued about what to get ready. What will be most wanted after the New Year and Christmas holidays? According to Tim it was photo frames, so

Millie's scar

people would be able to frame their holiday photos, as well as sets of tableware, because there were bound to have been a few casualties during the holidays. He also suggested they take two bedside tables and the usual souvenirs and costume jewelery. Pete thought everyone was getting at least one photo frame for a gift for Christmas, so he suggested taking cases and storage boxes so that people could stuff their dumb gifts inside and hide them under the bed. They all laughed. Then Pete picked up a cupboard and said he had to fix its leg. He took it away, sat down and started taking it apart with a screwdriver. Millie and Tim pulled out two chairs, photo frames, jewelery, glasses and tableware and began to polish them with rags.

"Everyone in Bath thinks you're a priest" she started. She had to understand what had happened to him, and why he had left the church. She also wanted to find out who Elza was, and her story, and she also about Liam, this ever smiling youngster.

"I know, I've been keeping this lie for four years." Then he paused, looked forward at Pete, and continued, while polishing a set of plates. "I was with the church for one year, but I was disappointed, it wasn't as I'd expected. Perhaps it's my mother's fault, she maybe encouraged me too much and wanted me to be a priest for the wrong reasons. I began to notice things, at first I said nothing, but then I shared them a few times with the wrong person. I thought of him as a friend, it was my mistake." Tim stopped, pulled out a cigarette and lit it, then, as it was in his mouth, continued polishing a set of glasses, pulled the cigarette out of his mouth, and continued, "Anyway, I saw things I did not like, then I found out about some, let's call it, mismanagement of money in the church and that made me angry. I decided to speak to the Bishop of the diocese, but he got angry, because I was meddling in things that were nothing to do with me. When nobody took any notice of my concerns, I got out of there. It was not for me and I was glad to be out. I don't dare tell my mother,

Millie's scar

you know how she is, and she's already 75, this is not a time to give her that kind of a shock. The disappointment would kill her. I go home once a year dressed in a cassock and tell her some lies so she can be happy. At the end of March, I'll go and see her, it's her birthday."

"I understand, and how did you end up at Elza's place?" Millie enquired gently.

"Everybody knows Elza around here, I had heard her quarreling several times with church representatives. She had seen the same things as me, that made me look for her when I left the church. I needed to talk to someone who saw the same things to make sure I was not wrong.

"Tim, what exactly did you see in this church?"

"I do not want to talk about it Millie. I'm a believer, a true believer. I try to live righteously, according to God's will. If I begin talking about what I have seen, people will lose faith in the church, and then their faith in God will be shaken. That's why it's a taboo subject with me" he said, biting his cigarette again, focused on the polishing.

"Okay, tell me about Elza then," Millie said returning to safer ground.

"Elza has had a hard life. She's a strong woman, she had to be. She was born in Poland, after her mother was gang raped by a group of soldiers from the Red Army during the Second World War. Back then gang rape was a frequent thing, it was used frequently in wartime to control and scare civilians. Her husband tried to save her but they shot him in front of her eyes, then raped her next to his body. To her mother's great regret, she became pregnant and gave birth to Elza. Her mother never knew if Elza's face was that of one of her rapists or had the eyes of her dear, dead husband. She could not forgive the child for the sins of her fathers and hated her from the bottom of her soul. She treated her with contempt and took out her anger on her. After a few years, Elza's mother married a Polish man who brought the family to

Liverpool. He wasn't able to have children, so he adopted Elza and cared for her as his own daughter. Within a couple of years her mother passed away, and he got married again. His new wife made life so intolerable for Elza that she ran away from home, so at 12, she's homeless. However, this was not the worst of it. Elza had a baby at 15, and her child was taken away from her and she was placed in an orphanage. She left the orphanage at 16, desperate to find her baby, and kidnapped a child she thought was the one. It turned out not to be and she was arrested for kidnapping and sentenced to a long custodial sentence. During her time in prison she got into all sorts of trouble and her applications for parole kept being refused. By the time she was released, her youth was gone, her record meant it was impossible for her to get a job and she spent the next 15 years living on the streets, helped by old contacts from prison, and surviving the long harsh winters by the kindness of strangers. A chance meeting and reconciliation with her stepfather led to her moving into his house shortly before he died, when he left her everything. With no income it was very hard for Elza to keep the house and there had been repeated attempts by the local council, electricity and water companies to take the house away from her, but she had fought back, refusing to let go of the one solid thing she had ever owned. To survive she started sheltering homeless people, their 'rent' being food, chores and most of all company. She finally had the family she had always craved. She's been doing this for years, I've been here 4 years."

"Truly, a hard, hard life," Millie agreed, feeling sorry for Elza's mother rather than for her. The memory of her rape was fresh, and for a moment she imagined what this woman had endured with multiple abusers. Then she chased away the dark thoughts and asked quickly:

"Well, finally, tell me about Liam, I need to know who I'm sleeping with in a room, right?" she smiled.

Millie's scar

"Oh! Liam is the best thing in this house. He's a joy, I admire him, and I would like to be more like him. He wakes up every morning reborn, full of life and having forgotten everything bad that's happened to him. What can I tell you, he has also had his hard knocks. His family were very poor, and his alcoholic father beat him and his mother regularly. One night when he was just 7 years old, he wanted to get money to buy food for his mother and bet a friend £5 that he could jump in front of a passing train. He was lucky to get out alive, but he lost his leg. When his father saw him, he called him a freak and drove him and his mother out. They ended up in a shelter and eventually Liam was placed into social care until he was 16. When he left, he couldn't find a job, and after his mother died, he was left on the street. So that's how he ended up at Elza's. He's a great boy. Now he's saving money to buy a prosthtic leg, but only I know that, not a word to Elza" Tim said, lifting his index finger towards his lips as a warning.

"My lips are sealed!" Millie said. She remembered how she had imagined she could fly, she was about 6-7 years old, as young as Liam, when he jumped in front of the train. Her mother saved her just before she was about to demonstrate her flying skills by jumping out of a 5m tree.

They both became silent. Pete walked back to them with the cabinet's foot fixed.

They cleaned up everything they had pulled out of the garage and started arranging it in the cart. On the way to the Car Boot, Millie offered to buy bread, salami and cheese with her money, and make sandwiches. They ate them on a bench and then went to hide the shopping cart. By two in the afternoon they were done. Tim sent Pete home and went with Millie to look for work He had thought of a few places she might try. No one they spoke to had any vacancies but said to try again later. At 17.30 they had were back at the house. Liam was ahead of them.

Chapter Ten

Millie felt very tired. They had not done much, but they were outside all day and the cold, the long walks and the sparse rations had sapped her strength. The fire was roaring and Elza's room was warm. Tim put a old saucepan on the fire and when it boiled he made tea for the two of them to get warm.

Liam and Pete talked quietly about something, and Elza read a newspaper. Millie sat in her place from the previous night. Her cheeks and hands were red from the cold, but she smiled to herself, cradling her cup, she sipped the hot tea, feeling the warmth spread through her body. Tim climbed the stairs when suddenly Elza turned a cold and piercing look and asked, looking at Millie right in the eyes.

"Millie, what did you bring for dinner?"

"Millie was startled, she had bought nothing. Tim told her that since she had provided lunch, he would provide the dinner, and she had agreed. "I'm so stupid" she thought.

"Well, Tim told me that ... he would get…." Millie panicked, widening her eyes, wondering where to look, anywhere but Elza's scowling eyes. She felt trapped, like a guilty child, a criminal, bruised with humiliation. She felt she had to buy something immediately. She thought she would clean up the place but even if she did, any good impression was probably already gone.

"Oh, Tim said so! Then Tim won't eat!" She raised her eyebrows and continued to stare at Millie. "Who do you think you are, some princess?!" I said clearly what you had to do, and what did you do?

"I'm sorry, Elza, at lunchtime I bought lunch for all of us, and he said he'd buy dinner."

"Ah, I see! Again, it's his fault!"

Millie's scar

"No, I'm not saying it's his fault."

"What are you saying then, stupid?" Elza shouted in her face, lifting herself with hands on the table, and getting closer to her. Liam and Pete looked at her, but said nothing, they were silent.

"It's okay, I'll go now and buy some food, the shop is still open." Millie stood up and walked to the door.

"You'll do no such thing, get back here and sit down!"

Millie did not know what to think. She knew she was in the wrong according to the rules of the house, and had to buy something, but now she was confused. She returned to her chair, her eyes on the floor.

"You'll stay hungry tonight to learn that the rules of this house are to be respected!" She let out a blood curdling scream that terrified Millie." Do you understand?!" she yelled.

Millie's heart was beating quickly and loudly. She shuddered. If she had any place to go, she would have immediately left, but before that she would definitely tell this old crone that she was out of her mind.

"All right," she managed to utter.

"Give me all your money! Immediately!" said Elza and hit the table with her fist. The two cups on the table bounced, and the improvised ashtray disgorged its contents all over the table. Elza pushed them back into the ashtray with one swing, and shouted again:

"What did you not understand about staying here?"

Where the hell was Tim? Millie thought, looking for help in the eyes of Liam and Pete, but they stared at the ground and were silent.

"Elza, this is the only money I have, I can't give it to you," Millie mustered the strength to defy Elza.

"Then you can get out of my house right now!"

Millie looked again to Liam and Pete for help, but they did not move. She was just getting warmer, she was very tired, away from

Millie's scar

Liverpool and the hostel, and she had money for a maximum of four overnight stays. Then Tim came in.

"What's going on Elza, who got you angry?" He smiled.

"Tell your tramp that she will give me all her money right now or she can leave my house!" Elza said furiously.

Tim, confused, sat down next to Millie on the chair.

"What happened here?" he asked

"What do you think? You told her not to buy dinner!" Tim looked Millie in the eye, saw her tears, and turned to Elza:

"That's right, I got dinner for everyone, I don't understand what all the commotion is about?"

"Everyone has to buy dinner, that's the rule. As far as I understand, you ate a good lunch with her money. And I eat left overs in the evening. Have you forgotten where you are? Take a good look around!" Elza shouted again, her gaze travelling to every anxious face in the room.

"Don't over dramatize, Elza!" Tim got nervous. "I said there's dinner for everyone."

"Did you buy me lunch then?" She asked.

"No, I did not buy you lunch!" He said irritably.

"Then I want all her money, here on the table, and since you defend her, she either hands it over, or you're both out of here right now!"

Her words were like a hissing snake in Millie's face. She got up, pulled her purse out of her backpack and placed all her money, £56, on the table in front of Elza, saying:

"It's not Tim's fault at all, you don't have to kick him out, here's my money." She sat down again in the chair and swallowed the bitterness and fear as she watched Elza take the last of her money and tuck it into a pocket in her waistcoat and went on:

"Let's move on to the second point. Who do you think is supposed to clean up after you, stupid? Me?" She laughed grimly. "Who do you think you are? You would go ahead and sleep in my

Millie's scar

bed covers, and I am supposed to clean up after you in the middle of the night?"

No, this was too much, Millie thought. She would clean the whole house after she had drunk her tea and warmed up. She had decided it the night before.

"I'll clean everything up today."

"Oh, you'll clean up, yes, but from now on you will be waiting for everyone to go to bed in order to clean up after them." You will not sneak away like some sort of princess and sleep while I clean after you.

Millie wanted to get up and slap her. Why did she believe Timothy's words that she was a good woman? Why had she not trusted her instincts and listened to her own heart? From the very beginning she saw that Elza did not like her. She should not have stayed here. And what now, she had no money, she couldn't run, she couldn't do anything.

"Isn't this enough, Elza?" Tim asked. "We're not here to serve you, what happened to our nice big family?"

"I'll tell you what happened – you brought a slut into my house and it fell apart. You're not here to serve me? Ha!" She shouted. "How long will we feed this good-for-nothing, she may not find a job for half a year?"

"We'll find work for her," he said. "She arrived yesterday, Elza." Tim tried to calm the situation.

"If you do not find a job for her in a week, she's a woman, she can sell her 'services', otherwise, she's out!"

Tim was shocked to the core and Millie just wanted to escape this hell hole. Her whole body was shaking. She couldn't believe how insulting and cruel Elza was being. Then Elza continued:

"What do you think, that she won't do it!" She laughed again maniacally. "Take a good look at her, idiot, she'll do anything to save her own skin, she'd bury us alive in a heartbeat. Look at her!" She shouted, and Tim looked at Millie, tears streaming down her cheeks.

"That's who she is, remember my words, she will use you and survive." Elza shifted her gaze to Millie and said, "You can't fool me with those tears, bitch. But mark my words, from now on you will go to bed last, so you can clear up after everyone else. And because you have not brought water, you will get up early tomorrow to go fetch water and if you do not start bringing dinner after a week, you're out of here."

Millie met Elza's gaze, through the tears her eyes were defiant pools of stone, throwing hatred and disgust at the old, fat woman. Millie wiped her face and began cleaning the house. Meanwhile, the others set the table for dinner. Tim had bought sausages and fried them in a blackened frying pan over the fire. The smell spread through the house and Millie felt hungry as she cleaned the bedrooms on the second floor, tears still spilling from her eyes.

Later, when she came down, everyone had started eating, and they had not called her. She went to her chair and sat down. There was no dish for her. She looked at Elza, who began again: "I found out that you wanted spaghetti, so *my* Tim," she emphasized, " has bought you a box of spaghetti, and since I also want to eat spaghetti, I left them for tomorrow for lunch."

Millie looked with sad and empty eyes, her cheekbones and eyes reddened from the tears, her nose leaking, and she hadn't got a tissue to wipe it. There seemed to be no one in the room that cared for her. There were only shadows. As Elza had stated, she would not have dinner, regardless of the fact that she was terribly hungry and she had polished plates and glasses for the good of the household, all day long. She had handed over all her money, and now she had to wait for everyone to go to bed in order to clean up after them, and even get up before them to bring water from God knows where. She swallowed and tried to get up, but Liam grabbed her hand and pushed her back into the chair. He put his plate with one sausage left and a few potatoes on her knees, put a slice of bread in her hand, got up and slowly left the room.

Millie's scar

Everyone was eating silently. Millie had a hard time swallowing her food and her tears dripped on to the plate, she sat with it on her lap, leaning down so Elza could not see her weakness. Tim and Pete then went up to their room.

Tonight, Millie remembered why she had never fallen in love with Tim in the past. He was a coward.

She waited for Elza to finish her food, cleaned the table, washed the dishes, and went up to her room. Liam wasn't asleep, but he didn't say anything to her. She undressed in the darkness, put on the pyjamas that Fran had bought her, covered herself and began crying silently. Liam waited for Millie to calm down and fall asleep, then he also fell asleep.

"Millie, wake up," Liam said, and put a hand on her shoulder. Millie opened her eyes startled, her heart bounced.

"What time is it?"

"Twenty past six."

"I overslept." She stood up quickly, felt dizzy and sat down abruptly on her mattress. He turned his back on her, heading towards the door.

"I'll show you where we get water from, I'll be waiting downstairs," he said, and closed the door.

Millie put on her jeans and her sweater, smoothed her hair, put on her shoes, and went down. He waited outside, leaning against the fence.

"Thank you for waking me Liam, I would have overslept, and God knows what would have happened then."

Liam smiled broadly.

"What could happen? The old woman will begin shouting and remind us that the house is hers, as if she lets us forget it." He looked at her and saw her smiling slightly, then continued, "I suggest you ignore her, you cannot punish her otherwise," he laughed again, and this time he saw her face relax, and her smile became more sincere.

"I don't know what I did to cause her behaviour yesterday.

"Well, you're probably not the most quick-witted" he joked. "It's clear as day to me. You are a woman, young, beautiful and you're loved by one of us, and she is just old and fat. It's jealousy, pure and simple!"

The two of them burst out laughing and turned towards Queens Road. At the bottom of the street there was a car wash, and beside it a small path that led behind. There was an external water tap on the back of the building. Liam explained that they would usually come late at night after the car wash closed and everyone had gone home. They rarely came in the morning, but if so, made sure that it was very early, so that no one would see them. Millie filled two five litre water bottles, then put them in an old backpack to hide them and returned to the house. Liam continued with the jokes, and this cheered Millie up for a little bit. Even the thought of going back into the house was filling her with dread. She didn't know what she was going to do, but she knew she didn't want to see Elza, but for now it was inevitable. She couldn't figure out how to avoid her, her malicious words, her cruel eyes. She already hated her voice, the way she talked about her as though she wasn't there, calling her a slut and a fool. Millie tried, but couldn't understand how anyone could ignore such insults. When they arrived back, everyone was up and drinking coffee. Liam noticed that Millie did not dare to enter the room and was hanging around the bathroom and the bedroom. He poured her a cup of coffee and shouted cheerfully to break the tension.

"Come on, Millie, coffee's ready!"

She entered the room and looked at him with grateful eyes. He's trying to make the situation better - she thought. Oh, Liam, you sweet boy, I have to try and behave like you, too, to pretend that nothing has happened. To smile, joke around and agree with everything. Millie took her cue from Liam, she would play nice

Millie's scar

until the next time Elza decided to hurl abuse at her, as inevitable as it was shocking.

Before she had barely touched her coffee, Tim and Pete got up and said they were leaving.

By 8:00 they had opened the stall. Tim and Pete hurriedly told her the prices and explained that they had something to do in the garage, and that they would return at noon. Millie saw a chance to ingratiate herself to Elza, if she could make a lot of sales, they would go home with more money and Tim and Pete would praise her in front of Elza. And if there is food, she would be pleased. So, another night in her house would have passed. By 9:00 o'clock people began passing by, there were many stalls and goods for sale. It was very cold, and Millie stood hopping from foot to foot, her hands pushed deep down in her pockets and a hood on her head. At first, she greeted everyone who passed by her stall, but she noticed that either there was no effect or that the greeting drove them away. So she stopped and watched what the other vendors were doing. Mostly they did nothing. Some of them were chatting, others were reading, and some were staring at their phones.

Time moved slowly, at 10:30 there were just a few people, it was, perhaps, too cold for an outdoor Car Boot. Two men stood in front of Millie's stall, but then moved on without buying anything. Millie was beginning to despair, and her worry of going home without money or food was growing in her until it became a permanent hole in her stomach that would not leave her.

At noon Pete and Tim returned. Tim acted as if everything was normal the night before. He showed no sign that he felt sorry for what had happened. This made Millie nervous. She thought that they would talk, that he would calm her fears or give her advice on how to handle Elza, but he simply didn't mention it. She thought of him as a friend, as the man who would help her and protect her. Perhaps it was pointless to rely on his past feelings for her. At least Liam had acknowledged the abuse and tried to raise

Millie's scar

her spirits and help her forget about what had happened. But she had to stay with them, she couldn't avoid the Car Boot, even if it was a failure. The day passed slowly and painfully. Millie could not feel her feet and her hands were extremely painful from the cold. Her head and shoulders were painfully stiff, and her lips were dry and cracked. Her stomach was growling but she did not say a word about that. She assumed that Tim and Pete had eaten, they didn't seem to be hungry. The thought that Tim ate secretly, away from her, that he had not even thought to keep something for her, made her despise him. She imagined in her head ways to escape this house, to flee from Elza and Tim, and all she could think of was to ask for Fran's help. And that was not what she wanted to do. All that remained for her was to hope that she would soon find a job soon.

They returned home having sold a Kilner jar for £2, a pack of cards for £1 pound and an old figurine for £4 pounds. A total of £7. This money had to feed all of them. They bought a loaf of bread, 18 eggs and a piece of cheese. Liam wasn't home when they got back. Pete made an omelette and served it to everyone equally. They sat down at the table and Millie placed her chair away from Tim's chair in the hope that this would please Elza. Perhaps she would see that Millie had no intention of them being a couple and would leave her alone. She was doing everything she could to remain nonchalant, but she couldn't meet Elza's gaze. She tried to make herself as invisible as possible. Tim said:

"It was very cold today."

"I can tell by the dinner," Elza answered.

The rest of the meal was in silence, Millie trying to eat as calmly as possible, controlling her ravenous hunger. Pete asked:

"Is there anything left to drink?"

"No." Elza answered shortly.

They had just finished dinner, and Liam stood with his big smile at the door:

Millie's scar

"Ah, bastards, you didn't wait for me!" He picked up a bag full of food and said, "Whoever is in a hurry will eat ..." he stretched his neck forward, looked at the plates, and finished with a loud voice and a huge smile - "...EGGS"!

All the faces shined, but Millie's the most. Liam filled her eyes and heart with joy. Liam approached the table, left the bag, leaned against the crutches, and sat down while placing them beside Elza's bed. Still, with a smile on his face, he looked at them one at a time and said in laughter

"What are you staring at me for, come on, open!"

Tim stood up and began pulling out of the bag - two bottles of wine, two big pizzas in boxes, the aroma of which filled the room, and a metal takeaway box. Tim began opening it, but Liam reached up, took it and said:

"This is for Millie," and put it in front of her on the table. Millie blushed and a shy smile spread across her face.

"Thank you, Liam, what is that?" Millie leaned forward and opened the box. It was Spaghetti Bolognese. For Millie it was a moment of pure gratitude followed by fear as she quickly glanced at Elza, who was looking at her maliciously, and who asked pointedly:

"What have you brought me, Liam?"

"I haven't forgotten you, grandma," he smiled at her, reaching into his back pocket, pulling out a pack of unopened Amber Leaf rolling tobacco. At the sight of this Elza perked up and she smiled at Liam.

"Oh, Liam, you know how to please me, not with crumbs, but with gold!" She stood up and pinched his cheek.

Millie, still excited by Liam's gesture, was looking at him, hoping their eyes would meet so she could thank him with her eyes, but he had begun an amusing story and everyone watched and listened as they munched on pizza.

Millie watched him as well, listening to his story, observing the ease with which he captivated his audience with his words and

Millie's scar

laughter. That smile. She wanted to be around more people like him, so she decided, tomorrow she would go back to Liverpool to look for a job. She could see that Tim would not help her, he had been enslaved by Elza, she gave him a roof and he did her bidding. Millie was, however, inspired by Liam's optimism, she told herself it was time to take control, find herself a job and get out of this damned house.

Millie saved half the spaghetti for lunch the next day, and when everyone had finished dinner, she cleared the table, washed the dishes, and put logs in the fireplace. She wished everyone goodnight. She went to her room and waited for Liam, in order to thank him. But he did not come. Warm inside the covers, grateful to Liam for the gesture and dinner, and pleased that she had avoided Elza's sharp tongue tonight, she fell asleep.

"How do I know when I have met my true love, Hugh?"

Hugh did not hear her. With small tweezers, he grabbed small screws and, with a tiny screwdriver, screwed them onto a computer board. Millie stood by the door watching him, enchanted by his movements. He selected one more small screw, but it fell. He tried again, but it slipped away. Millie held her breath. He gripped it tightly with the tweezers and placed it in the opening. With the other hand he began to slowly and gently screw it up. Millie waited for him to finish and repeated her question.

"How do I know when I have met my true love, Hugh?"

Suddenly Hugh raised his head. His irises were bloody red. Millie was startled and upset by his appearance.

"I don't have time for stupid questions, Milla."

Something was happening, Millie did not know what, but some tension was floating in the air. She looked around, as if everything was trembling. She again looked at Hugh.

Millie's scar

He abruptly stood up with his hands gripping his desk and shouted with the voice of the devil:
"YOU DON'T HAVE TIME!"

Chapter Eleven

Millie so clearly heard Hugh's monstrous, drawling voice in her ears that she awoke sitting bolt upright, her heart pounding, tears in her eyes, her mouth wide to take a deep breath. Acrid smoke tore at her throat and lungs. She spluttered and coughed. She jumped up and moved to open the window with effort. She swung half her body outside and took another breath. She coughed again. She saw the smoke coming out through the windows below. The house was on fire, a man engulfed in flames was writhing about on the pavement in front of the house. Millie recognized Elza, Pete and Liam, who were all trying to put the fire out, and there were other people some trying to help, some watching in horror. In the distance, she could sirens. Liam bent down and picked up something from the ground and turned with speed to throw it up at Millie's window, then he saw her and tossed the rock to the ground, shouting:

"Jump, Millie, jump!"

Millie saw the flames crawling up the front of the house, and thick black smoke belching upward. The flames were still far away from her, rising to the left above the front door and Elza's room. She took a breath of air and returned to the door, opened it, and immediately closed it. The fire had taken over the stairway and was rapidly approaching her room. The blistering heat hit her face and the smell of burning became unbearable. It made her retch. Everything she touched was greasy. Millie returned to the window, she leaned out and looked at the height and where she would fall. Straight down was onto a brick wall. Dark images of a cracked head or a broken spine passed through her mind. She glanced to the end of the street in the hope that the fire engines would come and save her, but the sirens were still at a distance.

Millie's scar

She frantically looked around the room for something to climb on but there was nothing. She saw her backpack, and stuffed her clothes and phone inside, pulling on her boots and jacket. She took another breath outside the window, her eyes were stinging, and running with tears. She threw her backpack out the window then grabbed Liam's bag, stuffing whatever of his she could find into the bag and threw that out the window too.

Liam shouted again:

"Jump, Millie!" Gathering the fallen things and looking up at her.

She took another breath and pulled herself onto the window ledge. Liam was standing below and staring up at her. Adrenaline coursed through her body, but fear prevailed, and she could not jump from the window ledge. Her whole being screamed, "Do not jump!" The burning man on the pavement was still. They had stopped the flames, but smoke came from his clothes, and he did not move. Millie struggled to control her thoughts, how should she jump, facing forward or with her back. She had to overcome the fear. To be burned alive was a more cruel death than falling from a height. Liam called two men who stood under the window, and one of them shouted:

"Jump, we'll catch you, jump now, there's no time!"

As the flames licked the building, ever closer to where Millie trembled on the ledge, she felt her feet and hands beginning to burn. She glanced toward the sky, there were stars, she said quietly:

"God, help me!" She turned onto her stomach on the ledge, inching away from the heat until she was hanging by her fingertips. She closed her eyes and let go. The men caught her, and all of them fell together. They got up quickly and moved away from the burning building.

Liam came to her with frightened eyes.

"Are you all right, Millie, I called your name for ten minutes, but you didn't hear me."

Millie's scar

Millie was coughing, her throat felt raw and she voice was a whisper.

"What happened, Liam, why is the house burning, and who is this man?" She was looking at the charred body on the ground, continuing to cough. Elza turned, took two steps towards Millie, and grabbed her by her hair and knocked her down next to the charred body, screaming:

"Look what you did, you wretch! I'll be damned, because I took you into my house! Foolish woman, you've killed Tim, you've destroyed my house! You've destroyed my life. Damn you to hell!" She did not stop pulling her head and screaming, bent over her.

Millie did not understand anything, hurt by the pulling, she was coughing, and she had no air. She was trying to get rid of Elza's grip. What had happened? How could she have caused the fire when she was asleep?

Liam grabbed Elza's hand and screamed:

"Let her go, Elza, it's not her fault!"

Elza began to push her even more fiercely. Liam lost his balance and dropped one of his crutches, leaned in and grabbed it. Elza tried to drag Millie on the ground, but Liam poked her into the ribs with his crutch, and she lost her balance, letting go of Millie.

"Did she turn your head as well, idiot? Didn't I tell you she'd bring trouble to us all? Idiots!"

The fire engines were turning into the street at speed and with blaring sirens. The noise was deafening, and the lights disorientated Millie. She lifted her gaze toward the house, flames had engulfed the ledge of her window. Then she looked at Tim's charred body and felt a deep sorrow for him. All she could see was his back, no one went near him and the ambulance hadn't arrived yet. Pete stared into space next to Tim's body, he was sitting on the ground, the flashing blue lights reflected in his face, wet with tears. Millie stood up. They all moved aside to make

Millie's scar

room for the trucks. Her eyes looked for Liam, he was behind her, he grabbed her elbow, and pulled her away from Elza, took her backpack from his back and handed it to her. About a dozen firefighters jumped off the trucks and began issuing orders. One of them went to Tim and squatted beside him, speaking gently to Pete. Liam took his bag from the ground and attached it to one of his crutches. A large ladder began to automatically rise from one truck. The other truck moved into position and its ladder also began to rise. The firemen moved the crowd about 20 metres away from the burning building. As everyone walked toward the end of the street, the firefighters began to extinguish the fire. Millie listened to Liam explain what had happened as they shuffled slowly away from the house. He spoke in a trembling voice, his eyes wide.

"We drank the wine and decided to go to bed, the fire in the fireplace was blazing, and Tim moved the logs to lessen the flames and make it safe to leave."

An ambulance turned into the street with the same deafening sound and stopped a few feet from Tim. One paramedic ran to where he lay on the pavement, and a second brought out a trolley, and took it to Tim. They put a blanket on the ground and rolled Tim over on to it. They picked him up with the blanket, placed him on the trolley and into the ambulance, and left again at speed, with the sirens blaring. Millie looked around and spotted Elza across the road talking to a woman. Then Liam went on:

"Tim raked the fire with the poker, I did not see exactly what happened, I was still at the table with my back to the fireplace. Pete said that Tim had spilt gasoline on himself while he filled the lamp earlier and that when he raked the fire a spark caught him. He began burning, and Elza threw her blanket on him to quench it. But the blanket was synthetic and turned him into a torch. The blanket stuck to him and he screamed as we all tried to pull it off him, but the melting blanket dropped molten fire everywhere and we took him outside. I was sure you had heard us. Tim was

Millie's scar

screaming so loudly, it was horrible Millie, I can't believe you didn't hear him."

Millie shook her head, walked slowly with him, and stared at the ground, her eyes horrified from the story and her mouth open.

As we tried to put out the flames on Tim, the fire took over the staircase, so I started calling from below to wake you up, but you still didn't respond. I decided to break the window to wake you up, to give you air, but then I saw you.

"My God, Elza is right, it's my fault, I built the fire up before I went to bed, I put more logs on because of her, so she would be warm, to get on her good side." If she hadn't put the extra logs on the fire this may not have happened. Millie placed her head in her hands and cried.

"You are not to blame, I have also put wood on the fire many, many times, and the house has not burnt down. What happened was just terrible luck. If Tim hadn't spilt gasoline on himself, the spark wouldn't have caught, and if the blanket had been wool, he would not have lit up like a torch.

They sat on one of the walls and stared at the house. Most people had returned to their homes. Elza was still standing on the other side of the pavement talking to the kind woman. She glanced at them several times and pointed towards them.

Extinguishing the fire seemed to take a very long time. One of the firefighters went to Elza and talked to her briefly. She nodded, holding her hand in front of her mouth, then began to cry.

"Millie, do you have anywhere else to go?" asked Liam.

She shook her head slowly, staring at the crack in a slab on the pavement. Then she asked him:

"What about you?"

"Me too, but we have to get out of here." There's nothing we can do here. Elza will kill you when everyone leaves.

"How will I live with this Liam? What happened to Tim is my fault, to the house, and even to you. How will I live with this?"

"It's not your fault, and now is not the time to talk about this. It's better to get out of here."

Millie lifted her eyes, looked at him, tracking his gaze. He was watching Elza, who looked crushed, weeping on the shoulder of a woman, and another one was trying to comfort her. Millie stared at her with teary eyes. Yes, Elza had been horrible to her, but she did not deserve to lose her house and be homeless at her age. She remembered her story about how luck had helped her get back her home which was taken from her. That luck would appear to have run dry. She felt a weight in her chest, it seemed to her that her heart and soul fell silent. Whatever she touched, everything was destroyed. Tim probably lost his life, and three people were left homeless because of her. Because of her desire to get on Elza's good side. "You're a hypocrite!" thought Millie, hating herself. Liam continued:

"I know Elza well. You have to get out of here, because when the shock passes and she regains her strength, all her wrath and grief will be directed at you.

Millie felt she deserved Elza's anger.

"And you? What are you going to do?" Millie asked him.

He looked away from Elza and said:

"I'll take you to a place I know for the night, for starters."

Millie got up from the fence, still in shock, and the walked silently into the night.

The first bus to Liverpool wasn't due for 3 hours. They decided to wait and go to Liverpool anyway, neither of them felt like sleeping, even if they found a suitable place. They sat at the bus stop in front of the only 24-hour shop. Liam bought them two coffees.

"There is a building site in Liverpool, not too far from the centre. I know the night security guard there, we're old friends, he'll let us shelter there. It has windows and it's not as cold as outside. We'll have to find blankets and some mattresses," Liam said, staring thoughtfully somewhere in front of him.

Millie's scar

Millie did not answer, just nodded. She was thinking of Tim, whether he would live and what his life would be like. Suffering until his last day, she was sure. They should go to the hospital and find out whether he was alive, and if not, when and where would they bury him. His mother would find out he was not a priest. Millie groaned at the memory of the frenzied and shattered woman who had buried her husband first, and now would have to say farewell to her only son. What would she say to her if they ever met - she would never have the strength to admit her guilt to her. Whatever Liam was saying, Millie knew it was her fault. She knew it, because while putting the logs in the fireplace, her thoughts had been selfish, hoping Elza would see how she was taking care of her.

Liam told her it was an unfortunate accident, but she had wanted only peace for herself with Elza,, she thought she could appease her with small, everyday gestures. She could not blame the gasoline or the blanket, she blamed only herself for her selfishness. Millie had thought Tim a coward, but she was the coward. She was selfish, she thought she was Elza's victim and had accused him of not defending her but how could he defend her? What was the benefit of Elza driving both of them out? No, he did the right thing, he intervened mildly so that they did not end up on the street. He did not keep silent as Pete and Liam had, but intervened. And what did Millie do? She despised him for not being her knight in shining armor. Then she despised him because she was hungry and believed he had eaten in secret, which probably didn't happen. The more she thought about it all, the more she was ashamed of herself. The guilt was eating at her soul and digging into the little self-esteem she had left. Her life had spiralled out of control, in short, she had no home, no money, no Bella, no dignity, parents who didn't care about her, she had caused a man's death, a man she had cared about. Tim, who had tried to care for her, had died and his essence had

Millie's scar

soaked into her clothes, her skin, her hair. She had lost everything. All she had was Liam. It was better to die than to destroy him, as well. She was afraid he might leave her. She stood up, took her jeans and sweater from her backpack and said:

"I'll hide somewhere to change clothes," and she pointed at the pyjamas she was still wearing.

Then she came back and lit a cigarette. It was getting lighter, and soon the bus would come.

An hour and a half later they were standing in front of the building site, and Liam was talking to Alex.

"Very bad situation, dude!" Alex agreed, after listening to his story. "I can help you, but from 6:30 in the morning to 19:00 in the evening you need to be gone from here, there are workers, and if they find out that I'm letting you in, I'll lose my job.

"Yes, my friend, we won't give you away, I promise." Liam said. "We'll come tonight after 7:00. Just one more question, is there anything to lie on? Everything we had was destroyed in the fire."

"There are wooden pallets and many boxes, just find some blankets because it's cold at night. Oh, I remember, there's also insulation wadding, you'll be fine" Alex smiled. "But in the morning, you must leave it as you found it, as if you were not there."

"Yes, of course. Thank you, and we'll look for another place to sleep in the future, not to bother you. Thank you again!" They warmly shook hands.

"Okay guys, go now, because my relief will be here any minute."

"Bye and thank you!" Millie said, holding up her hand in gratitude.

They headed for the city centre where Liam usually begged.

"Millie, you can't stay with me while I'm working, I'll make less money if you're with me." He smiled gently at her.

"All right, Liam, I'll look for work, and at half 6, I'll come and find you."

Millie's scar

"Cool." Liam reached into his pocket and gave Millie £2. "Get yourself something to eat."

"Thank you!" She said, and took the coins from his hands, up to her neck in shame.

They parted near the quay.

It was still early, Millie sat on a bench. The wind was blowing. There was a clothes store opposite her and she looked at her reflection in the window. Her hair was oily and specked with ash, she had ash smuts on her face and clothes and everything she wore felt itchy. She desperately needed a shower and a washing machine. The sweater that Fran had given her for Christmas was dirty and stained, the sleeves blackened. Her jeans smelt bad. She craved a bath and to put on clean underwear and clothes. She decided to go around the shopping centre toilets. In the baby changing rooms there were sinks, and hot water. She wouldn't be able to bathe, but at least she could wash parts of her body and hair, wash her underclothes, and then use the hand dryers to dry herself. This thought motivated her and she decided to find a shopping centre while it was still quiet.

She found exactly what she was looking for. A large spacious room with a nursing chair, a wash handbasin with hot water and liquid soap, there was also a hand dryer, and a plug. She pulled her things out of her backpack, she had a hair dryer and a tiny towel. It took her nearly half an hour to wash herself thoroughly, wash and dry her hair and scrub her dirty clothes. Everything smelt of smoke. She scrubbed her sweater but could only partially dry it, she'd have to attend to it later. By the time she had finished she was tired and sat in the chair and nodded off. When she awoke it was past noon and she felt refreshed, and more human. No one had disturbed her, and she would remember this place if she needed to come here in future. She felt she was presentable enough to look for work.

At half past 6 she went looking for Liam.

Millie's scar

"Look what I found," he patted a bag beside him on the ground. Millie looked inside.

"Blankets?"

"Sleeping bags, from a charity, very cheap, 4 quid each."

Millie had forgotten that they needed blankets, but Liam had not. He was a smart and responsible young man.

"Do you want to get a Maccy D?" He asked her.

"Whatever you want, Liam." Millie felt uncomfortable that Liam bought her food and added, "Look, as soon as I start a job, I'll repay you."

Liam laughed, patted her on the shoulder and joked:

"Should I keep the receipts?"

Millie blushed, and added quietly,

"I'm serious."

"Did you have a shower?"

"Almost," she grinned, telling him what she had done.

"There is another option, at the leisure centre. There's a coffee shop inside, if you tell the receptionist you're just going for a coffee, they let you in. Just wait for a queue to gather and for the receptionist to be busy and then go down the stairs to the pool. There are four cubicles with showers, unlimited hot water and at least fifty changing rooms. The only thing missing is shampoo, soap and towels."

"When can we go there?" Millie lit up.

"Tomorrow, if you want, during the day. Iit's open in the evening but there are more staff and it's much busier, more difficult to get into the showers."

They bought two double cheeseburgers with fries. They decided they would eat at the building site and headed there.

Alex showed them the room closest to the pallets, the boxes and the insulation wadding, and left them. It was dark, there was no electricity in the building, and they didn't have a light between them. The buildings around were all offices and they were already dark. A dim street light illuminated the room and they could see their silhouettes.

"Do you want to sleep together to keep warm Millie? I promise I won't touch you." He said and raised his hand in a mock oath.

"It had crossed my mind, but I didn't know how you would take it?"

They laughed shyly.

"Since we are officially co-habiting, it's best to be honest from the start, makes life easier for both of us," Liam grinned, leaning against the wall, and with only one crutch. Millie arranged the pallets together to form a bed. She lay a few flattened boxes over the top and said:

"It seemed a bit forward on our first night!!" she laughed, then went on. "I think we're going to get along."

Liam smiled.

Millie put the wadding on top, but it slid off the boxes and so they decided to use it only for pillows. Liam crouched, leaning against the crutch, sat on the improvised bed, and they started eating.

"What did you do today?" He asked her as he devoured his burger.

"Aside from my attempts at bathing," she laughed, "I went to several places looking for a job. I think I might have a chance in this one cafe. The manager seemed to like me very much, she said she had to wait another couple of days and then she'll call me. I'm really hopeful."

"It will happen Millie, even if it's not this one, you'll find a job at another place, there's no reason that shouldn't happen for you. You're young, you're, er, healthy" he stumbled over the words looking embarrassed, "Why would they not hire you?"

"Yes, there's no reason I can think of, but I've been here for over a week now and I've been to a lot of places and nobody calls back.".

Millie's scar

"That's no time at all, be patient, they'll call you soon."

"When I get my first wages, I'll look for a place, do you want us to live together there?"

"Ha-ha-ha," he laughed, "shouldn't we get married first?" Then they both laughed.

"I've never lived like this, Liam, I do not want to live like this," Millie said, wiping the tears of laughter from her face.

"Okay, you convinced me, I'll live with you if you serve me faithfully," he continued laughing and joking with her.

"Oh, OK, Mr Joker, then I will look for an apartment on the fifth floor, without a lift. Liam was about to spit out his fries from laughter. Their jokes continued for an hour and then they lay down, exhausted. A little later he fell asleep.

Chapter Twelve

The bed of pallets was extremely hard, it was as if she was sleeping on concrete. Whatever way she turned it was uncomfortable. She thought of Liam, of his cheerfulness. Where did it come from? How could a person live like this for years and be happy? She felt that their views diverged in this respect. She did not want to spend another night at this building site, although she was glad she wasn't sleeping on the street. But it was a building without electricity, water, furniture and she was sleeping on pallets and boxes in freezing conditions. She had never imagined anything like this happening to her. Whenever she saw homeless people on the streets, she thought that they had chosen their destiny, or at least done something to make them outcasts from society. She did not understand many things about their behaviour. Why were they dirty? Why were they constantly drinking? Why did they not do more to improve their circumstances? She knew she would do anything to get away and knew it would happen sooner or later. She would not stop fighting. She did not want and would not live such a life. If she could not get her life back on an even keel, and quickly, she knew it would destroy her. She knew she would not be able to accept this defeat and feared for her mental stability. She remembered when she was a little girl, she would lie in bed and ponder on what her future might be. She would think about all the possibilities. Her favourite adventure was travelling around the world on foot, she laughed at this insane childhood dream, she still wanted to travel, but certainly not on foot.

She feared losing her grip on what 'normal' was and drifting into mental illness. She did not find anything scarier than this. It had happened to her in times of great anxiety. And it scared her very much. Two or three times in her life, but felt she was losing her grip, so felt she must regain her equilibrium.

So, she determined in her head, as she lay awake, she did not want to live that way. She had to do her best to get away. She had seen enough bad things in her life, and she did not want to accept anymore. She was certainly not a spoilt girl, life had never pampered her, but she wanted a safe, warm place that was hers. Safe from Cloudy and Greg and Elza.

She stared into the dark and thought how her life had spiralled out of control. She thought if it weren't for Liam, she'd have eaten nothing for the last three days. First, he'd defied Elza to give her his sausage and potatoes, then he'd bought her spaghetti, and today he fed her again, twice. If not for him, she'd be sleeping on a freezing bench, alone, scared and hungry. She knew without his help she'd have no way of looking or feeling presentable enough to get a job. Without him, she'd have had to resort to putting Fran in danger or stealing food to survive and life would have reached rock bottom.

She needed Liam's help, not only to feed her, but he also gave her comfort. In his presence, nothing was as bad, she didn't dwell on her problems, she felt safe, lighter. She did not feel alone in this ordeal. As if his mere presence stopped time and the problems temporarily disappeared. He also made her laugh. She turned her face towards him and looked at him. Her eyes had grown accustomed to the darkness, and she could clearly see his face. He had a beautiful face. He also had charm and charisma. He would never have been in this state if he wasn't an invalid, she thought. He must buy a prosthesis and succeed in life. Or at least live a dignified life without begging on the streets.

In the morning, Alex woke them up at 6am, they returned all the pallets and boxes to their places and left. They agreed that Millie would meet Liam at lunchtime so they could eat together and then go to the leisure centre. She walked through the streets scouring shop windows for vacancy notices or just asking on the off chance if they might need staff. It was the middle of January and temperatures around 0 were normal during the day. It was tolerable if you stayed outside for a short time, but not walking around the city all day. Millie was angry and felt frustrated that her searching had yielded nothing. This was the second day that she wondered where to go to warm up. She wanted to drink coffee in a warm cafe, staring at the people outside, but now this was a luxury. The small backpack, which only contained a change of clothes, pyjamas and small stuff, felt heavy. It was constantly on her back. The feeling that she could not go home when she wished made her hate the situation she was in even more. Not only did she not have a home, she did not even have a room at the building site to get home to and get some rest. She could not take her shoes off all day, even at the site, because of the concrete, unless she lay down. She wanted to take a warm shower before bed, brush her teeth, cut her nails and file them into a nice shape. She had nothing to cut them with and was forced to tear them with teeth. These are all small issues, a patient with an incurable disease would say, Millie scolded herself, thinking of Tim. Small issues, but gathered together, they made her life grim and depressing. Things she had taken for granted before, which had now become a longing and a measure of a good life.

There was nowhere to go anymore, she had travelled around half the city. The other half was residential with hardly any restaurants or shops. After everything that had happened to her, she dreamed of finding a job in a small trailer. So small that no one would see her face when they bought something. She imagined it with a high, small window. She wanted to hide from people, not to be in front of them all day. She wanted to be alone, to be able to take off her shoes. Not to have to lie to colleagues about where she lived as she was too ashamed to tell them she was homeless. Her self-esteem had evaporated, and she needed to hide from the world. A small trailer, and inside it, Millie. That's

Millie's scar

what she wanted. Quietness and solitude until she could collect the scattered parts of herself. And not to talk to anyone. Solitude.

She went to meet Liam excitedly thinking of the hot shower she would take.

Everything happened exactly as he said. They waited a bit and went down to the showers at the pool. Millie turned on the stream of hot water, wanted to feel her body warm up, realizing sadly that she couldn't come here every day. Liam had bought body and hair gel and said to her:

"You first, don't rush, take as long as you want, I'll be here waiting."

Millie luxuriated under hot water, letting it run over her face and feeling the warmth. She could hear children's voices, excited by the games in the pool, and parents yelling at them.

After twenty minutes she came out clean and damp, having used only her tiny towel. Liam went in after her and showered as she dried her hair in the changing room.

They split up and Millie decided to go to the hospital. She thought she'd try to see Tim, and find out what his condition was, but she could not find the strength. It was a 20-minute walk and on the way she decided to light her last cigarette and call Fran. She found the conversation difficult as she couldn't tell Fran the truth about how bad her situation was. If she had, Fran would have insisted she returned to Bath, saying, "I'm sure if our positions were reversed, you'd do the same for me." And, of course, she was right. She told her that Greg and Cloudy were no longer a threat, so Millie would not be putting her at risk, and if she would only return, she could help her start her new life sooner. This suffering is unnecessary and so causes her to suffer as well. And maybe she was right. As far as the police and the court were concerned, Greg and Cloudy are criminals with a past. Millie wanted to believe that they wouldn't pursue her as it would land them in prison. Perhaps they have given up looking for her, but she couldn't be sure. There was also another reason Millie did not want to go back to Bath. She was 27 years old and she had to learn to live this life with all its ups and downs.

The realisation of what she had lost began to hit Millie. Events had put her on the street, and no matter how hard it was for her, she had to avoid running away again. She had to deal with it. After everything that happened to her, above all she wanted to deal with it in with as much grit as possible. By persisting, by not giving up, by not losing the battle. That's why the path to Fran was closed, not because she wanted to make life difficult for herself, but because she knew it would make her stronger. She knew that when she lay down on the hard pallets tonight, she would dream of Fran's warm, soft, fragrant bed, but what would she one day think of all this? They raped me and I ran away to Fran, then I ran away from her and maybe killed a man who'd loved me all his life? Then, when I found myself on the street, I ran back to Fran again, because it was the easy option, no matter what danger she would put Fran in. If anything happened to Fran, that would crush her. She saw that a small movement, a placement of wood in the fire, to soften someone's hatered, had destroyed a life. A life that could have been wonderful. Tim could have one day moved forward, had children, a career, he could have been happy. He could have, but no longer. That night she learned a bitter lesson. She had to think about every decision. She couldn't explain this to Fran, so she would just lie to her, and she was sure she would not be ashamed of that lie.

"Hello Fran, how are you?"

"Hey, Millie, I was just about to ring you. This morning, before work, a girl called Dariya phoned me?" Millie felt her stomach drop with fear. "I immediately felt that there was something wrong so I just listened to what she had to say. Oh, hang on." Millie heard voices in the background, and then the closing of a door. "She pretended to be very worried about you, but I knew no one knew where you were. How could she know about me,

Millie's scar

and let alone have my phone number? So while she was telling me she was a friend of yours, and very concerned about you, I made up a quick story."

"What did you tell her Fran?"

"I told her that you went to visit a girlfriend in Lisbon. I told her how you sent me a postcard and how you told me you loved the wonderful weather and the crazy Portuguese. After a long pause, she asked me if I were sure, and I told her: "Of course, I saw her off from Bristol Airport." She asked if I knew when you would return, and I said you'd had some trouble in your life recently and wanted to get away. Life there was calm, sunny and you'd just found yourself a job, so I thought you would stay." I said it was lovely for me to have a friend somewhere warm to visit. At that point she hung up on me. I hope I did the right thing Millie?"

"Oh, Fran, I don't know what to say, thank you." Millie fought back the tears as relief flooded her body. "Yes, I hoped I'd done well. Anyway, you're now free. Now, tell me how are you? What's going on with you? Did you start work? Where do you live?"

"Everything is fine with me, things are happening slowly, but it's a new place, and it's to be expected. I'm fine, I started work yesterday in a small cafe, it's shifts, working with another girl. The pay isn't great, but it's fine for a first job." She took a drag of her cigarette for the last time, tossed it to the ground, stepped on it, and continued, "I'm living in a shared house with three more girls and a boy. It's fine, I don't complain, it's a bit cramped but they're friendly enough."

"Okay, when are you going to tell me where you are? I don't think there's any more danger for me or for you."

"I'll tell you soon, I promise."

"But why do you hide it from me, I do not understand, don't you trust me?"

"Of course I trust you, it's just ... look, I've been through some terrible things, I just want to stay by myself for a while and incognito. I don't want to take any risks Fran. I just need to do

Millie's scar

this. Give it some time and I'll tell you where I am, and you can even come and visit me if you want, okay?"

"It's not okay, but it's your decision and I will respect it Millie. Listen, I have to go now, I have a lot of work to do."

"Bye, I love you, Fran! Thank you for everything!"

"I love you too, Millie!"

Millie could see the hospital now.

"Hello, I would like to visit a patient of yours, his name is Tim Clark." Millie said in a whisper, leaning down to the receptionist.

"One moment, please," the phone rang, and the woman held a brief conversation, then asked, "What was the name again?"

"Tim Clark."

"Are you a relative?"

"Friend." Said Millie quietly

"Ah, yes, Mr. Clark. He's not with us anymore I'm afraid, he's been taken to the Acute Burns Unit at Southmead Hospital in Bristol to be closer to his family."

"Can you tell me how he is please?"

The woman hurriedly searched in the computer in front of her. She had a lot of work to do, as was evident from the papers she had arranged on her desk.

"I'm sorry, but you'll have to ring the hospital or his family, we can't give you any clinical information."

The receptionist looked at the tears rolling down Millie's face and said "He wasn't doing well, but everything remains in God's hands, pray for him." She patted her hand gently and went back to her pile of papers.

"Thank you," Millie said, turned around and left. To pray for him - as if Tim had told her so - she thought. It seemed to her that it was not a coincidence, even though it was likely that all the friends and relatives of severely injured people were being told that by way of generalised comfort. But somehow, Tim and God, they were connected. She decided this was what she would do.

Millie's scar

She would go to church and pray for him. She just did not know what to pray for. For him to survive or to be put out of his misery. She decided she would pray for his survival.

She entered the first church she saw and stayed inside for three hours in prayer. For Tim, for herself, for Liam. She prayed for mercy and for forgiveness. She came out with eyes red from crying. It was her most genuine period of prayer ever.

She and Liam went back to the construction site and she told him about Tim. He had bought tea lights so they didn't have to sit in the dark. Both were extremely careful with them. Liam watched Millie in the flickering, golden light and thought how beautiful she was, and so sad. Under different circumstances, he would indulge his desire for her, he would have tried his luck, but he felt a tenderness towards her that made him go slowly. He wanted to protect her and love her, gently and truly. The connection they had was strong and he wanted to make sure she felt it too. When she suffered, he suffered, he felt every tear. He wanted her close, beloved, cherished.

Chapter Thirteen

"I'm so sorry, Liam, I did what I could. You've slept here for three weeks, but after my colleague made a call, I can't let you stay anymore. I hope you find some place. I was on edge all night long, that the inspectors would sack me on the spot."

"It's okay, Alex, thank you, you've helped us a lot, we'll be fine," Liam smiled, but inside he was worried. It was not easy to find a place to sleep at this time of year.

"Yes, Alex, you've been very kind, thank you." Millie said.

"I feel bad, but you know, I have a kid, I can't risk my job. I'm really sorry."

"It's okay, man, don't worry, we'll be fine. Watch yourself now. I appreciate everything you did for us," Liam said again jovially to ease any sense of guilt, then went on. "Okay, come by and see me some time, you know where I am, I'll be glad to see you, to have a chat over a beer."

"Agreed, maybe in a few weeks," Alex replied.

"Whenever!" Liam winked at him and they left.

Alex's colleague from another construction site had rung to say that there had been a spot inspection in the early hours. He was on edge all night that he would be next. He waited until 5:30, then woke them. They put everything back into place and left. They were both very tired, the cold and the hard pallets made sleep fitful. They both ached from the hard surface, from the cold and from walking endlessly during the day. The general fatigue they both felt made them skittish and grumpy, but they never took their bad mood out on each other. On the contrary, they were both trying to make their everyday life as comfortable as possible. When one of them started to complain about the harsh conditions, the other one made a joke to ease any self pity. Millie

Millie's scar

now knew why Liam was constantly laughing, it was not from happiness, he had learned to turn everything into irony, and tried very hard not to take himself too seriously. In this way his life was a little bit more acceptable. In comparison to the other homeless people, Liam looked as if he came from another world. And she was glad that she had stumbled upon him in this situation. The life she was leading now, with anyone else or by herself, would have been unbearable. Liam was her friend, her companion and her talisman. Millie managed to find a job for two hours on Friday and Saturday at noon in a small but busy restaurant. She was peeling potatoes, onions, avocados and carrots. She carried cooked meals into the hall, she did general cleaning, she washed dishes. Whatever the need was. They had promised her that if they were satisfied with her, they would hire her from Monday to Saturday, but only at noon for 2 hours. So she worked as hard as she could. The pay was £8.75 per hour, she would earn £35 for four hours, and if she was hired for the whole week, she would earn £105. Too little to pay rent, but maybe she could save money for a deposit and rent a room. Soon, the weather would get warmer and things would sort themselves out, as she kept saying over and over in her mind. She would also find another job, and life would again become more acceptable, gentler. £35 a week for now was too little money, but it was enough to eat and for her to not entirely depend on Liam, even for purely feminine needs.

On the day Millie found the job they decided to celebrate. It was unusually warm for February, and they bought beer and crisps and drank on a bench next to the harbour. Giddy from the beer, they then bought a bottle of rum and. They sat there as it grew dark, the alcohol loosening their lips and they admitted how happy they were to have found each other. They admitted they liked each other very much, then promised that they would never ruin such a friendship with sex. Alone at last they shared the most passionate and gentle love that they had ever made. They would remember that night until their last breath. The memory of it would make them long for one another and ask themselves why they could not experience the same with anyone else. Perhaps the long absence of tenderness, love, closeness brought out of them the most real and fragile manifestation of love. Or maybe they really were soulmates, Liam wondered. In the morning they were completely sober, but charmed by what had happened, and promised that whatever happened between them, they would do their best to preserve themselves as the best male and female friends in history. Nothing had changed. Their life was still inconvenient, hard and gloomy. But they found enchantment in one another, masking the ugly face of reality. Millie saw that others had done it with drugs, alcohol, and fantasizing, but they did it with love.

During these three weeks, Millie watched the homeless people. Not everyone had resigned themselves to this life. A big portion of them were people who had ended up there and could not get out, but fought for an escape. People with bad destinies. Hated, rejected, forgotten by their loved ones. Sick, dirty, frozen, wrapped in everything they had and huddled on the pavement. Unable to eat because they did not have teeth, cripples and orphans. And worst of all, the most degraded vagrants led the parade. The drug addicts and alcoholics. They did not want to leave this cruel world, they felt strong. Most of them had a normal life once, but they had lost it through addiction. Millie hated drug addicts. In general, they seemed quiet, but they were scarily unpredictable. At any moment they could decide to do something brutal, such was the nature of their cravings. They were followed by the alcoholics who were openly aggressive. But the most downtrodden were those with mental health issues. They did not understand what was happening at all. They usually served as entertainment for the alcoholics. They did all the dirty work, and endured abominable mockery. Millie would never forget how one

Millie's scar

night she saw a boy with Down's syndrome, cleaning up after an alcoholic who'd just taken a shit on the pavement. The others were laughing their heads off. Millie felt the most sorry for this boy. He was a good guy, she saw him crying several times. She felt sorry for all the other people who did not belong to any of the three groups. They were horrified and shocked by everything they saw and experienced. They were like her, ending up there simply by luck and bad experiences. Each of them had a hard and painful story. A story filled with hatred. Hatred of those who passed by them and who thought it could never happen to them. Liam told her about the fate of several of them. They were normal people, there were college graduates, working people, once with families, homes, careers and worthy struggles behind them. They could not always bear this reality they had found themselves in. Some of them had struggled, but they had lost. Others had surrendered before they ever thought of struggling and waited for their happy day. What kept them going was the thought of one day finding their 'home'. Stark reality had darkened and gripped the mind just like a spider entombing its victim, watching it struggle. Something more than a strong spirit was needed. What was required was endless perseverance and strength to bear the darkness around and within themselves. Silently and without stepping back from the goal, to gain their freedom. The horror of their thoughts was visible when they were alone with themselves.

Millie and Liam were different. They loved each other as if they had felt that love for their entire lives. They kept themselves to themselves. If they felt cold, they wrapped themselves in dirty blankets on the street or they would go somewhere to warm themselves for a little bit. They were allowed everywhere because they looked like normal people. They bathed and washed themselves at least twice a week. They avoided contact with the homeless as much as possible, but despite their efforts, communication with them was unavoidable. They were a part of that desperate community, no matter how much they tried to distinguish themselves. They saw Liam begging every day, they knew who he was, knowing his destiny and being annoyed that he had a girl and that he was distancing himself from them. And now, when there was nowhere to sleep, they would have to seek shelter with them.

"One of our options is to spend the night at the Labre House night hub. You will not like it, we will still have to sleep on the floor, they give you yoga mats and everyone is crammed into one room," he laughed, although he did not find it funny at all, then went on, "but there is breakfast there and showers, laundry, computers."

"There are computers, but no beds?" Millie looked at him, puzzled.

"Yes," he continued laughing.

"Any other options? And, please, stop laughing, "she said, smiling.

"There are several homeless centers, where they can accommodate us for one or two nights. We cannot sleep on the street. First, we'll freeze to death, then either we'll get robbed, beaten up, or arrested, or all three. The final option is a hostel, £19 per night, it will clean us out"

Liam was right, the option of sleeping on the sand or asphalt in February, waiting to get robbed, beaten or arrested was unthinkable.

"Alright, I have £10, how much do you have?" Let's sleep in a bed for at least one night, and tomorrow we'll think again. The day after tomorrow I'll get £17.50 from work.

"Okay, but I have to warn you that these hostels are sometimes harder than the street. There are beds, you are alone in the room, there are showers, but it is full of drug addicts and crazy people. We might not get any sleep, on a bad night they scream and shout, beat each other up, vomit everywhere. It can be terrible."

Millie's scar

"I don't care Liam, let's give it a go, at least we can have a warm shower and sleep in beds for as long as we need. This sleeping for only an hour has exhausted me. I'm falling apart, my entire body is hurting, I don't want to sleep on the ground again."

"Don't say I didn't warn you," Liam said, leaning forward and kissing her lips. He would agree to anything as long as it was what she wanted. He had lived on the street for 12 years. He had seen a lot, he had slept in all sorts of places.

They went to McDonald's, drank coffee and agreed that she would go to City B&B hostel and check in as early as possible at 2pm, she would try and get some sleep. He would beg until 17:30 and would meet her at the hostel after that.

Millie found the hostel easily, located beside the Mercy River and the Kingsway Tunnel, and she rented a room. The hostel seemed decent at this hour. How much worse could it get? Millie asked herself.

Millie then went back to church. She went every day, ever since she did it the first time. She felt relaxed there. Rarely did she have to share the space and it was warmer than outside. She prayed for Tim every day. For his salvation, for his pain to stop, for his sins to be forgiven; him leaving the church and lying to his mother. She prayed that the Lord would forgive her too. She was praying for the strength to get her life back on track and for her and Liam to live a normal life, like everyone else. She imagined him already with a prosthesis. She imagined his happiness when he would have the prosthesis and could walk by himself and without crutches. She imagined that they would both find jobs, and they would have dinner in front of a warm fireplace. She imagined that she would light it on every winter night. They would initially live in a room, but then, when they had saved some money, they would get a house with a garden. One day we will have children. "A boy and a girl – perfect" she said to herself. Liam mentioned that they could sign up for a government assistance program. Someone would meet with them every week. He said it was for

Millie's scar

drug addicts and alcoholics, but she hoped it was for everyone who was in difficulty. She would question him later today in detail, so she could go and sign up. They might be able to help with finding jobs and affordable housing. It was the most important thing, if they found work, they would be able to get a place to live.

She sat for a little while in the church, she bought a dinner that consisted of pitta bread, lamb kofta and coleslaw. She also bought cheap beer. They would relax tonight. It was over a month since she had found her job and they had had a drink together. She sat on a bench waiting for two o'clock. She dreamt of them settling into the hostel, taking a shower and spending the rest of the day and night in a soft, warm bed, wrapped in each others arms.

Liam had bought her tobacco and papers and she learnt how to make her own cigarettes. She didn't smoke much, because the tobacco was strong and she made one packet last over a week and a half.

As 2pm precisely, she checked into a very small room with two beds, which she pushed tightly together. The beds had springs, Millie sighed, lay down and let her body sink into the softness. She lay there looking at the cracked and peeling ceiling, took a deep breath, then got up, unloaded the luggage, put the koftas on the radiator to warm them up a little for dinner, and she put the beers on the window sill to chill them. She plugged in her phone to charge it. She looked at her clothes, and took almost all of them to the bathroom to wash them. They had until tomorrow to dry, the radiator in the room would help. She stood in the shower for half an hour, washing herself thoroughly and enjoying the sensation of being warm. She used the tiny towel she carried, then dressed in her cleanest clothes and arranged her washing on the radiator. She lay on the bed again and pulled the covers over her clean, damp body and fell deeply asleep. Liam would come at six o'clock. She had two and a half hours to sleep.

Millie's scar

Millie awoke just after 5.30 PM. She tidied the room, rearranged her clothing that was almost dry, brushed her hair and sat down and waited for Liam, her excitement growing. By 7pm he was still not there. It took about half an hour to walk from McDonald's to the hostel, maybe 45 minutes for Liam. Even allowing for the slow going at rush hour, he should have arrived by now. She decided to wait another half hour. At 7.30pm she put on her jacket and went downstairs to smoke and wait for him. She decided that if he did not come until she smoked her cigarette, she would leave a note and go looking for him at McDonald's. Maybe he'd met a friend and that's why he had been held up. She smoked her cigarette outside. It was already dark outside and there were already a lot of people in the hostel, and the noise level was rising, as Liam had said it would. She asked at reception for a piece of paper and a pen. She wrote a note for him to wait for her at the hostel and left it in the room. She left the key at reception, and described Liam, so they would give it to him if he arrived after she'd left. There were fewer people on the streets. Millie thought about what route he may have taken. He liked shortcuts, but in the dark he would stick to the main roads. He was not in front of McDonald's, nor anywhere on the entire shopping street. Millie began to worry about what might have happened to him, hoping it was nothing bad. She had a habit of looking on the dark side, but Liam was a fun guy, and there were more funny stories associated with him than bad ones. She was telling herself that everything was fine and that when she went back to the hostel he would be waiting for her there. She imagined how she would scold him that he had scared her. She decided to go try some of the back streets, John Street, then Hackins Hey, and Pall Mall after that. It began raining lightly, it was cold. Millie walked quickly, looking around and trying to recognize Liam and his crutches through the pedestrians in the distance. He wasn't there. As panic rose in her chest, she began running. She changed the route, from Hackins Hey she turned

Millie's scar

left towards Chapel Street, but then decided to go back onto Pall Mall. It started to pour, the streets became totally deserted, just passing cars, people in a hurry to get home. She walked all over Pall Mall, he was nowhere to be seen. Arriving back at the hostel, she looked enquiringly at the receptionist, who looked back at her blankly

"Did the guy with crutches come?"

"No, I haven't seen a guy with crutches."

"Were you here all the time?"

"Yes, I only went to the second floor for a little bit, but I did not spend more than 2-3 minutes there."

"Okay, can I have the key for room 12 please?"

The receptionist handed her the key and she ran upstairs. She unlocked the door and rushed towards the phone. Maybe he'd called her from somewhere. He had lost his phone three months ago, and he never bought a new one. He had written down her number in the notebook he wore in his inner jacket pocket. No one had called. Millie sat on the bed with the phone in her hand, staring into space and thinking. Besides the hospital and the police, she did not know where to look for him. She decided she would go to the hospital. The hospital was 30 minutes away on foot. It was past eight-thirty, and she didn't want to waste any more time. She was cross with herself for coming back to the hostel, she should have gone directly from Mcdonalds, the hospital was no more than 15 minutes from there.

She arrived at Accident and Emergency and went to the reception.

"Good evening," she said, breathless, her throat dry and croaky. "I'm looking for my friend, he's missing so I decided to check if anything had happened to him? Maybe he's here? He'd disabled, he only has one foot, uses crutches, so may have had a accident?"

"OK, can you tell me your friend's name?"

"Liam Blake."

149

"Date of birth?"

"Ah," she thought, he had told her that he was born in the beginning of October – "ah, yes - 3rd of October 1986."

The woman began typing on the keyboard, then began reading.

"Yes, your friend was admitted today just after 6pm."

Millie's eyes widened, her heart began pounding harder. Relief and fear hit her as one.

"How is he? Why is he in hospital? Can I see him?"

"He was found in the street, badly beaten and unconscious. He's in ITU and we'll keep him under observation for now. You can visit tomorrow from 10.00 to 12.00."

"Please can I see him, just to let him know I know where he is and will come back tomorrow? He'll worry.

"I'm sorry, it's too late. Please make room for the patient behind you."

Millie turned, behind her stood a visibly sick middle aged man.

"Excuse me," she said, allowing him space, and headed for the door, she stopped to think if she could possibly see him somehow? What kind of monster would beat up someone disabled? Bastard! She cursed in her head. As she left A&E she saw the main entrance to the hospital and walked in. It was dark inside, just a light from a back corridor. She saw a number of signs ahead of her and walked over to see where she was supposed to go. But the security guard came from the room on the right.

"The hospital is closed, ma'am, please come back tomorrow morning."

"Look, my friend was admitted as an emergency to ITU. I just want to see him" The man shook his head, and gestured towards the door.

"Go and get some sleep, you can't do anything now. Good night."

He told her, sending her towards the sliding doors and out of the hospital.

Chapter Fourteen

Millie felt dispirited and flat. She didn't feel like sleeping, she didn't want to be by herself in the hostel. What kind of beast could beat a disabled man? "God, Liam, how sorry I am! I should have come to pick you up, if we'd been together this wouldn't have happened. Unconscious!" She could not stop the thoughts racing around her mind. "What did they do to him? And why couldn't I see him?" The rain grew heavier and Millie began walking faster. She arrived at the hostel, wet through. There were two men out front, one looked visibly drugged or drunk, and she couldn't see the other one's face. They looked at her as she went inside and they followed her to her room, and then continued along the corridor to the right. Millie stripped off and took her dry clothes off the radiator and replaced them with the wet things. She lay down in her underwear, shivering, staring at the ceiling and thinking about Liam. "He had not told her he had any enemies. How could Liam have enemies?" She dismissed it as an option. "They must have been muggers. They probably saw him begging and decided to beat him up and take his money. But why would they beat Liam? He can't stand upright without his crutches. It would be enough to push him over and take his money. Why would they beat him? And so badly that he was unconscious?" She stood up and removed the kofta from the radiator. Her stomach was rumbling, but she had no appetite. She forced herself to eat a little, sitting on the bed she made a pocket out of the pitta bread and filled it with the warm kofta and the coleslaw. She knew she had to stay strong for Liam and going without food would not help her look after him.

She decided that she should try and get some sleep, but this was not an easy task. Down the corridor it sounded like a battle was

Millie's scar

waging. She could hear shouting, screams, banging, the sound of things breaking. But Millie was far enough away from them, and she thought she would not hear them in her sleep.

She was on the verge of sleep when a heavy blow on her door scared her. She jumped out of bed and scuttled to the door. For some reason she thought it was Liam. She opened and looked, there was nobody. With a pounding heart, she locked the door and went to bed. She must have dreamed it, she thought, looking at the phone, it was twelve forty-five. The shouts in the other room continued. She laid down and then drifted off again.

A loud bang on another door woke her again. She got out of bed and stared at the door in the dark. No footsteps were heard. She lay down and waited. After another 15 minutes a new bang was heard on another door. Millie was feeling scared and disorientated. She needed to sleep and these crazies would not let her. She turned her back to the door and rolled the blanket over her head. Again, she was drifting off when she heard scraping metal outside her door. Millie got up again, put the light on and approached the door. She heard something, but she did not know what it was. She was shivering from fear and cold and went back to bed. She decided to leave the light on. "What did they want? Why couldn't they just stay in their own rooms instead of roaming the corridors? "

Bang. Another door again. Millie covered her head and tried to ignore the sounds."

"What's up, man? Don't hang up on me because I'll find you and cut your throat, understand?" someone was screaming into a phone just outside her room.

The screams were aggressive and hysterical. Millie covered herself to the neck with the blanket as she sat with her legs bent and leaning against the wall. Her heart was racing. She was staring at the door with fear. She was very nervous. She wanted to sleep and she wanted Liam.

Millie's scar

She slept fitfully and awoke to the noise of her key falling to the floor. She jumped and screamed:

"Get out, leave me alone, what do you want from me!" There was no answer, only steps outside the door were heard. She ran to the key, grabbing it and replacing it in the lock, turning it horizontally, so it couldn't be pushed out. She went back to bed and sat down against the wall. She was trembling.

"Don't say I didn't warn you," Liam said in her thoughts. "Of course you warned me, my love!" she thought, but she admitted she did not expect the crazies to bang on her door all night long. She had not expected them to bully her, she knew they would be noisy, and she thought she would sleep in a warm, soft bed, next to his naked body. But he was gone, beaten and unconscious, while she was alone with a lunatic trying to get into her room. She tried to calm herself down, they're stoned, they just want to scare me, she kept telling herself.

A strong bang from a fist hit her door three times. Millie froze. Her heart was about to burst out of fear. What did they want and wasn't there anyone in this hostel to prevent the other guests from being harassed? The old Millie would have gone down to the reception and made a scene, but she did not dare. She held her breath, trembling under the blanket, waiting. She decided it was best to get her stuff together and packed her backpack. If she had to flee, she would be prepared. The radiator wasn't warm enough, her clothes were not yet dry. She gathered all the rest and sat down again in bed. About half an hour passed. There were no noises. Millie slipped under the covers and fell asleep.

Bam! Bam! Bam!

It was like some form of torture, she couldn't stand it anymore. If it didn't stop, they would bring her to madness. She could hear a strange hissing noise and her befuddled mind thought they were trying to gas her. She shivered and wept with exhaustion and fear. She covered her head and prayed. She was praying to be left

Millie's scar

alone. She just wanted a little sleep. She was barely breathing. After a while, she drifted off yet again.

Bam!

Millie kept the blanket over her head. This nightmare seemed endless.

In the morning, Millie timidly opened the door, stuck her head out, saw that there was no one and ran all the way down the stairs. She could hear someone running after her. She threw the keys at the half-sleeping receptionist and ran through the door. She ran with all her strength, turning twice, to check if someone was chasing her. She saw a figure, but she was not sure if he was chasing her or it was a passerby. Her chest hurt, she had no air, and tears streamed down her cheeks. She could not stand it anymore. This was beyond cruel, it was unbearable. She struggled to survive every single day. She took a turn onto a quiet street and leaned against the wall, bent double, gulping air. She could barely swallow, her throat was so dry. She looked around the corner, there was no one suspicious, just people on their way to work. She calmed down and began walking, limping, with her backpack on one shoulder. Someone targeted her, they banged on her door every half an hour, denying her rest, inducing terror, scaring her by trying to break in, the incident with the key. She had not had such a bad experience since the rape. She was exhausted and spooked, her head was aching and she thought she might be going crazy. Her mind was a shambles. She had to stop thinking at once. What she needed above all was sleep. She rolled up a cigarette, while shivering, and sat on a bench to calm down. She waited there, smoking her cigarette, watching people hurry to work. It was only 7:30am, it was ages before she could see Liam. She wanted to find a quiet and peaceful place, a park, to sit on a bench and wait in silence. The noise of the city early in the morning, in the past it had given her strength to start her day off filled with energy, and now it made her crazy. She wanted peace and silence. She pressed her palms in her ears and stayed like that for a little bit. She could not isolate all the noises, but for a moment she drowned out the city's morning hubbub.

At 10am, the hospital entrance was open to visitors. Liam had been moved to a side room. Millie spoke to the nurse in charge, who explained that he had sustained two cracked ribs and a broken finger on his left hand. He had also had a nasty crack on the head but had recovered consciousness just after they brought him in. He was having a CT scan today to ensure there was no internal bleeding, but this was just precautionary as he had spoken to the nurses last night and seemed lucid. They had sedated him and he was on a lot of painkillers, so would probably sleep for some time. She sat beside him in a chair and held his hand. He looked good, there was almost a smile on his lips. She had expected him to be blue and swollen, but his injuries were all to the back of his head.

She stayed for 20 minutes in the hope that he would wake up, but he was in a deep sleep. "Too much has happened to us my dear Liam, rest, and I'll come again tomorrow." she spoke to him in her mind. She kissed him gently on the lips then got up and walked out. She asked the nurse to tell him when he awoke that she had visited.

She had £4, nowhere to sleep, and she was utterly alone. It couldn't get any worse. Millie walked along the corridors like a ghost. She was weak and exhausted and no longer cared what was going to happen, she was at a dead end anyway. She stepped out of the hospital and walked without direction. She wanted to find a park, lie down on a bench and at least rest. If the sun came out to warm her, she would be grateful. But there was no time to rest, she had to figure out something before the night came.

Millie found the city hall and headed straight for the first employee she saw.

" Hi, my name is Milla and I'm homeless. I need help, I have nowhere to stay tonight."

Millie's scar

" Come in and get your ticket, ma'am." - the security guard said. A middle-aged man with a greyish hair and beard and a slightly tight suit.

Millie followed the advice and waited for her to be called. She felt that it was written on her forehead the miserable condition she had found herself in. She felt so exhausted. She looked at the people waiting with her, there was no one like her, no one so broken down. They seemed happy, clean, carefree, with no danger for their lives. They looked as she should have looked. She who had done no harm to anyone. She did not deserve what was happening to her. The one to the right of her deserved it because he had left his child on the ground to roll on the dirty floor while he was just staring at his phone. He was not interested in anything but his rotten phone. Or maybe that blond „doll" with the fake lips and nails who was standing on insanely high shoes. She deserved it because she looked like a spoiled brat. Because she had gotten everything on a silver plate and probably had never worked in her life.

And why not the woman in her 40s who was standing next to the counters and was cleaning up the otherwise impeccably arranged hall. She wore a stylish suit with a slim sky blue jacket and a straight skirt over her knee, and a dark gray light scarf wrapped impeccably on her neck. She just stood there looking at the hall, and if anyone spoke to her, she smiled hypocritically, pretending to want to help. Or not, it was not hypocritical but she rather seemed to be entertained by the fact that others were waiting their turn, and she was being paid to just stand. It was her job, was it not, to watch during the entire day how others were waiting. She would receive a solid paycheck and go back to her cozy home, to her stupid husband, pour herself a glass of cold wine, get her feet on a stool, and complain about how exhausted she was and what a busy day she had. God, she had no idea what a busy day really was. Millie felt an abhorrence for these people, wishing they could at least be in her place for a little while to see if they would behave and look like that. They knew nothing about life. She felt her eyes beginning to fill with tears. She didn't deserve all this. At the very least she deserved to have a bed to lie on. She quickly wiped away her tears and at that moment she heard her number. She went to counter 5.

" Hello, my name is Milla and I am looking for help, because I have no place to spend the night."

" Hello" - said the young employee, reaching in a drawer on his desk and taking out a form. He passed it to Millie and continued – "fill it in and we will get back to you in a week."

Millie's eyes widened.

" You don't understand, I have nowhere else to sleep tonight."

" I understand, ma'am, but there's nothing more I can do for you today. Seek help from a shelter if you wish."

" But it's awful there" - Millie rasped in tears and her tears began dripping directly onto the desk. Hot waves covered her whole body. The clerk grimaced pursing his lips and lifting his eyebrows, which made it clear to Millie that he did not want to waste his time with her. A bitterness stuck in her throat and tears filled her eyes and blurred the image of him. Powerlessness came over her and she didn't know what to say, so she stood up, put her hands on his desk, leaning toward him, and yelling in his face – " Why don't you go to a shelter, asshole, go to hell "- then she went towards the exit, feeling all eyes looking at her, and seeing that the guards were coming towards her angrily, and reaching for her to take her hand in order to bring her out, she pulled her hand away so that he would not catch her and passed him, trying not to listen to him.

" Ma'am, you have no right to engage in any form of aggression against employees, leave the building."

Millie ran through the entrance and went down the stairs. This night would probably be her last night. She was done, her life was coming to an end before her eyes, forming a puddle on the tiles of

Millie's scar

the city hall, and she couldn't do anything to stop it. Her hours were numbered. She felt dizzy and sat down on a sunshine bench in the city hall courtyard. She put her hands in her palms and screamed in anger. Her tears didn't stop. She didn't want to die that night. She wanted to curl up in Liam's arms. She didn't want to die. She was hungry, her throat was dry and she didn't even have a bottle of water with her. She could feel people passing by, but she was no longer interested in anything. She was crying out loud, at least she had that right, to mourn her inglorious death.

At one point she felt a strong female perfume and a hand on her back.

" Are you all right ma'am, may I help you? "

Millie was startled and looked up towards her with her red eyes, saliva running from her mouth and down her hand. Millie wiped herself with the back of her hand and said:

" I'm going to die tonight" - then the tears came running down again, and she hid in her palms again. The woman hugged her and said:

" Come talk to me inside, I work in the city hall, I will do what I can for you." - Millie looked at her and believed her words. They were sincere and full of concern for her, she stood up and walked to the entrance of the city hall with her.

" I have no place to sleep, I will probably be raped tonight, then they will kill me and you will hear this on the radio tomorrow "- she said as they walked to the entrance.

" Don't worry, I'll take you to the right person." - said the woman, and they entered the city hall.

"Welcome, come in, take a seat, Amelia will be right with you ...", the woman said, opening the door.

"Thanks," Millie said, and walked into the room. The woman closed the door behind her, and Millie looked around. A bright office with a desk in front of which there were two low armchairs. Behind there was a bookcase, which at the bottom had a cupboard with three doors. Several large planters with leafy green

Millie's scar

plants were scattered around the room. Millie sat down and stared out the window to the left of her. She could see the tree tops and the sky. Millie loved green, swaying trees, she felt relaxed when walking in the woods near where she grew up, but it was a long time since she'd been able to enjoy nature. She watched the naked branches move in time to the song the wind was humming outside. They looked like skeleton fingers, reminding her of death and loneliness. The door opened and Millie jumped, turning towards it. A young woman came in, dressed smartly, smiling and friendly she extended her hand to Millie and took hers, shaking it gently.

"Hello, Millie, I'm Amelia and I will be your mentor." She sat down behind her desk.

"Hello." Millie said quietly, feeling embarrassed and exhausted.

"How can I help you?" Margaret told me a few things, but why don't you tell me in your own words," she smiled.

"Well, I'm homeless and I have nowhere to go tonight." Yesterday I slept at a hostel, but it was such an appalling experience. I felt like I was going to die, there were a lot of drug addicts, they kept banging on my door every few minutes and tried to break in. I was so scared. And even if I wanted to go back there, I have no money. I'm just hoping the council can help me?

"Yes, of course, we'll help you, do you work?"

"Yes, but it's only 4 hours a week. That's why I need help. I've been looking for a job for more than a month and this was the only one I could find."

Amelia wrote something down, then raised her head to Millie and asked:

"How long have you been homeless and what caused it?"

"I have been homeless for a little over a month. I moved to Liverpool because I wanted to work here, but ..."

"Where did you live before that?"

"In London."

Millie's scar

"Why did you decide to move to Liverpool?"

Millie knew she had to tell the truth because Amelia was working for the council, and she would be able to see the statements Millie had made to the police in Bath. But she felt so exhausted she didn't think she could go over it all again. All she wanted to do was lay her head down and sleep.

"Look, this is a very difficult and long story, I'm exhausted, I have not slept properly for days. Is it possible for me to go somewhere I can sleep and tomorrow afternoon when I finish work, I will come and tell you everything?"

"I do understand Millie, but I must have answers to a few questions before I can help you." Amelia said gently.

"I was raped and they threatened to continue raping me, they stole my identity and took all my money so I fled London."

Amelia's eyes widened, then she nodded slowly and said:

"Okay, you're right, it's going to be a long story, now I'll call a few places to check where we can place you, and tomorrow we'll continue our discussion. I have to first establish that you're entitled to our help though Millie. Do you have a passport proving your nationality?"

"Yes, I managed to get a new one." said Millie, digging in her backpack and handing over the new passport.

"Did you report the crimes against you to the police? Do you have a crime reference number?"

"Yes I do, it's on my phone."

"OK Millie, that's fine. I just have to check you are unintentionally homeless and a UK citizen. I'll have a ring around and see if we can find you somewhere for tonight."

Amelia searched her phone for a number and dialled it while Millie powered up her mobile phone.

"Hello, Kate, it's Amelia from the Housing Department at City Council. Do you have a place for a young, homeless woman?"

"OK, thanks, I understand, I'll give Adelaide House a ring then."

Millie's scar

Amelia hung up, looked for another number, and dialed it.

"Good afternoon, I'd like to talk to the deputy. Yes, I'll wait" there was a short pause during which Amelia looked at Millie, "Hi, my name is Amelia Preston and I work in the Housing Department at City Council" Again there was a pause. "Yes, Megan retired last week, I'm her replacement. I look forward to meeting you too! I'm phoning because I'm looking for a place for a young homeless woman, do you have room for her? That's wonderful, thank you. Is it possible that she can be accommodated in a separate room? She's vulnerable, with no criminal record and has been the victim of bullying and abuse. Yes, I do understand, but in this case I feel she needs our protection from the more disruptive residents if at all possible? Can you help?" Amelia listened and a smile spread across her face.

"Thank you so very much! Yes, I will send you all the documents along with her. Oh, is that right? Fine, I'll come with her then. Thank you, see you soon."

Amelia hung up the phone and smiled at Millie.

"It's done, Adelaide House will take you. The women there are mostly on probation, my advice would be to keep yourself to yourself.

"Oh, yes, I just need a place to rest and will keep my head down." Millie said. Amelia opened her laptop and said:

"I see that you're tired, so we'll keep this brief." We'll complete the minimum I need and tomorrow we'll complete all the remaining questions. What time tomorrow can you come in?"

"Thank you so much Amelia, I promise I'll be here tomorrow at 1.30pm after I finish work." Millie said.

They completed the basic questions for 20 minutes, and Millie wondered how much time it would take to fill in all the details.

"You worked and paid your national insurance until two months ago, I see your last job was "Fly" in London." Amelia was staring at the computer as she spoke. "If you had to leave this job through fear and intimidation, and we can investigate that thoroughly, I believe you are entitled to Job Seekers Allowance. It looks like, given our information, as you're over 25 you can get around £72.40 a week from the state. Millie's eyes widened in surprise. She couldn't believe she'd been through so much before seeking help. Amelia continued.

"You can't stay at Adelaide House for a month. During this time, we will help you find accommodation and a job and see what we can do as far as benefits are concerned."

Millie nodded approvingly, listening intently and excited to at long last hear some positive news.

Then Amelia continued: "Look, Millie, it's my job to help you. I'll do my very best, you seem like a good person and my intuition is rarely off, but you have to help me. I want you to be open and honest. You need to tell me everything, but we'll leave that for tomorrow.

"Yes, of course I will be. Thank you so much for your help and your time. It's rare that someone wants to really help. I am so grateful. Thank you Amelia"

Millie smiled, feeling like a huge weight had been lifted. Amelia was a very pleasant woman, and she felt she would really help her recover. She felt grateful towards her even before anything had happened. Her kindness was such a relief. Amelia printed off the completed forms, Millie signed them and they left. Amelia drove them to Adelaide House, which Millie felt so grateful for. They were there in a little over 10 minutes

Adelaide House was a smart, well maintained building. The staff inside had uniforms, and looked more officious than kindly. Amelia and Millie entered the deputy's office, a woman named Caroline Buckettt. Miss Buckettt was not an attractive woman, nudging 60, she looked gaunt and slightly bug eyed, and was wearing a shapeless black dress that skimmed her ankles. Her refusal to smile did nothing to soften her harsh appearance.

Millie's scar

Amelia introduced Millie.

"This is Milla Bloom, she's been through quite an ordeal, I'm so glad you could accommodate her. Here's the paperwork Miss Buckettt." Amelia handed a buff coloured folder to Caroline, who nodded.

"Thank you, Miss Preston. The usual stay here is up to a month, but this can be extended if necessary."

"Yes, I understand. Millie hasn't slept in several days, maybe she could be shown to her room where she can rest and you and I can finalise the arrangements?" Amelia suggested.

"Yes, of course." Caroline reached into her desk and pulled out a small booklet, handed it to Millie and said, "Milla, this will explain everything about Adelaide House, especially our rules. We're very strict about the rules here, be sure to read the booklet carefully and ask if you don't understand anything. We make no exceptions, if you cannot follow the rules, you cannot stay here."

"Thank you Mrs Buckett.!" Millie said quietly, taking the booklet and beginning to read. There was an hourly timetable, with proscribed times for breakfast, lunch, dinner and bedtime. There were rules about behaviour, noise, visitors, dress, smoking, alcohol and drugs, to mention a few. The stay was paid by the council, no visitors were allowed, there was access to a kitchen where residents could prepare their own meals, but only with permission. Millie's eyes wouldn't focus, and she closed them as the words floated in front of her.

"I hope you will be an example to the others Millie?" Caroline said sharply. "The women residing in here are mostly ex-convicts, recovering addicts and alcoholics, they have had their troubles but by enforcing strict rules we help them rebuild their lives . That said, they can sometimes prey on newcomers. Amelia has asked me to protect you as much as possible, but you have to look after yourself too. Can you do that Millie?" she asked, staring at Millie questioningly, expecting an answer.

Millie's scar

"I don't want to get involved in any trouble, I just need some time to rebuild my life as best I can," Millie said humbly.

"Well, the cost here is £35 per day, full board. If you want to prepare your own food, your stay will cost you £25 a day. Our cooks are superb, and the menu is varied." Millie looked at Amelia who added, "The City council will meet Millie's expenses, and I will organise the transfer as soon as the paperwork is all finalised." Caroline looked at her, then went on:

"There is a shared laundry, living room, dining room and a media room with several computers for common use. Each bedroom has a TV and a private bathroom. You have to keep your room and bathroom tidy and clean, it will be inspected daily. We also reserve the right to enter your room at any time of the day and to search your personal belongings without permission. If we are suspicious that you are undertaking any illegal activities, we are obliged to report this to the police and your mentor and you will leave Adelaide House. Do you understand everything I've said?"

"Yes, I understand," Millie said, thinking only of how she wanted to lie down and be left in silence for a while.

"Please sign here." Caroline said, placing a copy of the rules on her desk and pointing out the place for her to sign."And print your full name here," she went on, pointing to the line under the signature. Millie finished and stood up.

"One of our most important rules is 'no guests', if you bring anyone into the house without permission, you will be asked to leave." Caroline finished, and Millie nodded her understanding. Then Caroline picked up the phone and said: "Scarlett, would you take our new resident to her room? Thanks."

Less than a minute later, Scarlett, a round, bustling woman who creaked as she moved, entered Caroline's office and asked that Millie follow her.

"Millie, I will remain with Mrs. Buckett to finish up the paperwork, and tomorrow I'll see you in my office at 13:30," Amelia said to her with a smile.

"Thank you for everything, I'll see you there," Millie said and followed Scarlett down the hallway.

"Your room is on the third floor, at the end of the corridor," Scarlett said to her, walking towards the stairs. "Be strict with the program, Mrs. Buckettt gets very angry with those who are not. If you are going to be out during the day, make sure you notify us so that no food is cooked for you. Mrs. Buckett does not like food to be wasted. And you should be precise with the hours, the house is locked at 11:00pm sharp, after which noone can enter.

Millie listened and absorbed the information. She felt this was like a cross between a hospital and a prison, but she didn't care, it was warm and comfortable and safe here.

"When you leave your room, lock the door and hand your key to the security person at the entrance if you leave the house" Scarlett continued.

"All right, thank you for the information Scarlett." said Millie with genuine gratitude.

Scarlett unlocked the room and Millie followed her in. It was a small, bright, neat room with a big window overlooking the garden, with bright orange curtains. There was a single bed adorned with a duvet cover with large flowers in orange, white and green. A small pine wardrobe and chest of drawers were against the far wall, with a small TV on top. The floor had a fitted carpet with a small green and grey pattern and beside the bed was a soft, brightly coloured rug. An angle lamp rested on top of the bedside cabinet, while several well-read paperbacks were neatly stacked below. The bathroom had a shower cubicle, toilet and sink. There were towels and toiletries. Just like at a hotel, thought Millie.

"I'll leave you, girl, dinner is at 7pm, see you soon!"

Millie's scar

"See you soon, Scarlett. Thank you so much!"

Scarlett closed the door, and Millie sat on the edge of the bed, tears rolling down her face with relief. Within 5 minutes she was fast asleep, still wearing her clothes and shoes.

That evening she went down to the dining room to have dinner. She was early so sat down at a table and waited. The room began to fill up with everyone taking a tray and queuing up by the counter from where the food was served. There were about 15 women, a variety of different shapes, sizes and ethnicities. Their ages were just as diverse and one of them was pregnant. Some looked at her with curiosity and some with open animosity, but their attention didn't last long and they went back to chatting among themselves. She had decided to stay away from them, she didn't need anyone here. She just wanted a bed, a shower and food. She had dinner by herself at her table and then went back into the room. She watched some TV and fell asleep again

Chapter Fifteen

"I made so many choices and all were wrong, Hugh. Was this the crossroads you showed me?"

"There are no wrong choices. There is a way towards the goal. You can pass by it hundreds of times without noticing it. It is only revealed when you have eyes for it."

"What is the goal then? I just want to survive and be happy."

"The goal is known only by the Almighty, we all fulfill his goals, we are his disciples. Don't worry, you can't miss your goal. It is the meaning of everything, it has been a part of you since birth."

She was awoken by a noise in the corridor. She looked at her phone and saw that she had three minutes to get down to the dining room for breakfast. She got up, threw her clothes on and ran downstairs without even washing her face. She didn't want to be late for breakfast on her first morning. After porridge and toast and coffee she went back to her room, made her bed, took a shower, got dressed and left the house. She wanted to be at the hospital at 10:00 precisely because she could only stay for 20 minutes to see Liam, she had to be at work for 11.00 and she couldn't be late. Millie walked quickly towards the hospital, although she had plenty of time. She wanted to see him, see how he was, see that beautiful smile and also to tell him where she was sleeping now. So many things had happened in such a short time. She needed to understand what had happened to him, tell him about the night in the hostel, how she feared for him, and then for her own safety. She missed his smile so much, she just wanting to hug him and stay like that forever. The memory of the warmth of his body excited her, and she began walking even faster. What would they do when he left the hospital? Only women were allowed to sleep at the shelter. She did not want to leave that

Millie's scar

place. Amelia would help her find a full time job, and after a while she would rent an apartment and they would live together, but until then, Millie had to convince him to find a shelter himself."

At 10.00 the doors opened and Millie almost ran into his room. He was awake, his face lit up when he saw her.

"Oh, Liam, I was so worried about you!" She said, leaning toward him, kissing him and putting her head on his chest, sitting beside him on the bed. He flinched and quietly groaned.

"Oh, sorry, did I hurt you?" Millie asked him. He smiled and pretended she didn't.

"A little, but worth it!" he took her face in his hands and began kissing her lips passionately.

Millie gently pulled away and said breathlessly.

"I don't have long, I have to start work at 11am."

"I thought you wouldn't come," he clasped her hands and kissed her several times.

"The first night I came they wouldn't let me in and then yesterday when I came you were asleep, I didn't want to wake you, they did tell you I came didn't they? I was so worried…"

"I'm fine, my ribs hurt a little when I breathe, but I'm fine," he said, lifting his hand and showing her his bandaged little finger. "The scan of my head came back and there was no bleeding, so it's just a matter of rest and waiting for the wounds to heal. They want my head to heal before they let me go. It'll be a few more days."

"What happened to you? I waited for you until seven, and then I went aroundsearched all the usual places in the city for you, and then I thought to come to the hospital, but I was too late and they sent me away. I was beside myself with worry."

"There's this idiot, Mario. Years ago I played him at poker and won big. He accused me of cheating and has never let it drop. He saw me and just flipped. He had two mates with him, I didn't stand a chance. But I'm fine now, don't worry."

Millie's scar

"If you know who he is, you have to report it to the police."

"Nonsense, that would just make it worse. He's a junkie, even if they find him and lock him up for a while, he'll just get out and find me, and I might end up in a worse state next time."

"But he could just beat you up again!" Millie said in a tone of insistence.

"I know, but it's unlikely. In general, I rarely see him. I expect he's got it out of his system now, he took my money so hopefully feels the debt has been paid. Tell me how are you? Where did you sleep last night? I dreamed all night of how you were on the street, being attacked, I kept waking up, I don't think I slept at all."

"I went to a women's refuge, it's fine there, I can stay for a month and I'll get help with finding a job and benefit payments. You were right about that hostel, if you only knew what a nightmare I went through, I thought I was going to die, I didn't get a wink of sleep all night. Every few minutes they just banged on my door. I barely got through that night. They tried to get into my room, I just shivered in a heap in the corner!

Liam pulled her to him and hugged her as hard as he could, stroking her head, and said:

"It'll be over soon, Millie, I made a decision. How about we go to Oxford, I always wanted to live there, a very beautiful city full of young and smiling people?"

"But how? We barely survive here?" Millie did not understand what Liam was suggesting.

"I told you I have collected money for the prosthesis, it will wait. What do I need a prosthesis for, if I'm dead, they could have killed me the other day. And all night I did not sleep, thinking about you, if something happened to you, I do not want to even think of losing you. We'll start afresh, we'll find jobs and I save up again for my leg."

Millie's scar

"Oh, Liam , I won't allow you to do it, not for me. You said you needed only a little bit more. Amelia, the mentor they appointed to me, said she would help me find a job, and I am entitled to benefits, it's not much but enough to find a place to live and things will be alright. You've saved for so long, I won't let you give up.

"No, Millie, I made my decision. Now go, you're going to be late, we'll talk again. I'll see you tomorrow?"

Millie looked at her phone, it was 10:25, she leaned over, kissed him and stood up.

"Tomorrow I will come again for a little bit, but the day after I will stay as long as they will let me in this place!"

"Give me another kiss," he asked her, smiling.

Millie leaned over to kiss him, and he wrapped his arms around her. For a minute they held on to each other, kissing gently and touching fingertips. It took all Millie's determination to drag herself away.

At work, they told her that a guy called Derek was leaving and they needed a replacement. They said if she got on OK she could take his hours, six days a week from 11.00 to 20.00 in the evening. It was minimum wage, but came to around £400 pounds a week. Millie smiled.

"When do I start?" She asked enthusiastically.

"What's today?" David began looking at his phone, then he said, "Derek leaves on March 15th, so after that." he looked at her and added, "Let's see how you get on, it would be much easier for me if I don't have to advertise and do interviews!" he smiled. "Don't let me down Millie."

"Oh, David, thank you, I promise I won't let you down!"

Millie was in a hurry to meet Amelia, she was so happy that her life was beginning to fall into place. Amelia greeted her with a smile and invited her into her office.

"I have some good news for you, Millie, I found you a job. The company is a subcontractor of the council and has a position that

Millie's scar

is perfect for you. They are looking for an associate in their supply department. I've already sent them basic information about you and I've spoken with Greg to arrange an interview."

Millie was startled when she heard that name. She felt shivers and began trembling. Amelia saw her reaction and asked her:

"What is it Millie, are you not pleased?"

"Oh, no, I'm glad, it's just that name, Greg ..."

"It's a common enough name. I know Greg well, he's a very responsible and decent man," she said.

"That sounds good, I've got experience with supply-handling, as I said before, but today I was offered a job in a restaurant, and now I'm going to have to choose," Millie smiled in embarrassment.

"Greg offers a long-term contract of employment with many extra benefits. Of course, there will be a probationary period of 6 months, but if you do well, you will have a nice, safe job, with a starting salary of around £17,500." She took a breath and continued. "besides, you will have 20 days paid annual leave and sick pay. These are very good conditions these days. The office is located outside of Liverpool, and the company provide transport and a subsidised canteen. I think it's a great opportunity."

"Oh, yes, it sounds really good. The restaurant is minimum wage and cash in hand." Millie smiled, not believing the opportunities that had opened up to her in a single day. This was her happy day. God had heard her prayers. She had awoken rested, in a soft bed, had eaten a full breakfast, took a hot shower, had spent a happy half an hour in Liam's arms and had two job offers. She had waited for a day such as this for so long. Her eyes were full of happy tears.

"It just sounds incredible!" Millie continued, laughing and saw that Amelia was also joyful.

"Okay, now we'll write a fantastic CV for you and I'll send it to him, and then we'll get to work. You have to tell me everything,

Millie's scar

Millie, it's the only way that I can help you" she said, and saw Millie's eyes cloud over.

"I swore I wouldn't go back to this moment, but I'll tell you," Millie said.

"I suppose it was terrible, but you don't have to go into details, just tell me what you can.

Millie nodded and they began writing her CV. The women talked for a long time, Millie told her story starting with the rape and finishing with the night at the hostel. She told her everything. She felt she could trust her, it proved cathartic, letting go of the story and the guilt that went along with it. She was ashamed of everything, but mostly her inability to protect herself from Greg. She spoke of the video they had shot, she said it probably seemed that she was acting voluntarily. She was ashamed of the fact that her body could be abused by anyone simply because she was weak and defenseless. Amelia's face changed with every new horror that Millie was sharing. There was compassion, but also pain and anger on it. She didn't comment she just listened, with her elbows on her desk, leaning forward. When Millie fell silent, exhausted and crying, she got up, went to her and held out her arms for a hug.

"You poor girl, Millie, you have been through so much, but it is all in the past. I can refer you to a program for people who have experienced violence. There are very good psychologists working there and they can help you cope with the trauma you've experienced. She continued to speak, holding her tightly in a hug, then let her down and sat on the armchair beside her, and continued, "On top of this, we can look to backdate your benefits. I'll see what we can do but it might be enough for a deposit on a room."

Millie wiped her eyes, feeling the warmth and compassion in Amelia's embrace.

Millie's scar

"Thank you so very much, Amelia, I know everything will go well, I need a helping hand to get back to normal. Without money it's simply impossible to turn yourself around.

"Everything be alright, let's fill in the forms now."

"I have one question," Millie said, concerned. Amelia nodded, giving her a sign to continue. "I'm worried about Liam, he'll be discharged in a few days from the hospital, and he'll have no place to sleep. And he has broken ribs and a broken finger. Is there an equivalent place for him to stay? Like Adelaide House, but for men?"

"I understand. There are hostels, but nothing like Adelaide House. I'll have a think about what we can do for him, but he also has to be registered as a homeless person with us. When can you come on Monday?"

"At any time, I'm not working that day."

"All right." She walked past the desk and looked at her chart, then went on. "Let's say 2 o'clock, and we'll think of something for Liam then. You said that Liam is disabled? He is missing a leg? You do know that Liam can get any operations that he needs and a prosthetic limb through the NHS?"

Milly gasped, clapping her hands, a broad smile on her face and tears in her eyes.

"Oh my goodness, this is just incredible. I cannot wait to tell him. Thank you for everything Amelia!" said Millie, and they began filling in the mountain of forms.

An hour later Millie headed for Adelaide House.

The next morning she could not wait to see Liam and tell him everything.

"Hey, handsome!" Millie said, peering through the door beaming at him. Liam turned his head to her and beamed back.

"I could hardly wait to see you, my love!" He said, kissing her urgently. He was up and leaning against the bed frame. He

173

Millie's scar

removed a strand of hair from her face and started kissing her everywhere, holding her face in his palms.

Millie pulled back a little and began telling him all her news.

"Really, oh, that's wonderful, I'm so glad!" Liam smiled at her, enjoying her excitement.

"I have more news Liam. They told me that you do not have to pay for your operation or your prosthesis, the **NHS** will fund it. You can use the money you have saved for a deposit on somewhere to live. You'll also find a job and we'll live happily 'til the end of our days," Millie laughed and kissed him. Tears filled his eyes as he wrapped his hands around her waist, with his eyes locked on hers, kissing her at every opportunity.

"Honey, I'll have to go," she said, looking at the phone. "Tomorrow I will stay longer."

Liam leaned toward her and said,

"I love you, Millie, you are my day and my night, I want to spend the rest of my life with you!" Then he kissed her passionately. Millie was a little shocked by his statement but replied happily:

"I love you too, Liam, I'm so glad I met you. You're the best thing in my life." They kissed again, and she left, walking on air, excited by their declarations of love.

Chapter Sixteen

The shrill alarm sounded throughout the entire apartment. A startled Liam stopped it hastily and slumped back into bed. He looked at Millie, who had not even heard it. He lifted himself up on an elbow and kissed her tenderly on the cheek. Millie moved and asked:

"Is it time?"

"Aha" he said, and began to kiss her neck moving slowly down her body. Millie smiled, closed her eyes again and wrapped her arms around his shoulders.

It was the beginning of July, and the apartment they had rented had been bathed by the sun during the last month. The bedroom was warm and bright and they slept naked, wrapped only in a thin blanket. Millie took his face in her hands, pulled him close, kissed his lips and said:

"There is no time for this, I have to go, work!" she said but didn't move.

Liam pretended he did not hear her, his lips exploring her.

Millie a willing recipient of his kisses, decided there was no better start to the day than to make love with her beloved man.

Afterwards Millie made coffee, while Liam prepared breakfast, exchanging tender kisses all the while. Millie sat down at the table and turned on the TV. As she finished her coffee and went to put the mug on the draining board, she heard the morning news report mention a murder. She turned to look at the TV and saw a young Dariya smiling at her.

Millie searched for the remote and turned up the volume.

"The trial continues today for the murder of Dariya Easton, whose mutilated body was found by a cyclist in Richmond Park a month ago. The two men arrested at Heathrow Airport the next

Millie's scar

day as they attempted to board a flight to Lisbon have been charged with rape and murder. The case continues." Millie knew in her heart the men were Greg and Cloudy. She slumped into a kitchen chair as the realisation that they were behind bars sunk in, but Dariya's death hit her hard and she could feel the tears coming. The news went on "Data on sex crimes all over the world is frightening. The largest number of sexual offences for the European Union are registered in England, Germany, France and Sweden. According to Rape Crisis, about 85,000 women and 12,000 men are raped every year in the United Kingdom. That's around 11 rapes every hour. For the year 2012-2013, 22,654 cases of sexual abuse against persons under the age of 18 were registered. According to a report by the Ministry of Justice, only an estimated 15% of the victims of rape report it to the police and only 5.7% of registered rapes in the UK have led to an effective criminal conviction. 8% of the rapes ended with murder. Rape and sexual abuse is often carried out by relatives and individuals who are close to the victim's entourage. The increase in rapes for the past year is 14%. According to UN data, 250,000 rapes per year are registered, data covering 65 countries around the world. If these registered cases are only 15% of the crimes committed, the figures will show that over 1.5 million people are the victims of rape worldwide in a calendar year."

Then they continued with international news.

Liam saw Millie shivering and approached her.

"What is it, sweetheart?"

"I knew this girl," she said, and walked to the bathroom, feeling the bile rise in her throat.

"Lisbon?" Thought Millie, looking at herself in the mirror, shaking her head angrily. "The bastards were coming after me to replace Dariya." Millie felt shocked and relieved. The news of Dariya's death pulled her out of balance, and the report on rape left her devastated. The illusion that we live in peacetime crashed and burned for her. She had thought her rape was a rarity. But the fact was that more than a million women were victims of rape each year. Millie washed her face and brushed her teeth and threw on her clothes in a hurry. Liam had warmed croissants for breakfast, Millie grabbed two and was about to go when she said:

"See you tonight, I must hurry, I'm late."

Then she slammed the door and ran down the stairs. She was not late, but she wanted to think about Dariya on her own. She had not told Liam her story, she was ashamed and besides what could he do? Nothing would change if she told him and it might taint how he felt about her.

For three months now, she worked for the city council's subcontractor. Amelia was right, the job was perfect for her, and Greg was a very good boss. It wasn't just his name that reminded Millie of the Greg she hated. They both looked good and she would have never thought that either of them might be a rapist. Both were charming and smart. Except that Greg, her boss, was an extremely well-read and nice person, unlike Greg the rapist. She felt relief that Greg and Cloudy would now be behind bars, probably for life. They got what they deserved, but at what price? Now, if Millie wanted to, she could go back to London, and probably one day she would be able to walk peacefully past the house with the loft apartment.

Throughout the day she performed her duties mechanically, thoughts of Dariya and her murder plagued her. She was terrified by the thought that she could have been in Dariya's place. What had Dariya been through? They had probably raped her dozens of times, beating her to a pulp each time and eventually killing her. It was monstrous and cruel. The memory of Cloudy beating her, and masturbating and urinating on her lifeless body shook Millie to the core. No woman deserved that. She knew that before it had happened to her, she would have been asserting that the victim of such a crime should report it to the police immediately. It was logical, she would have prevented subsequent rapes. But

Millie's scar

having been through it, she knew that it wasn't so easy. Shame was eating her away from within. She was ashamed that someone had used her body without her consent. They had made a mockery of the most intimate part of her person. How would you report that a stranger used your body for his enjoyment and shared it on social media while you were contorted in disgust? How would you share that he hit you and threatened you and you got scared? How would you explain that you have not fought back for fear of losing your life? No, she did not fight because she was very scared. She knew they could kill her and so she shut her mind off from what was happening to her body. How could she admit this? Her flawed logic and shame made her acquiescence feel like consent. She would never forget how the forensic doctor had dismissed the little bruises she had, and how she could read in his eyes the question: "Did they really rape you?" He had not seen how they abused her. He had not seen how they hit her, he had not seen the tattooed tear, had not heard the threats. He was not there when they forced her to take drugs, nor when they made a video with her and then shared it. He saw only a few small bruises. Prior to the examination with him, Millie felt shame and pain, and after the examination she began to feel guilt. The guilt of judgement. The guilt of a victim. How many victims of violence had not shared their story because of this shame and guilt they were experiencing? On TV they claimed that only 15% admitted to being raped, so the remaining 85% were silent. They were afraid that they would be killed, and they had endured everything in the hope that they would live.

During her lunch break, Millie found statistics, rape news and resulting murders, and forums where people were discussing the topic. On one of the websites she read something that confirmed her thoughts. 60% of the women felt that if they did not resist the rape they would not feel it as such. 60% of women thought that if they did not fight they would save their minds and bodies. They were all victims, and they had accepted this fact to save themselves.

Women are almost always physically weaker than men and are constantly aware of trying to keep themselves safe. Women pray that they will not end up in the wrong place at the wrong time with the wrong person. Even the law doesn't protect them. The maximum penalty for rape is 5 years, but agreements are reached and after a year or two they are at large to commit further crimes. Rapists are not stupid people. They are intelligent and manipulative. They know how to keep their victims silent. They know how to stay under the radar and remain unpunished. Otherwise, more than 15% of raped women would report the crime.

The more she learned about the subject, the more deplorable Millie found the situation. She also came across articles of mass rapes in past years. Rapes of many women by many men in front of their families. The children were also not spared. Millie found a book in which a daughter told how she was raped with her mother in the same room, many times. The titles were shocking: "10 men raped me for six months," "Mass rapes in nursing homes in the US," "Rape as a military tactic," "Imposing Islam with rape," "Mass protests after raping a 7 year old boy, "Mass rapes of tourists in Spain", "Brazil is shocked by a rape video"!. There were countless pages of countless stories. Millie was horrified. She read about a famous female athlete who was raped and the public was up in arms. "The death of one is a tragedy, but death of a million is just a statistic." she thought of Marilyn Manson's song. She felt discouraged and betrayed. She would never forget the rape, but that was not the worst of it. Her fear was that given the statistics, there was absolutely no guarantee that she would not have to go through it all again. Nothing protected her, nothing gave her safety and the imprisonment of her rapist would give her peace of mind. It was not just him. If the UN statistics were

Millie's scar

correct, that 250,000 registered rapes per year in Europe, and unregistered over 1 million, that meant that millions of rapists were walking freely in the streets of Europe. And she had no chance of shielding herself from them. No one had a chance. It could be every single person she met.

Her colleagues came back from their lunch break, and she got back to work. But her thoughts were there, with the victims. The rape had broken her life. It was not just the act itself, the violation, humiliation and abuse. It was a broken life. She was chased from her home, she lost her job, her friends. She was stalked like an animal, running for her life. She experienced death threats, enslavement threats, her identity was stolen along with her savings, she was humiliated, lost an old friend in a fire, she was homeless. Rape has nothing to do with sex, it is just a way of humiliating and controlling. Rape was her ruined life and that of Dariya's. That's what the lives of all the raped women in the world look like. The rape had left a deep mark on her soul and mind. Millie wiped the tears away quickly and went outside for a cigarette.

Her anger grew in direct proportion to the despair she felt with every word read on the internet. Something had to be done. Women from all over the world needed to unite and resist this insanity. They were not dolls, they were not slaves, they even gave birth to the rapists. Didn't they have mothers, sisters and daughters? She could not wrap her mind around it all. Or perhaps they did despicable things with them too? She had the feeling that if Greg was right in front of her at this moment, she would strangle him in cold blood.

No matter how small the chance was for this madness to stop, she had to try. Millie had to figure something out. She remembered an old teacher telling her: "No question can resist long and focussed thinking on it's solution!" Millie was about to do just that, she would find a solution to stop or at least reduce the number of rapes. For that, she needed a lot of information.

She had to look at the problem from all sides, and then she would find a solution. There was a solution, and it certainly was not an increase the prison sentence. Millie realized that overcoming the male physical force was not the whole answer. We could not turn all women into fighters. The struggle had to be with something else. These people had a weak spot somewhere. And it must be obvious, she thought.

After work, Millie went home. Liam was working on the computer, and when he saw her, he stood up and greeted her with a smile.

"How's my princess?" he brushed away a wisp of hair from her face and kissed her softly on her lips.

"I'm fine, just shattered, we were really busy today," she replied, taking off her sandals. "And how is your job going?"

"Great, I'm getting faster all the time and earning more," he told her, walking into the living room in front of her.

Ever since he had stopped begging, he had changed so much. Millie noticed that he had become a little more nervous, but he was already starting to make plans for the future. He had become ambitious, and in his head he was mostly thinking about how to make money. He wanted to earn enough money to be able to support them, and he always said he felt bad that it was her who had made their lives better and not him. He had found work on several advertisement websites and he mostly wrote texts and edited pictures. He also maintained three websites.

Millie realized that most men thought like this, and she was delighted to see ambitions in him for a better life. Though she did not see his smile so often, she knew that their common future required them both to be responsible and ambitious. Their life had changed for the better as soon as Amelia appeared. Besides finding work for Millie, she helped them get a substantial sum in allowances, which they used as a deposit for a flat. At first Millie began working at the restaurant, but three weeks later she went

Millie's scar

for an interview at the company Amelia had recommended and Millie began working there after giving a weeks notice to the restaurant.

Little by little, their lives changed, they loved and took care of each other, and the money they earned made life comfortable. Fran was very happy for her when Millie told her where she was and that she had a new boyfriend, a job, and had rented a flat. However, she told her the sad news that Tim had died after 25 days of struggle. His mother met Fran and asked her to tell Millie that Tim's last wish was for Millie to be included in his mother's will. Tim, on his deathbed, had thought of her. She, who felt partly responsible for his death. Millie, full of guilt, called Tim's mother to express her condolences and asked for her part of the inheritance to be given to a charity for the homeless. Millie tried to redeem her sins by helping one person. The boy she had seen who had Down's Syndrome. She spoke to Amelia, and then to social services, explaining where he was living and the bullying and mockery that he was subjected to. The same day, the boy was located and taken to a safe house to be assessed. Amelia told her he would most likely be looked after in a council care home going forward.

Over time, they were able to buy clothes and essentials for their new home. Their life was on the right track and they were happy. Until this morning, when Millie heard about Dariya's murder.

Liam had prepared dinner and set the table. Cold roast chicken with potato salad and cherry tomatoes. He opened a beer because he knew this Millie's way of unwinding after a tough and tiring day and they sat down at the table.

"My dear, something is bothering you, I saw it this morning. Are you upset about the murdered girl?" He asked her.

"Yes, Liam, I'm just so tired now, I promise to tell you everything, but let it not be today. My head will burst. I feel exhausted."

Millie's scar

"No problem, I just worry about you and I thought that if we talked, you'd feel better."

Millie looked at him with an adoring look. This was the most magnificent man in the world. He was so kind and caring towards her. So smiling and so positive. Beautiful and sexy, passionate and loving. There was nothing more she could want in a man, except maybe to walk hand in hand.

"Did you contact the clinic today?" She asked him.

"I contacted them, yes, and I've got an appointment in three weeks. There is a long waiting list and I have to have a review first. I will probably need an operation on my stump and physiotherapy before they can fit the prosthesis. It's not an easy task. Will you come with me Millie? You may have to help me with the exercises."

"Of course I'll come with you Liam, I'll help you in any way I can." She kissed him and squeezed his hand.

"Listen, I'm exhausted, I know it's only 8 o'clock, but I'm going to go to bed. Don't feel obligated to come with me just now, besides, I want to be by myself for a little bit."

Liam looked at her with a full mouth and nodded in agreement. Millie got up, rinsed her plate, wished him a good night and went to bed. Liam continued to eat, lost in thought. It occurred to him that Millie was keeping secrets from him. He thought they had shared everything of essence with each other. She had told him about her life in detail and he had the impression that he knew everything about her. But he now knew there was something else. Or maybe she's just upset about the girl being killed and was tired after a hard day at work - he chased away his anxious thoughts. Whatever it was, she'd tell him in her own time.

The next day, Millie spent the day in front of the screen, entering data. Every free minute she had, she read more about rapes, punishment, prevention and victim's stories. She still had no solution to prevent or at least reduce the number of rapes. She also began to feel a little naive. People studied for years and specialised in how to prevent crime and she thought she could just work out an overarching solution in a few days? But still, she also couldn't get Dariya out of her thoughts. She had found a few articles, and learned from them that her death had occurred as a result of strangulation. They had strangled her, presumably, while they were raping her. Millie closed her eyes, imagining the situation. Greg and Cloudy were huge men, big and heavy. Dariya had no chance of saving herself. Millie was thinking and trying to remember if Dariya ever mentioned how long she has been abused by them. It may have been going on for years, but she could not remember Dariya telling her or Nicole about it. The only thing she remembered was the expression of consummate fear when they had rushed into her loft, and Dariya saying out loud: "How did they find me?!" Nothing else. Nicole had told her that they had been pursuing Dariya, but not how long. The police did not know that, they probably thought the rape was a random, singular occurrence. Millie could tell them, and she could even file criminal charges about her rape. Officer Porter had dissuaded her from filing a complaint against them because there was no evidence. Back then the incident was fresh in her mind and she was still frightened, and she just wanted to be safe and not reminded of it all. Now she felt secure. Dariya's death gave her confidence, these bastards had to pay for everything they had done. She could look for Miguel, Isabella and Kate, they were witnesses, they saw Greg and Cloudy crashing into her home. They saw how they destroyed her home, they saw their aggression. Millie even remembered Greg hitting someone, probably Miguel. Then Nicole could testify, she had found her in a terrible state. None of these things were, however, evidence of rape. Millie then remembered, she had to find the video, even if she appeared to have sex on it voluntarily, with the other testimonies from Miguel, Nicole and the other girls, she would be able to convince the jury that they had raped her. Moreover, they

Millie's scar

were already accused of rape and murder. She would tell Dariya's story and that her rape was not accidental. Fran and her mother could be witnesses that they had chased her and lied about her, that they had looked for her in Bath. Millie felt strong and full of cold determination. She might not have been able to convict them herself, but to be able to increase their prison sentences and see justice done made her more decisive. If she had been killed, she would have wanted Dariya to testify against them. She would want everyone to understand what monsters they were and how they tortured her. She still did not know how to find the video, but she knew she would be ashamed of it. She knew everyone would see it. But what worried her the most was that Liam would see it. She had to tell him what had happened and she was afraid of his reaction. If he saw the video, his attitude to her could change. She could lose him, and she had just found him. But for the first time since the rape, she had the courage to face them. Everyone needed to understand what she and Dariya had experienced. And how big and brutal the problem of rape is. By the end of her working day, it was all she could think about, and that's why she came home with a heavy heart. She was afraid he might stop loving her. He was lying on the couch reading a book. Several books had been left in the apartment, probably from the previous tenant, all were crime novels and he had read them all, this was the last one. When he saw her, he left the book and sat down on the sofa, tapping the sofa beside him to invite her to sit next to him.

"Come beautiful," he said to her with a wide smile.

Millie sat beside him, her heart beating wildly, her face seemingly worried and frightened. Liam noticed this, put a hand on her shoulders and asked her:

"What's going on, Millie? I'm starting to worry, something happened yesterday. Please tell me what's wrong."

" I have to tell you something, but I'm worried about how you'll take it," she looked at his eyes and saw that he was puzzled.

"Tell me." - He said softly, taking her hand.

"Do you remember that I told you I came to Liverpool because the company in London fired me and I was out of work?"

"Yes, so?"

"That's only half the truth. In fact, I fled from London and left my job and left everything I had there."

"Is that so? Why?" He asked, still not understanding anything.

"Because I was brutally raped!" she whispered, and did not dare look at him, staring at the floor in front of her. Liam leaned toward her and pulled her into his chest. Millie cried. They stayed like that until Millie stopped weeping so hard, and she leaned back and continued.

"This is not all. Let me tell you the whole story." she said, turning her body toward him. I was with a girlfriend at a party, it was boring and a girl we'd just met suggested we go to another place to continue partying. The girl's name was Dariya, the same girl on the news this morning, the one who was murdered. Me, her, two more girls and one boy all went to my flat. Everything was fine until two huge and terrible men, Greg and Cloudy, broke down my door and rushed in. The others fled, only me and Dariya remained. Cloudy beat her to a pulp, kicked her, struck her, then masturbated on her bloody body, and finally he urinated on her. I wet myself with fear and the guy called Greg dragged me to the bathroom, where he beat me and raped me under ice cold running water. I tried to escape but they caught me. They hit me so hard on the head I fell unconscious. When I woke up, Dariya and Cloudy were gone. Greg forced me to smoke some kind of drug with him, and then I do not remember much else. Nicole, a friend of mine, found me. Dariya had waited for her in front of her home. She told her to warn me to run, that they made a video of the rape, and put it on the internet and that they would pursue me, the way then had her, and make me a sex slave. I was very frightened, Liam, besides, my home was destroyed, I could not stay there. They had taken everything, my passport, my bank cards and money, everything. So I fled."

Millie caught Liam's eye, he was crying. He caught her again in his arms and said:

"My God Millie, I'm so sorry this happened to you, I'm so sorry. You should not have been afraid of my reaction. I have seen rapes on the streets more than once and know how awful it is." He held her in his arms and stroked her hair with one hand. Millie pulled away again. She was compelled to finish her story.

"They killed her Liam, and I am thinking of testifying against them," she said, staring at him tentatively.

"Of course you should testify, did you report it straight away?"

"Because a policeman dissuaded me, he told me I had no evidence. And he was right, but I remembered there were a lot of people who could testify about everything else. If I find the video that they made, I will be able to prove it."

"These cops are good-for-nothings, he was probably too lazy."

"No, he was not, he was a friend of Fran's husband, he wanted to help me, but I had taken a bath. My period had erased all traces, and back then I was ashamed that everyone would see the video. I managed to file charges against them for my broken home only. And they were charged with paying for the damages."

"But still, this is not the only way for a rape to be proven. Idiot, he just misled you and scared you. Have you seen the video?"

"No, I haven't, I only heard how it started" Millie said, her voice barely audible, sinking in shame, wondering what it showed, and whether it would not change Liam's opinion of her when he saw it. "Look, Liam, I probably did not resist during it. I could not move because they drugged me. When I fled to Bath, I went to Fran, but she was not there, and I slept at a hostel. I don't remember exactly what day it was, but I went to see my mother and before I got there I saw Cloudy talking to my step father.

Millie's scar

They came after me. And in the evening they even slept in the same room of the hostel. But they did not see me, and I escaped after they fell asleep. I heard them watching the video and laughing, it started with: "Swallow!"

She did not dare look up at him. She was so ashamed.

"Damn the bastards, let them rot in jail, of all criminals I hate rapists the most! They are vile, pathetic scum!" Liam said, took his crutch and stood up. He moved to the kitchenette and pulled out two glasses into which he poured red wine. Millie stood up, took the glasses and put them on the table, sitting in the chair in the dining room.

"Liam, I'll be honest, I'm afraid of what's going to happen. I'm afraid if you see the video, you'll hate me."

"My sweet Millie, I'm sure to hate someone, but it will never be you!"

Liam was very upset and angry. Millie did not expect this to happen. She thought he would accuse her.

"Of course you will testify against them!" Liam continued, standing, leaning against the kitchen counter. His eyes were full of rage. Millie did not know how to comfort him.

"I have to find the video first, without it I can't prove anything."

"I'll find it, when was it uploaded on the internet, do you know?"

"Around December 20-21, I think," she told him.

"I'll find it! He sipped the wine and sat down on the couch with the laptop in his hand.

"Let's have dinner now," she said trying to diffuse the atmosphere.

"I'm not hungry now, you eat if you want," he said, not even looking at her.

Millie went out onto the terrace and lit a cigarette. Then she called him for dinner again, but he refused. She was very hungry, so she ate.

Millie's scar

"Do you want to come to bed?" She asked, sitting beside him on the couch, but he did not look at her and did not answer her. He was focused. She glanced at the monitor. He had opened a few porn sites and browsed video files.

"Liam, please ..." she whispered, he raised his head to her and said:

"You have nothing to worry about, you are not to blame for anything, I'm very angry and I will find this video if I have to search for it for a year, I will, because these men have to get the severest of punishment. Go to bed" he gently stroked her neck and pulled her to him, kissing her lips gently. Millie calmed down and stood up.

"All right, good night, do not stay up late, please."

"Good night, I'll be in in a little while."

"I forgot to tell you," she said, "I have long hair on the video, I cut it to disguise myself when I ran. Also Dariya mentioned that the video was uploaded to some group, if that helps."

Liam turned his head, with anger-clenched teeth, and began to look even more focused at the monitor.

Chapter Seventeen

In the morning, Millie found him in the same position.
"Liam, did not you sleep?" Millie asked.
"No, but I found the video," he said. His eyes were red.
Millie froze. She didn't know if she wanted to see the video, or if she wanted Liam to continue talking. She stood and stared at him.
"Come see it" he told her, but she did not move, and he continued gently. "It's OK Millie, I'm with you, this thing can't make me stop loving you, nothing can. Come sit beside, I'll be with you, we'll watch it together." Millie sat down on the sofa beside him and he played the video.
The camera showed a penis entering her mouth with rapid, forceful thrusts. Her eyes were closed and she looked as if she was unconscious.
"Swallow, whore, swallow I told you!" It was Greg's voice. Semen dripped from Millie's mouth. The camera panned to the left, and for a split second another man was seen entering her forcefully from behind . Hands were seen on her hips, digging fingers into her soft flesh. The frame moved again. Greg was ejaculating onto her face. She was still unconscious.
"Dude, did we kill her?" Cloudy's voice sounded amused and he continued slamming himself as hard as he could into her lifeless body. The camera turned to Cloudy, his large body was visible up to his chest as he continued to rape her.
Liam paused and pointed to a small tattoo on the side of Cloudy's belly.
"Look, this is proof of who this bastard is. They never show their faces. I watched it thirty times, this is the only proof.
Then he played it again.

"Ha-ha-ha!" Greg's laugh was heard. "No, she's very high, I gave her a lot. What are you doing?" Greg shouted, the camera moved down, and for a fraction of a second you could see Millie was vomiting on his leg. Then the camera shot another second from the floor and the recording ended.

Liam looked at Millie, she was crying. He reached over and gently took her chin in his fingers, lifting her up to look at him. There was bile in her throat and tears blurred her vision.

"You will convict them, Millie, you will convict them, do you hear me, they will pay for everything! In jail they will get what they deserve! They'll curse themselves for the rest of their lives for not having kept their cocks in their pants!"

Millie pulled back, and without looking at him she went to the kitchen cabinet, took two tissues and blew her nose. She turned and looked at Liam, he had left the laptop and was sitting on the couch, staring at the floor, his elbows on his knees.

"Do you want coffee?" Millie asked in a hoarse voice. She blew her nose again, wiped her tears with her hands and put the kettle on.

"Yes please" he said. Then he took his crutches and went to the kitchen table, sat down and leaned the crutches against the table. He was watching her. She was beautiful, she was gentle, she was pure. Despite everything she had experienced. If he had ever seen her pass by while he was begging, he would never have guessed that she had ever been through such terrible experiences.

Millie stirred the coffees and left the spoon in the sink, then turned and sat down at the table across from him. Her eyes were moist and puffy, cheeks red from crying. Looking at him, her eyes filled again with tears. Liam did not know what to say and what to do to comfort her. She was not looking for close contact, every time he touched her, she pulled away. Perhaps she needed to be alone for a while, to ponder things, to remain alone with the pain. They took a sip from the coffee and he said:

Millie's scar

"When do you plan to file charges? I want to come with you, I don't want you ever to be scared again."

"I don't know, I'll have to ask at work for days off, it takes so much time, it can take a whole day."

"Why not call now? Maybe tell them you don't feel well? I don't think you should go to work in your current state of mind sweetheart."

Millie knew he was right. She really did not feel well. She picked up her phone, searched for Greg's number, and dialled.

"Hello, Greg, it's Millie... Yes, thanks, nothing serious, I'm just very upset today." Her voice became hoarse with the rising bitterness in her throat. "Can I have the day off? Yes, I understand, I'll come then... Oh, okay, great, thank you, maybe in the next days I could work overtime, I'll stay after work to make up the time. Thank you Greg, you are the best boss in the world!" She hung up the phone and explained:

"I can't take any annual or sick leave until after my probationary period, but he said not to worry, I'm going to work overtime to make up the time." She took the cup of coffee and her cigarettes and headed for the terrace. "I need a cigarette," she said, and went out.

Liam rose from the chair, took his crutches and went to her on the terrace. He closed the door and put a hand on her shoulder.

"My darling Millie, I want you to be strong, I'll be with you all the time. I will not leave you. It's clear on the video that you're high, even they say it, Greg says he's given you a lot of drugs. You will win, I'm sure, you have to convict them."

"I know, Liam, I know, it's just difficult to see what they have done to me. I can't remember anything from that day. They brutalized me, Liam. And you know what scares me most? That it can happen to me again. They can still rape me today. You saw how huge they are, how could I fight them off? You know the humiliation I experienced with the police when I was giving my statement, and when the doctor examined me, they doubted my

Millie's scar

story. They thought maybe I was exaggerating. This wasn't about sex, it was brutality and control, you get that don't you?" Millie cried softly, her hands trembling, as she furiously puffed on the cigarette, then went on. "But I will go through it again. Dariya deserves for these men to receive the longest possible prison term. I will do it for myself and then for her."

"You will, of course, and I will be right beside you. Whatever happens, I will never leave you!" he stroked her hair, then pulled her towards him and held her tight. They stayed like that for about a minute and he said:

"Now, let's get dressed, we have a job to do."

40 minutes later they were in the police station.

"Good morning," Millie greeted the woman behind the counter. "I have information about the victim, Dariya Easton, who was found dead in London."

"One moment, please," she said, then picked up the phone. "Detective Cunningham, a lady says she has information about Dariya Easton, the woman found at Richmond Park. Yes, thank you!" Then she looked at Millie and said, "Please take a seat, Detective Cunningham will call you when he's ready."

They had just sat down when a man in his 40s appeared. He leaned through the open door to his colleague, told her something, and she stood up, pointing to Millie and Liam. The detective approached them:

"Hello, I'm Detective Cunningham, please follow me."

They followed him into a small office, he gestured to two chairs in front of his desk and sat down himself.

"I understand you have information about the murdered Dariya Easton?"

"Hello, I'm Milla Bloom, and this is my friend Liam Blake. I knew Dariya Easton briefly. I believe the two men you have in custody for her murder are the same men that brutally beat her in front of me and then beat and raped me also. I know them as

Millie's scar

Greg and Cloudy. I can't say precisely how long they terrorised Dariya, but I know she ran away from them repeatedly and they found her and kept her against her will as a sex slave. She warned that the same might happen to me. I want to bring charges against them also."

The detective raised his eyebrows and said:
"When did this happen?"
"On December 18th."
"All right, I'm listening, tell me everything." Liam grasped Millie's hand and nodded, to steady her.

Millie told everything from beginning to end.

"I understand and I'm sorry for what happened to you" said the detective. "I'll call my colleagues in London, they'll want to speak to you. I'm sure they will want to bring a second case and so they'll be tried for both crimes at the same time. Please return to the waiting area and I'll call you when I'm done."

Millie and Liam returned to the corridor and the chairs they had sat on before. Liam bent down and kissed her cheek.

"You did well, but keep in mind that you'll probably have to tell it at least 20 more times."

"Yes, I know," She smiled and looked at him. "I'm gonna handle it, I got to this point, I'll handle everything so they get what they deserve."

Millie felt they were waiting forever when eventually the detective called them.

"I've spoken to the colleagues, they want you to go to London immediately and make a statement."

"But I have to work!"

"Don't worry about it, we'll explain, and they will release you as required."

"But I'm on a probationary period, I don't want to lose my job, it was so hard for me to find it."

Millie's scar

"Please don't worry, we'll send an official letter to your employer, under law then can't penalise you for being a witness to a crime."

He handed a note to Millie, on which he had written down a name, phone number, email and address.

"This is Detective O'Neill, he will be waiting for you tomorrow morning at 9.00 at this address. We'll arrange for a car to collect you tonight at 18.00 and for accommodation overnight in a hotel in London."

Millie's eyes widened, she did not even know what to ask. He turned to Liam and said:

"Sir, if you wish, you can accompany her."

"Yes, I will do it." Liam said, shocked by the situation.

"Your case is not in my jurisdiction, but if you have any questions, do not hesitate to contact me." He stood up indicating that the interview was over and shook Millie's hand and then Liam's.

"Thank you," Millie and Liam said at once, then smiled at each other as they left the office.

When they got home, Millie called her boss.

"Hello Greg, it's Millie .... Oh, really, that fast?" Millie listened with her mouth open, and Liam raised his eyebrows questioningly.

"Well, I don't know how long it will take, I hope... Oh, I understand, are you sure that ... well, okay, thank you. Bye, I'll keep you posted. Thanks, I'll keep safe." Millie hung up the phone smiling and surprised at the same time.

„You will not believe it, they called him from London, he's already received an e-mail explaining that I will be a witness in a trial and will be absent indefinitely." She left the phone on the table and sat down in the chair, and Liam sat down as well. "So quickly, how did they know where I work, where I live, that happened so fast?" Millie was looking at Liam, and him at her, as

Millie's scar

if thinking together." Greg told me not to worry about the job, he would distribute my tasks to others until I came back." The two of them were still stunned. Then each of them sank into their own thoughts.

Millie looked at the watch - it was 1:30.

"We have to pack our bags, but let's eat before that, I'm starving."

At 17:30, the bags were at the door and they were waiting with their coats on. At precisely 18:00 Millie's phone rang.

"Yes, okay, thanks, we'll be right down!" she hung up and said: "They are at the front door, they have my phone number, and maybe yours too," she laughed. This had all begun to feel like a crime movie to her. They took the bags and went downstairs. A black BMW 5 was waiting for them. The driver came out, walked around the car and stood before them, looking at Millie.

"Milla Bloom?"

"Yes it's me!" she said, he turned to the car, opened one of the doors and motioned for her to enter, explaining:

"I'm your driver, Mr. Adler. I'll take you to the hotel in London, and tomorrow morning I'll take you to the police station."

Mr. Adler also introduced himself to Liam, helped him get settled into the car, then took the crutches and put them in the boot with the bags. He then got into the driver's seat and said:

"Get comfortable, we'll be in London in about four hours, and tomorrow you'll meet Detective O'Neill and he'll explain what you need to know." He then raised the privacy screen and set off.

When they entered the hotel room, there were two pizza boxes on the table, a bottle of orange juice and a fruit bowl. Millie and Liam smiled at each other. They had dinner and went to bed.

At 8:30, as instructed, they met Mr Adler at the front of the hotel. By 9:00 am they were in Detective O'Neill's office, a tall, bulky man of about 45, smoothly shaven, wearing a dark gray suit.

Millie's scar

"Hello, Miss Bloom! Then he turned to Liam, shook his hand and said, "You must be Mr. Blake, I'm Detective O'Neill, and I'm conducting the investigation into the death of Dariya Easton."

"Hello," they both replied, then Millie caught Liam's hand and he put his other hand on hers. They looked at each other.

"My colleague Mr. Cunningham showed me the statement you made to them." Millie and Liam looked at each other again, the detective saw it, smiled, and said, "Don't worry, this is standard procedure, we make records that have no value in court, but they serve us to recall the stories of witnesses and eyewitnesses. The victim had dozens old injuries on her body, she had obviously been in an abusive relationship for some time. Some were made just before her death, others at different times before. Your story confirms this. Greg and the man you know as Cloudy had repeatedly raped her. Their names are Greg Davis and Alfie Miller. I want to ask you, have you seen the video they did of you?"

"Yes," Millie said, looking at Liam, who was taking out his phone. He found the video and reached across the desk to hand over the phone to the detective. He played it, and the room sounded with Greg's shouts. The detective watched it, then made a phone call, and only a few minutes later a young employee entered the room.

"Download this file and send it for analysis!" O'Neil ordered. The young man took the phone and left.

"It's good that you found the video, now you have to tell me the whole story from the beginning. This time, with every detail that you can remember, even if it seems to you to be insignificant. This time, however, I warn you that I will be recording what you say and this video will be seen by their lawyers and the jurors."

Millie started her story. When she finished, the detective pressed a button and then spoke.

Millie's scar

"It is clear from your story that no one can prove your rape, but we have a video, we have witnesses who have seen them breaking into your home, and there is a witness who will confirm what condition she found you in and who has spoken to Dariya. Can you tell me any more personal information about these witnesses?"

"I can give you Nicole's phone number, and also the man who invited me to the party. He may be able to connect you with Miguel, Kate and Isabelle. Francesca and my mother's husband can also confirm that Alfie and Greg came after me in Bath."

"Excellent, let's get to work then!" he said, then stood up and took them to another room where Millie had to describe everything in detail again, and, with the help of a sketch artist, they sketched every significant scene as she remembered it. It took forever. They had lunch, then drank coffee and she continued to write and do sketches. At the end of the day the video was processed and they had spoken to all the witnesses she had mentioned in her statement. The next day they would have to attend the police station and do everything that Millie had done today. Millie was instructed not to see any of them or speak to any of them on the phone. Everyone was warned about this.

Mr. Adler took them to the hotel, stopping on the way for fish and chips.

They had dinner and laid on the couch.

"You are a very strong woman, Millie, you don't appear as such, but you are. From what you've been through, you haven't gone crazy, you're not embittered, you're not angry. You have incredible self-control and you behave calmly. Today I was so proud of you while I was watching you. You stand steady as a professional. You look steadfast and unshaken. You astonish me with every passing day and I love you more and more."

"Is that so?" Millie smiled, searching for his lips, and handed him the crutch, going towards the bathroom.

"Fancy a bath?"

Millie's scar

"M-m-m, you've twisted my arm" he said with a wide smile and glittering eyes. He opened the fridge and saw that there was a cold bottle of white wine, cheese, milk, bread and four cans of beer. He took two wine glasses, opened the bottle, and went to undress. Millie had filled the bath and was waiting for him, her eyes shone as he came to her.

They spend the next day at the hotel. They were thinking of going out for a walk, but it rained heavily all day. Millie felt anxious, she didn't know how the interrogations were going and whether they would all agree to testify. She had no doubt about Fran, but everyone else was in question. Her mother's husband was a petulant, lazy man. He would resent having to travel to London, and he had never had any time for Millie. Her only hope was that as a former military man, he would feel it his duty. She also wondered what her mother had felt on finding out what had happened to her, would she apologize to her for the message she had left? Nicole must be 7 months pregnant, and she didn't know Miguel, Isabelle and Kate and she tried to predict what their reactions would be.

Mr. Adler brought them food and said he would collect them at 8:30 the next morning. Liam was also tense, he suffered from phantom pains in his amputated leg and spent the day lying down. He was trying to work, but was moody and silent. He saw that Millie was worried, but the pain did not leave him, and he preferred to keep quiet, work or watch television. From time to time he sighed and re-positioned himself. He had told her that the sensation of these pains was different to normal. Sometimes he felt his missing toes hurt, as if he had been wearing a shoe several sizes too small. Another time it felt as if his ankle was sprained or his calf was stiff, or that something was crawling on him or that he had been splashed with hot water. Nothing helped, but he did know that distracting himself with work did ease the intensity of the pain. That's why he refused a wheelchair. It would be easier with it, but the muscles would become weaker and, moreover, sitting down, he would feel depressed. Seeing the world from below would make him feel even more disabled than he was.

Liam had left the wheelchair of his childhood behind and had learned to walk well with crutches. In most cases, especially at home, he used only one, but he took both of them when outside.

Millie smoked an unusual amount of cigarettes that day. Time was passing so slowly. She had no idea what was going on or what progress they were making, and her mind kept going over the scenarios again and again. She hadn't anticipated that she would be this nervous just sitting around waiting. After dinner, Liam told her it was better for him to spend the night on the couch, for he would probably not be able to sleep and he would keep her awake. So, Millie, reluctantly went to bed by herself.

"Hello, Miss Bloom!" Detective O'Neill said, pointing to the chairs, then went on." Yesterday I held all the interviews and everyone is ready to cooperate. They confirmed 100% of what you said. So we are ready to build the case.

"Great, I'm very happy, I was afraid that there would be people refusing to cooperate. Nicole is pregnant, and my mother's husband," her voice faded.

"Don't worry, everyone will gladly help. I did not notice your friend Nicole being pregnant, otherwise I would have said she could provide written testimony. I'll call her today to check this out."

"Oh, is that so? That's strange, maybe she's already had the baby?" Millie was working the dates out in her head. Nicole should be about seven months pregnant, but maybe she'd got her dates wrong and was already a mum..

"I'll ring her, I don't want to put any stress on a pregnant woman in such a case." He glanced at his watch, lifted his head, and said, "You can go back to Liverpool, the prosecutor will call you when he finds out the date for you to testify. The case is scheduled to start on the 6th August, I'm guessing you'll need to be here on the third day, but we'll find out on the 6th. Mr. Adler will take to meet with the prosecutor and then you can go home after you check out of your hotel." He picked up the phone and said: "Come and collect Miss Bloom and Mr. Blake please!" Then he hung up, looked at them and continued: "Don't worry about anything. The prosecutor and the defence attorney are already working on your case and this afternoon the prosecutor will take you through everything and explain what you need to know and do. Relax, he knows what he is doing."

The young man from two days ago entered the room, waited for them to stand up and follow him, then the detective said:

"From now on you will work with the Prosecutor's Office, I won't see you again until court.

"Thanks for everything you've done for me." Millie said, shaking the detective's hand, she was just getting used to him, and they had to part ways.

"Goodbye," Liam said. Then they followed the young guy out of the office.

After a quick sandwich they were taken to meet with Attorney Richard Brady. She was surprised that he was so young, in his early 30s, tall and thin, with red hair, blue eyes and freckles. His suit looked too big for him. He spoke quickly, and Millie had the feeling that he was looking right insideher, right into her soul. He had seen the recording of Millie's story and the video that Greg had recorded, several times.

"You will appear in court somewhere around 8-9 August. The defence will try to make you feel as uncomfortable as possible, asking questions that will unsettle and confuse you. They will try and discredit you as a witness. For example, they could ask if you take drugs regularly or if you enjoy rough sex. They might ask if you always do as you're told when someone tells you to, in relation to the drug taking."

Millie's scar

"But I was frightened, they had already raped me and beaten me unconscious before that."

"I understand Millie. Don't worry about these questions. Don't let them confuse and mislead you. You will get the opportunity to explain everything that happened, other witnesses will confirm what you said, and the video will show what the act was. Put yourself in the hands of the jury. A jury of 12 people is hard to be lied to when there are so many witnesses and so much evidence. The defences questions are to confuse you. They rarely mislead the jury.

"What's the probability that they will win the case?" Millie asked.

"They have pleaded not guilty. They are unlikely to win the case, we have CCTV footage proving their entry and exit from the park, which coincides with the time of Dariya's death. There is forensic evidence on her body from both of them. We have your testimony and witnesses. In addition, they tried to escape to Lisbon, which actually turns out to be about wanting to find you." He scratched his head and then went on. "You are free to go, Miss Bloom, you can go home, I'll keep in touch with you and we'll see each other at the case hearing. Mr. Adler is waiting for you out front." He looked at his watch and continued. "I will send you further information tonight on how to prepare for the case."

"Thank you." Millie replied quietly, as they walked from the office.

Chapter Eighteen

Millie went back to work the next day. Her colleagues asked her questions, but she said she wasn't allowed to discuss the case with anyone, saving herself from the many questions circulating. She was aware that sooner or later everything about the case would be known. The press would continue to report every detail of Dariya's murder as it was revealed in court, with the more salacious dailies seemingly enjoying the drama of the case. She knew they would find out about her too, and this scared her. She did not want the whole of the UK to know about her experiences, she had put this far to the back of her mind when she had decided to testify but now it was becoming a reality.

At home they opened a bottle of white wine, pulled out nuts and chips, and tried to relax as bests they could. Liam told her about his day, then they discussed the information that the prosecutor had sent her regarding the case, they had supper and went to bed.

Six days remained until the case hearing, and although Greg was likely to be punished for what he had done to her, Millie kept on thinking about how to prevent rapes in general. Everything in her everyday life urged her to think about it. She watched people in the streets as she went to work, as she returned, anytime she was out. Life seemed tidy and calm, there was no evidence that around the world, that night, there would be thousands of rapes. Millie made an estimation that if the raped people per year were about 1,500,000, as they said on TV, that meant that 4,109 people were raped in a day, of which 274 were in England and Wales. The numbers frightened her, they did not give her peace, they spurred her on. This had to be stopped or at least reduced. She had to figure something out. In the evening she shared this with Liam, and he laughed.

Millie's scar

"Ah Millie!" He stroked her head, then kissed her. "How do you think you can do this?"

"I don't know." Millie said ashamed. "I just know I must try."

"You're not the first person to try and tackle this issue Millie. There are specialists who have devoted their lives to this problem and have hardly made a dent in the numbers. You can't stop this, Millie, but you can punish the person who did this to you."

She felt downtrodden. Liam was right, he didn't believe she could make a difference, but she wanted to have his support anyway. If she knew she was not alone in this, she would have felt more secure. They could have both thought about it. He had free time and could look for information which would help them. But it was not his cause. Instead of giving up, Millie began to think even harder about the problem, it was becoming an obsession. The next few nights after work she spent in front of the computer with headphones in. She watched documentaries, movies, read analysis and reports by experts in the field and watched the stories of many victims. She did not know what she was looking for, but she was sure she would find it. From all the research she was doing, she almost forgot about the case. She received a call from the prosecutor on the afternoon of August 6th.

"Hello Milla, this is Prosecutor Brady."

"Hello, Mr Brady. Has the case begun?"

"Yes, today was the inaugural meeting, setting out the case, there was no testimony given. You will be summoned on 10th August. The case begins at 10:00 am, so please be there at 9:00 for us to make final preparations."

"Yes, of course, but I have to check how I can get there that early."

"You can come down the night before and stay at the same hotel, we'll pay for your expenses."

"Yes, okay, is there anything else?"

"Actually there is, it's a difficult subject Millie. I have received information that Dariya and you are not Greg and Alfie's only victims. Unfortunately, they are too scared to testify against them in court, even though we have assured them that we will protect their identities, they refuse to comply. We think that you may be able to give them courage."

"I'm sorry to hear this, of course, how can I help?"

"If you waive your right to privacy before the trial, they will see that they are not alone in this and I'm hoping they will find the courage to testify."

"What does that mean Mr Brady? I'm sorry, I just do not understand."

"Victims of rape have their identity protected by law, the media cannot name you unless you give your permission, without that permission I don't think the other victims will agree to testify."

Millie was torn between strengthening the case as it stood and protecting her privacy. How much humiliation could she stand? It was as if she were going to be assaulted all over again. She needed time to think about it all.

"Look Milla, others like Greg and Cloudy enjoy their liberty because a lot of victims do not report the crime of rape. We have an opportunity here to put these criminals behind bars for a long time. Please think about it very carefully."

"I understand, let me think about it and I will ring you."

"Of course, please take your time, it's a big decision, and let me know before the 10th August so I can try to gather the additional testimonies."

"Thanks Mr Brady, goodbye." said Millie, hanging up the phone and staring out of the window. She had not considered Greg and Alfie's other victims until just then and that there were more girls surviving the same pain as she had experienced caused her huge sadness. She was ashamed of having been raped and not reporting it to the police, keeping it a secret, but now all the people who were important to her knew about the rape. She had nothing left to lose, nothing at all. She felt she wanted to keep

Millie's scar

fighting and to do everything she could to bring Greg and Alfie to justice. She was among the 85 % who did not report the rape, had Greg and Alfie raped another girl after her? Maybe more? If so, then she was partly responsible, because she has not stopped them by reporting them to the police. Dariya, she might still be alive, maybe Greg and Alfie would have been in jail if she had reported the rape sooner. Again she remembered the logs she had placed in Elza's hearth before the fire and how her actions has been partly to blame for Tim's death. "Every decision is important", Millie said quietly to herself. She would waive her right to privacy before the court. It would be an example to all women of the world. She would tell them, "There is nothing to fear nor to be ashamed of, let's put these criminals in jail before they can find their next victim."

She had a little under an hour left of her shift when she went to Greg's office to tell him about her impending absence.

"Hello, Greg, forgive me for bothering you," she said, leaning her head round the door.

"Come on in, Millie, just give me a second to send this email…" Millie sat down opposite him and waited for him to finish.

"There we go, how can I help?"

"I got a call from Prosecutor Brady, I have to be in London from the evening of 9th August, I'll give my testimony in court on the 10th."

"Okay, don't worry, what day is that?" he looked at the calendar and said, "Oh, the 10th is a Monday, okay, I'll arrange for someone to cover for you. Do you know when you'll be back?"

"No, I'm sorry, they've given me no idea how long it might take."

"Okay, if they forget to send me an official letter, I'll remind them," he smiled at her. "Well, I wish you good luck, a very brave act, testifying against murderers."

"Actually, I wanted to talk to you about that. I'm afraid word will get around and I do not want you to be unprepared."

Millie's scar

"What is it Millie?" He asked her gently but his brow twisted in surprise.

"Aside from testifying about the murder, I am actually filing charges against the same perpetrators for rape." Millie was silent, waiting for his reaction, but she did not dare to look at him, so she stared at her feet.

"Oh, Millie, I'm so sorry to hear about that," he told her, and she looked at him, and his face was filled with sadness.

"I'm worried how everyone here will react. You know this is not a topic of conversation for the afternoon break."

"Don't worry about it. I will make sure no one worries you."

"I'm worried about the company's image too. I may be in the papers, and where I work might be made known."

"Oh, that's the last thing you should worry about. Go to London and punish these bastards!" said Greg with passion.

"Thank you!" Millie managed a smile.

"It's fine, if I can help with anything else, don't hesitate to ask me."

"Thank you again!" Millie said, and left his office.

The next three days seemed like an eternity. She stayed awake until two or three o'clock in the morning, re-telling the story that she would tell in court thousands of times in her head. That is why she got up several times to smoke. And when she fell asleep, she had nightmares. She had no appetite and the anxiety was crippling. She watched several lawyers' films and tried mentally to imagine how the trial would go. She was afraid of the questions the prosecutor had told her about, and she saw how in the movies, the victims were made to look ridiculous. The lawyers confused the victims, twisted their words, refuted them, though the viewer knew that they were telling the truth. So one night she wrote the entire story on her computer. Then she read it several times. She had to use specific and precise words. She mustn't use phrases like "I think", "it seemed to me", "I'm not sure" but "I

Millie's scar

saw", "I'm sure" and "absolutely". She believed she would give everything she had and she encouraged herself to be brave. Liam was also busy, he wanted to make up for the days he didn't work, and he edited photos and wrote texts until late. There was a bug in one of the websites he maintained, and he wanted to fix it as soon as possible. It took him a long time and made him very anxious. They spent Saturday and Sunday at home, despite the nice weather outside. And on Sunday afternoon they took the bus to London. Both were silent. Liam was reading his book, and Millie stared out the window, quietly. She was exhausted from thinking, insomnia, and worrying. She wanted to stop thinking at least for a little bit, so she enjoyed the view through the window and tried to clear her troubled mind. She loved the countryside. It was always green in the UK mainly due to all the rain, the warm summers and temperate winters. The only thing she would have added were mountains. When she was about 10 years old, she had visited Scotland with her mother. Her first view of The Grampians had delighted her and one day she dreamed of living in a mountain house and carrying water from the nearby spring. To live in the forest and spend her time communing with nature had been her childhood dream.

As they travelled, her thoughts jumped around her head. She decided she should visit Tim's grave. She felt bad for not continuing her visits to church after she left the streets, and she thought it was necessary. God had heard her prayers, and she had stopped going to church. That was wrong. We should not pray to God when we are unhappy, but forget about him when we are happy, she reproached herself. She had to thank him every morning after she woke up, for being alive, for being with Liam, her love, for having work and food on the table. That would not be forgotten, she promised herself. She looked at Liam and kissed him. He looked away from the book, smiled at her, and kissed her in turn.

"A little more, my dear, and I'll finish it, I have..." he looked at the last page, "...60 pages left and I am all yours."

"Keep reading, I don't miss you." She joked, giving him one of her best smiles.

"Ah, ok you, then I'll sit by that blond in the front row," he reached out his head and looked ahead. Millie followed his movement, after which he poked her gently in the ribs and said, "You fell for it, huh?" They both laughed.

After an hour and a half they arrived at the hotel and settled down. They ate the kebabs they bought from a small shop outside, drank beer, Liam watched TV, and Millie ran a bath, hoping it would relax her and help her sleep. But when they went to bed, she tossed and turned for another two hours. Her mind was racing and would not stop. Tomorrow was the day she had to pour out all the details of what Greg and Cloudy had done to her. She was desperate not to make mistakes, she was telling the truth and she shouldn't be afraid. She knew she would see him, and knew she would look into his eyes while she accused him. She hated him from the bottom of her soul. He had tried to ruin her life. He left a lasting scar on her, and she would not forget that until her last breath.

At 8:45, she and Liam were in front of Snaresbrook Crown Court, expecting prosecutor Brady to meet them. The building itself was magnificent, looking more like a country house than a crown court, with large wings on either side of a central tower featuring two domes. The building was surrounding a small courtyard and looked as if it had grown copiously over time, resulting in a warren of buildings and outhouses. The prosecutor appeared at the main entrance and motioned for them to enter. He greeted them with a wide smile and a handshake, and walked down the corridor to the left, and they followed him. He climbed the stairs at the bottom two at a time, upsetting Millie that he didn't take into account Liam's disability. He seemed to be

Millie's scar

rushing them, and she wondered why they hadn't asked them to be there earlier. They climbed to the second floor and entered a small office stuffed with documents and folders on every surface, a bookcase spanned the entire back wall and a mahogany desk was just discernible under the clutter. Curiously the office had only one chair.

"I'm sorry, there's no place to sit, but there's really no time for that."

Millie looked at him and said, "I have decided to waive my right to privacy." she said, and looked at Liam, who nodded approvingly.

"That's wonderful Millie, and very brave of you. I'll speak to the other victims and let you know how we get on," He pulled a form from a folder on the cluttered desk and handed it to Millie, pointing out where she should sign it. He continued:

"Right, very quickly, the defence maintains the position that Dariya loved rough sex games and they are trying to convince everyone of this. Speak loudly, calmly, and look mainly at the jury, me and the judge." The prosecutor stood opposite her, gesturing lightly with his hands and speaking quickly. "Today they will also question other witnesses. The jury is already familiar with your story."

"But what am I going to say then?"

"You'll answer questions," he told her and Millie frowned. Her heart shrank, this was the nightmare that frightened her the most. She enters, sits down and they begin crucifying her with questions. The day was starting badly.

"Don't worry, Millie, everything will be fine. You need to wait outside hall number 6." He looked at his watch and went for the door. "In half an hour the hearing starts. Until then." Then he waited impatiently for them to leave and ran back down the stairs. Millie wanted a cigarette. So, her and Liam left the building by the front entrance and she lit up. She was nervous and Liam was trying to reassure her.

Millie's scar

"Try to calm yourself my love, you haven't even entered the court room yet, and you're already shaking like a leaf. Think about it, everyone in there has heard your story, you will come in and answer questions. Then all the others will come in and they will confirm everything you say. Don't be afraid, you are not a criminal, and you are not lying." He pulled her towards him and hugged her with one hand.

"What if I make a mistake, or freeze, or say something stupid?"

"That's why you need to calm down," he told her, pulling away and looking at her face. "If there was a way I could speak for you, I would, but I cannot. Gather yourself, go in there and destroy those bastards, Millie!" he raised his voice to give her more encouragement.

"They'll be inside, seeing them, I'm sure I'll begin to shake even more."

"Of course they'll be inside, but with handcuffs and guards. They are the criminals and they killed Dariya and raped you. Do not forget for a second why you came - to bring them to justice, that's your goal!"

Millie nodded, smiled uncertainly and headed for the door.

"Come on, let's go in, I don't want to be late." Then she put out her cigarette in the ashtray at the entrance and went in. The signs showed them where the hall was located, and after 2 minutes they were in a wide corridor with several benches. There were a lot of people. Millie saw Fran, Nicole, her mother, her husband and Miguel. Fran rushed to her and hugged her.

"Ah, my dear, Millie, I'm so proud of you! Now they will get what they deserve! Then she let her go and looked at her. Millie was nervous, looking at the corridor in front of her. Her mother rose from the bench and waited, watching her.

"Thank you, Fran, I'd better go and see my mother and then we'll talk."

Millie's scar

Fran turned to Liam, they introduced themselves, speaking earnestly to each other.

Millie went to her mother and when she approached her she saw that she was crying.

"I'm sorry, Milla, I didn't know what you'd been through, can you ever forgive me?" Then she reached out to her for a hug.

"Hello, Mum, thank you for coming," Millie said, pulling away. "I'm waiting to be called and I'm nervous, we'll talk about it later. She glanced at John and said, "Thanks for your help, John!" Her mother looked at him and stroked his hand.

"It's my duty to serve justice Milla," he said dryly.

Millie approached Miguel. "Hello, Miguel, thank you for your cooperation!"

"I'm sorry about what happened, Millie, I didn't know that's the way things went. I fled like a coward back then, but I was pretty drunk and anyway I would not have been much help."

"Oh, don't think about it, it's in the past now, we can't turn back the clock. Are Isabelle and Kate coming?" Millie saw many people entering the hall, one of them being the prosecutor. Then the door closed. Her heart pounded in her throat, and she felt she needed to go to the toilet, she looked at the corridor hurriedly, seeing that there was a toilet further down. "Excuse me, I'll be back in a minute."

By the time she got back Isabelle and Kate had just arrived, panting and reddened, speaking excitedly to Miguel. Millie went to Liam and Fran, they looked up at her from their conversation. She gritted her teeth and shook her head, showing how afraid she was.

"Oh, Millie, we are all here for you and everything will go well!" said Fran, hugging her tightly.

The door opened and a man cried out loudly:

"The court summons witness number 3 - Milla Bloom!"

Millie closed her eyes for a second and walked away without looking at anyone. She could feel all eyes were on her and her heart was racing. When she entered, everyone was looking at her again. The hall looked exactly like in the movies. Two rows of benches, the judge in front of them, with a recorder below, in front of him. To the left of the judge was the jury, and to the right, the witness box with her in it.

"Please repeat after me!" The man told her, handing her the Bible and showing her how to hold it. "I swear by Almighty God!" Millie repeated "That the evidence I shall give shall be the truth, the whole truth and nothing but the truth."

As he moved away, Millie took a quick glance at the court room. To her surprise, Greg and Cloudy were at the far end of the hall. Seated, with two security guards either side of them. Both of them stared blankly at her. She wanted to go and spit in their faces, she hated them, they were rapists and murderers. She turned her gaze toward the jurors, then to the prosecutor and the defence lawyer. The prosecutor stood up and began his speech.

"Your Honor, honorable jurors, this is Milla Bloom, the victim of a cruel and brutal rape. The victim was subjected to violent sexual acts by the two suspects, she was raped, beaten, forced to take drugs and threatened with life as a sexual slave. All this you have seen in her taped evidence. And then you saw a video of one of the rapes of this witness, even when she was unconscious. Since we have witnesses who prove her words before and after her rape, but not the rape itself, it is imperative to leave no cause for doubt that the victim has been raped. That is why I will concentrate precisely on that period when there were no witnesses, and we will ask the victim to tell us again what happened. The prosecutor looked at the jury, then the judge, and finally turned to Millie.

"Miss Bloom, could you tell us again how the first violent act against you happened?"

"My house had just been broken into and I watched as Cloudy or Alfie beat up Dariya, he then masturbated over her. I was so scared I urinated on myself. Then Alfie said that Dariya was his

Millie's scar

whore, and I now belonged to Greg. Greg said he didn't want me because I had pissed myself and I stank, and Alfie told him: "Go and wash her, then, do I have to tell you everything?" Greg dragged me to the bathroom by my hair. Inside, I tried to reason with him, I told him he seemed more normal than Alfie and begged him to spare me, and I would not tell anyone in return, if they just left. But he struck me hard across the face and I fell to the floor. Then he told me that I had offended him, saying he was softer than Alfie. Then I saw that there was a tattooed tear next to his eye. I remembered this as a symbol of a murderer. That's why I stopped resisting, I thought he was going to kill me. He switched on the shower and held me under the cold water. After that he raped me, penetrating me from behind."

"What did you do next?"

"He left the bathroom and told me to clean myself up and go to him completely naked. I tried to postpone this as much as possible, but after about five minutes I entered the room where I saw that Alfie was peeing on Dariya's lifeless body." Millie looked at the jury, she felt like her heart would burst, her hands trembling. Everyone was watching her. She took a breath and went on: "I went back to the bathroom because I was nauseated by the smell and the sight, and they laughed at me. In the bathroom I decided I had to try to run away or they would kill me. I thought Dariya might be dead already. I ran down the stairs completely naked. My goal was to get to a busy junction and get help from other people. I heard someone running after me. But when I opened the front door of the house, someone hit me on the head. Everything went black."

"Do you think there was any other way to escape or resist your abusers?"

"Absolutely not!" Millie said.

"What happened after you woke up?"

"Only Greg was there. Dariya and Alfie were gone, he told me that I could not escape him and that it was better not to try again.

Then it became clear to me that the rape was just the start and that I would be raped by him many times. He made me warm up a spoon with a lighter on which he had placed a drug and was smoking from it. Then he told me to smoke and I told him I did not want to, he threatened me again and I realized I should not contradict him. So I smoked from the drug with him. Then I felt that I couldn't move, talk, and a little later I blacked out. I cannot remember what happened afterwards. I vaguely remember that I was vomiting, that Alfie had returned, that there was a phone directed towards me.

"Thank you, Miss Bloom," the prosecutor turned his back to her and sat down in his chair.

"I call the defence!" said the judge.

The defence lawyer stood up and approached Millie, then began:

"Miss Bloom, you say that Greg Davis has raped you and forced you to take drugs, is this so?"

"Yes."

"At what time did that happen?"

"I don't know, but certainly after midnight. We didn't leave the other party until after 11pm."

"Dear jurors, Honorable Judge, I have just received evidence and I apologise for not presenting it to the Prosecutor's Office. At the time when Miss Bloom claims she was raped and forced to use drugs, Mr. Davies was not in her house. Four licensed video cameras shot Mr. Davies at 12:55, 2:05, 3:34 and at 5:15 at Wimbledon Station in south London, which is 5 miles from the crime scene. Miss Bloom has accused him of destroying the property, and for that he has received his punishment in another case. But then he left her property and the rape and drug use did not happen aat that time" The attorney's assistant handed photos to the jury and the judge. Millie was dumbfounded, this was not happening. Her heart began skipping. She was burning all over.

Millie's scar

"Miss. Bloom, why did not you file a complaint about Mr. Davies's rape with the case for your damaged home?"

"Because back then I thought I didn't have evidence, I had taken a bath, and my period had erased all traces of the rape. I was advised by police in Bath that it was unlikely there would be a conviction."

"Miss Bloom, in that case why did you come forward now?"

"I decided to testify after I saw that Dariya Easton had been murdered . I knew in my heart it had to be by Greg Davis and Alfie Miller."

"So are you saying that once you knew of Dariya's death, new evidence has emerged?"

"No! "Millie hated their lawyer.

"Then what?"

"I remembered there were witnesses who could confirm my words. I found the courage to testify. I felt I owed it to Dariya."

"Miss Bloom, did you see Greg Davis in Bath?"

"Yes."

"Where did you see him?"

Millie thought about it, she had seen Cloudy in front of her mother's house, and he had gone to Fran's house as well. She had seen Greg only in the hostel.

"At the hostel where I spent the night."

"Dear jurors, Honorable Judge! Alfie Miller was registered with the hostel in question. Mr. Davies has not stayed there. That night he celebrated a friend's birthday in London, and three witnesses can confirm it. Officer Porter from Bath also confirmed that he has seen only Alfie Miller. Besides, two of the witnesses mentioned by Miss Bloom will confirm my words, they saw Mr. Miller, not Mr. Davis."

Millie looked desperately at the prosecutor. He was leaning back in his chair and was thoughtful. Their eyes did not meet.

"Miss Bloom, according to the video analysis, the video was shot at 3:40am, as I said, we have a photo at 3:30am from a camera

Millie's scar

where Mr. Davis is located 5 miles from your home. You say that you were unconscious, and that you do not remember anything. Can you prove that the video which was recorded involves Greg Davis?"

"No." Millie wanted to get out of the hall and run away. She did not dare look at either the jury or the judge. She was desperately looking for the prosecutor's eyes, but he looked even more overwhelmed than her.

"And one last question! Since Mr. Davis was 5 miles away from your home and could not force you to use drugs, then do you accuse Mr. Miller of forcing you to do something?"

What the hell, she had to answer! Millie was silent. No, Cloudy had not done anything to force her, he had only pulled on her hair. How was she to accuse him of pulling on her hair, she would become a laughing stock. She was unconscious when he raped her, he didn't force her to do anything. She was doomed.

"No."

"I do not have any more questions."

"Mr. Brady?" The judge asked.

"Honorable judge and jurors! Prosecutor Brady stood up. "Attorney Anderson has just shown evidence that the prosecution is not aware of. I would like to ask for a short break to review this evidence."

"A thirty-minute break! "The judge knocked on his desk, and they left the court room.

Millie was walking, not seeing anything. How could cameras have shot Greg five miles away? The only chance that this happened was when she was unconscious after the blow. She did not know how long she had been unconscious after the strike. And after he got her high, she totally lost sense of time. She walked out into the corridor. Liam and her mother rushed to her.

"Did you destroy them, Millie?" Liam asked enthusiastically, but he stopped immediately, seeing her expression and the tears in

Millie's scar

her eyes. She shook her head in denial. Prosecutor Brady came out, grabbed her arm and pulled her aside.

"I'm sorry, Millie, I had no idea about this evidence. I'm not sure what we can do. I think somebody is protecting Greg, the CCTV footage is pretty convincing and he can't be in two places at once. With this evidence it looks like he will get away with the rape charge against you. But don't worry, he won't get away from Dariya's murder. I will have to release all the witnesses except Nicole, she will confirm that Dariya told her they had been pursuing her for a long time. We can also prove that Alfie was in Bath and he was looking for you. Miguel and the two girls will confirm that he has commited breaking and entering, but they have already been convicted of this. Alfie has made up a story. I was thinking of not telling you for now, but I think I have to."

Millie looked up at him, in anguish.

"Alfi claims he's in love with you, you were having fun that night, and he fell in love, but you went missing, so he decided to look for you in Bath. He claims you told him it was your home town. Right, I have to look at these pictures from the cameras, they're suspicious."

Milla could not believe any of what she was hearing. Alfie's story was just lies. She could feel the conviction slipping away. It wasn't enough that they had raped her, that they had tried to destroy her life, stole everything she had, murdered Dariya: but now they were laughing at her. Millie waved her hand and walked towards the exit without saying anything to anyone. But everyone followed her.

Chapter Nineteen

Millie stood in front of the newspaper stand in a stupor. Her face was on almost every front page of every daily newspaper. The headlines read:: "Raped Milla Bloom testifies against her abusers!", "Another rape victim testifies against the murderers of Dariya Easton!", "A shocking video of Milla Bloom's rape spread all over the net!", "Milla Bloom rape – fact or fiction?", "Why do women lie about rape? – Milla Bloom on the stand." The news stand looked like a photo gallery with her picture and name plastered everywhere. People stopped and stared at her. Millie hid behind the bus stop and waited for the bus to work. She was trembling all over. Officer Porter was right when he warned her to think how much she could handle the publicity from such a case. When she saw the bus stopping, she ran and climbed on in the hope that no one had recognized her at the bus stop. It was almost full. They all fell silent when she boarded the bus and most stared at her, some averting their eyes out of respect. Millie kept her eyes down, she knew everyone that would be on the work bus, she had worked with them for several months now. She sat down in the first available seat and heard behind her back:

"Poor girl!" She clenched her teeth in anger. How will she ever look these people in the eye again? Curiosity and regret were evident in their eyes at the same time. "Damn the tabloids!" She whispered softly. Everyone would recognize her. But the bad thing was that they would recognize her as a rape victim and a liar. What did people imagine when they looked at her? How many times had they already watched the video? How much had they seen of what Greg and Cloudy had done to her? How many had called her a nasty, lying bitch? Millie buried her face in her hands and her tears began to fall, bile rising in the back of her

Millie's scar

throat. She was shaking and sobbing quietly when a gentle hand touched her shoulder. She lowered her arms quickly and turned back. It was Carla.

"I'm sorry, Millie, be strong, we're all with you!"

Millie just wanted to disappear into the ground. She did not want anyone to talk to her now, she did not want anyone to feel sorry for her. She just wanted to be invisible and be left alone! She held up her hand to thank Carla for the sympathy and turned back. She was thinking about the office, how would she be received there? She remembered that Greg had told her, "Leave it to me!" But what could he do. Except to warn everyone not to talk about it? Nothing. Everyone would watch her and recall scenes from the video they had seen. And if Greg had read that she was a liar, would he still be so gracious towards her?

The bus stopped and Millie stood up, she wanted to get out first and walk into the building before everyone else. She wanted to try and avoid sorrowful eyes and good intentioned pity. The last thing she needed was to have to thank people for their pity. Millie walked quickly to the entrance but at the last moment turned to her right, and finding a quiet spot she lit a cigarette. She needed to compose herself, she was shaking all over. She lit up and took a quick puff. Why did they have to use her picture? She wouldn't have been so recognisable with only her name. People on the streets did not know her name, but they could see her face. And now it was written on it in large letters: "RAPED AND LIAR!". A lifetime label. That was her big shame. This was why victims of rape do not report the crime. Because they carry the mark of being raped their entire lives. People question their integrity, look at them with pity, and some of the more perverse ones would even imagine depraved things with them. How was she to live with this? Arghhhh! - she wanted to scream.

"Damn you, Greg, I hate you!" She said aloud. "I hope you rot in jail!" she continued in her mind. But what did it matter to her that he was in jail? Nothing. She was not safe. There were a million others like him. And he was unlikely to suffer there. He won't be hungry and homeless, on the contrary, prisoners are looked after. Millie even found out recently that the rapists were separated from the other criminals in separate units. They would not feel their lives were in danger as she had. And with behaviour, their sentences could be reduced to a year or two. Was this justice? It was her taxes that would pay the cost of imprisoning her own rapist. And then she would pay for his integration back into society, because criminals should be given a second chance. Greg and Cloudy had abused her, stolen from her, drugged her, raped her and left her with nothing apart from the kindness of friends and strangers. The justice system had made her out to be a liar. It had mocked her. How much did Greg enjoy himself while watching her being made to look like a fool in court? And this man was to be given a second chance? Millie felt bitter towards the police, she did not feel they protect citizens and the court was intent on releasing the prisoners. And Greg was one of those 94% of cases, he slipped through the net without due punishment. That was the harsh reality. No one cared for honest citizens. They could not defend themselves, they expected the state to protect them, and believed it was doing just that until they fell into the hands of unscrupulous people. What, in fact, was the state doing to prevent the ever increasing number of rapes? Millie looked at her watch. She had another ten minutes. She took out another cigarette and lit it. She didn't feel like going in just yet, she didn't want anyone to feel sorry for her. She didn't want sympathetic eyes and whispers behind her back. That's it, she suddenly realized. It came to her in a flash, she suddenly knew how the rapists should be punished. Prison didn't work. They were expensive and overcrowded. It occurred to her that in the way her photo had been plastered all over the papers, they should have their crimes recorded on their faces, for all the world to see. Just as the tattooed tear indicated a killer, a tattooed forehead

Millie's scar

would warn the world about the type of person they were dealing with. Everyone had to be able to protect himself, the state was protecting no one but the prisoners themselves. The abusers had to be the ones to carry the mark of their crime, not their victims. They had to be recognisable by everyone. People needed to be able to recognise them and be capable of protecting themselves. And children could protect themselves like this. This was a universal mark with which to brand criminals. Would there be so many rapes in the face of being branded? The abusers relied on their cruelty to remain secret and used intimidation to do so. In this way it would not remain a secret. Everyone would recognise them at first glance and could decide on their level of interaction.

Millie put out her cigarette in the ashtray and walked into her office. Inside everyone had gathered at the meeting table. When they saw her, Greg stood up and shouted:

"Let's welcome the bravest woman in this company!" And he reached his hands out to her. Everyone stood up and turned to her, applauding. Millie's eyes filled with tears. She approached them and said, raising her hand for them to stop.

"Thank you, but I don't feel like a hero. They did their best to humiliate me. It's been so hard." Then one of her colleagues presented her with a large bouquet of flowers. She took it and said:

"There's really no need for this. Thank you, you've been so kind but I'd prefer to try and put it behind me now, please."

"Of course we will not talk of it again. We just wanted to tell you that we are proud of your courage and your bravery. You are a very strong woman and we are proud that you're a part of our team. Now come and sit with us because we have a lot of work and we need to discuss an important issue about changes in supply procedures."

Millie sat down and, in the course of the conversation, managed to get away from her thoughts. But an hour later, when she started working on the computer, her thoughts returned to the injustice she'd suffered and the appropriate punishment she imagined. Millie believed that the branding would not only make the world a safer place as you could see danger coming your way, but it would reduce the number of crimes in the first place. Millie did not doubt that many potential abusers would think twice about committing rape when faced with the danger of being branded and recognised by everyone. We had all seen how Greg and Alfie hid their faces from the cameras. They didn't want to be identified. Millie did not doubt that a large number of the women who had been abused would have the courage to report of a rape if they knew that this shame would be borne not only by them but also by the abusers themselves. What did it matter for the victim if the abuser spent a year or two in prison? This did not solve the problem, it was not a real punishment. They had to bear the same shame. Millie would use social media to disseminate her idea quickly, supporting it with clear and concise arguments and facts. Every man walking on this planet had a right to be able to see and protect himself from a criminal since the state does not adequately protect him. Everyone had the right to preserve their integrity, physical and mental health. Millions of pounds are spent on crime prevention and further millions on looking after criminals, and finally enormous sums were spent on the re-integration of criminals into society. There were those who change for the better, but for many it is straight back to a criminal life. She wanted them to be punished not with pain, but with humiliation. That was the just punishment. She was humiliated and wanted the same punishment for her abuser.

That evening, Millie shared her idea with Liam. He was surprised.

"I admit that your idea is very good. It is fair, after all that you experienced, it is a just punishment. But is it legal to mark people?"

Millie's scar

"I'm thinking of ringing Victoria, a classmate of mine. She graduated with a degree in law, she might be able to advise me."

"Yes, definitely get a legal view. If there is a small chance, and if you gather a lot of people to support you, that could solve many problems related to crimes." Liam said, then leaned down, kissed her, and continued. "My clever girl, how did you ever come up with this? Your idea is genius and I'm sure it will attract many followers."

"The hard way. After seeing my picture on all the front pages of today's newspapers. Everyone on the bus was watching me, they all recognized me. They had seen the news and had seen the press. It was terrible, I had the feeling that I had: "Raped and disgraced!" written on my forehead. I cried, and they pitied me. My workmates were truly kind though and that got me through the day, and my idea for branding." Liam hugged her and kissed her head, then said:

"The good thing is that the video has been removed from everywhere it had been posted. It was actually only there for a few hours. Apparently they realized it was rape, and it's been taken down. This is tacit acceptance of your honesty Millie."

"I'm so upset about what happened in court, Liam. They made me out to be a fool and a liar. How did they do it? How did they fabricate so much footage, it must be high level corruption. He was there, I know he was there! There's a video for goodness sake."

"Stop it, Millie, stop thinking about it, we have been discussing this for so long now, you'll go crazy. You know you told the truth. His brother has money and gangland connections, he probably managed to buy some pictures. We cannot fight this. Not with such rich and influential people."

"But that means he'll get away with it." He will not pay for what he has done. He tried to ruin my life!" Millie dropped her head into his lap and sighed deeply:

Millie's scar

"You are right, I will try not to think about it. I have to accept that life is not always fair. It remains for me to hope that God will judge him! Then she stood up and smiled. "They applauded me in the office and said I was the bravest woman in the company. They were all very kind to me, and we carried on as usual, just getting on with work. Apart from that stupid Anabel, but she doesn't like me, so I wasn't surprised."

"Don't think about it, leave them, let them think what they want," Liam told her. "I am proud of you."

"Easy for you to say, I tried and feel I failed, it's not that easy to forget," said Millie with bitterness.

"Okay, why don't you act on your idea? I liked it very much. You could use social media to spread the message. It will gain popularity."

"Yes, I thought of this too, I can put it on Facebook both publicly and in groups. Perhaps it is better to start a petition? If it gets enough votes, it will be voted on in government."

"Consult your legal adviser first."

"Yes, I will write to Victoria right now, we are friends on Facebook."

Millie got up and took the laptop. She turned it on and wrote a message to Victoria. She explained her idea to her in a few words and waited.

Victoria managed to be a geek and cool at the same time. She was the best student in class and a complete party animal. She was noisy, fun and talented. She graduated with first class honours and was one of the youngest people to be admitted to the Bar.

An hour later Victoria responded. She was aware of what had happened and offered her sympathies.

"On your question," she wrote, "I don't want to be the bearer of bad tidings but I'm pretty sure the European Convention for the Protection of Human Rights bans people from being branded.

Millie's scar

The European Charter for the Protection of Human Rights, the UN declaration, also possible discrimination as a consequence. I have always been of the opinion that someone's rights, especially criminals, could be reduced to the benefit of the common good. But that will not happen. I'm sorry, Millie, but your idea is not feasible."

Over the following days, Millie read these conventions. She saw the biggest obstacle was Article 5 of the UN Declaration of Human Rights, which stated that no one could be subjected to humiliating punishment. Victoria was right. The idea was impossible to implement. Again her hands were tied. The statistics were chilling, but no one cared about the statistics. No one read them, and no one knew what the real picture was. We live in a male world and men would never agree to brand the perpetrators of rape. However, Millie decided that hope always exists. She wanted to diseminate her idea, she had come to it through a lot of pain, and she wanted everyone to know about it. Thousands of theses and theories have been rejected over the centuries as false or impossible, and then they have became reality. However improbable her idea was, it deserved to see the light of day. Perhaps someone there in the world would read it and they would have the strength, influence, and means to turn it into reality. Millie had nothing to lose now, she had every reason to share with the world how she believed crime could be reduced. How to prevent people from being victims of twisted individuals.

So she started by sharing her idea on several groups on Facebook to see what the response was. She drafted a statement incorporating all the information she had found because she knew that people were living in some kind of falsely safe world where bad things were happening only to bad people. She spent a lot of time on the statement, detailing the statistics, provided links to each piece of information, and eventually presented her idea of branding, which she called "Millie's Scar". Once the statement was completed, she uploaded it to ten groups.

Millie's scar

Her words were shared 1287 times in 24 hours.

"Will I succeed, Hugh?"

"You've already succeeded," he said, and got up from his chair. His desk was empty. He bent down and took a small briefcase in one hand. He was smaller than Millie remembered. He stood before her and said:

"There are people who give birth to ideas, some people follow them, others oppose them, but there are some who make them happen. Everyone in this world is called to serve a higher purpose. And you have served yours. Leave the rest to Him now."

Hugh left the room, and Millie never saw him again.

Prosecutor Brady had tried to reach her, but Millie had turned off her phone, so he had left her a voice message. "Hello, Millie, it's Prosecutor Brady. The case is over. Alfie Miller was sentenced to 25 years in prison for the murder and rape of Dariya Easton. Greg Davis was sentenced to 4 years in prison on charges of raping Dariya Easton. I'm so sorry, I wanted to tell you personally. It's all over the press."

Millie put down the phone. For a long moment she stared into space. Then she got dressed up and went to work.

Chapter Twenty

Liam got back from work, closed the front door, and put his coat on the coat hanger. He sat down in his chair, took off his shoes, put on his slippers and went through to the kitchen. Millie was feeding Bella. He bent down and kissed them one after another. Bella was falling asleep in her mother's arms. For him, they were the two most beautiful beings that existed in this world. The next day, Bella would celebrate her first birthday. They had decided to spend the morning at Bella's playgroup with several other mothers and babies, then have a little party at home with cake and presents. And in the evening, after Bella had fallen asleep, they would leave her with the babysitter and take themselves to their favourite Oxford restaurant.

Liam went upstairs, undressed and took a shower. He grasped the handles he had carefully mounted in the cubicle and let the hot water pour over him. He had to be careful in the bathroom, his prosthesis was one of the best on the market, but it wasn't designed for wet tiles. So he had fitted handles in the wet rooms and put rubber pads on the ground. This was after several tumbles in the early days. All his dreams had come true. He was in love with the most beautiful woman in the world, and she loved him too. Their love seemed to grow with each day and his daughter had given him fulfilment in a way he could never have imagined. They lived in a beautiful city in the small, sunny house they had found together, and he had found his dream job, that of a travel agent. He travelled every day, sometimes he had to spend a day or two away from home, but the benefit of cheap travel to exotic destinations excited them both. Millie started working at the library in one of the city's universities. She enrolled in a Sociology degree, but then Bella was born, and she had to put her

Millie's scar

studies on hold. Liam could not believe his luck. His memories of his poor father's family, the beatings, the hunger, the accident, the death of his mother, and then the twelve years of homeless life. Now he was the most grateful man in the world. The last 4 years, he often pondered over fate. If Millie had not been raped and chased out of London and Bath by Greg and Cloudy, none of this would have happened to them. He suffered beside her, but they would never have met and fallen in love. They would not have the most perfect daughter. Millie would not have thought of the idea of the scar and for half the world to read about it and hear her story. Her idea had become so popular that her followers managed to demand a vote in the parliaments of several countries around the world. The proposal of the scar was not approved anywhere, but that was not important. The response was the important part. Liam often thought of it, and once again he was convinced that the suffering in our lives is always to teach us something and open doors invisible to us.

He finished his shower, and saw that Bella and Millie were asleep in the bedroom. He picked up his clothes and walked quietly out of the room. He went downstairs, dressed, and began to prepare supper. Chicken with steamed vegetables and mashed potatoes. And for dessert - fruit salad with chocolate mousse. He sliced the chicken, rubbed it with a little olive oil, seasoned it with salt, black pepper and a pinch of oregano, placed it on a baking tray, covered it with aluminum foil and put it in the oven. He prepared the vegetables and put them in the steamer which Millie had bought when Bella started eating solid food. He put a few potatoes on to boil. He chopped the fruit, put a handful into ice cream bowls, he then whipped up the chocolate mousse and poured it over the fruit, placing the bowls in the fridge to set. Then he laid the dinner table and poured himself a glass of red wine. He sat down on the couch, lifted his foot onto the stool, switching on the TV. He flicked between several channels and

Millie's scar

found a discussion "Nanotechnologies in the fight against crime." The guest explained in a lively, excited manner:

"The justice model of depriving an offender of their freedom in response to illegal activity is no longer sustainable. The prisons are overcrowded, and therefore the practice of early release for good behavior is rising and this raises a number of questions. Are criminals really being released because they have been rehabilitated and in the anticipation that they will no longer commit crimes? Or is it just too expensive for the public purse to keep funding their incarceration? Is it fair that there is free education of criminals in prisons when our young people, who have committed no crimes, have to pay excessive college and university fees? More money than ever is being spent on criminals' re-integration to society, all at the expense of the taxpayer. Is there another way? These are pressing issues that Governments have to decide on and nanotechnology can help with this problem. The idea that garnered attention four years ago that criminals should be branded so that each person can protect themselves makes a lot of sense to many. This is nothing new. In ancient times, criminals were taken out to the square to be seen by everyone and publicly mocked. These days we live in large conurbations and this kind of display is no longer possible, but it is possible to mark criminals after they leave prison, meaning a brand-new kind of punishment for petty to medium crimes. We are not talking about branding the criminals, support for which was great 4 years ago, but Article 5 of the Human Rights Act expressly forbade individual humiliation or discrimination. No, we are talking about humane and temporary physical identification of people who operate outside the justice system."

"But how can we allow killers to walk around the streets? What kind of benefit will that bring? They will be free to kill us!"

"We are not talking about them. We are not talking about shutting down prisons. We are talking about petty crimes, thieves, rapists, stalkers. They have short sentences and with good behavior, far too short in many people's opinions. They do not come out of prisons rehabilitated, very often they leave prison with better nefarious skills than they had before. Therefore, they need to be identified, temporarily branded and tracked. Electronic tracking devices went some way to doing this, but they can be removed in extreme circumstances. What we offer are tracking implants that will be under the skin. We can combine a tracing device with a marking symbol. On the one hand, law enforcement agencies will be able to track their location, and on the other - criminals will be immediately recognisable by the population. People have a right to know who stands up against them and if they wish, they can protect themselves appropriately. For example, if someone walks into your shop with an initial showing that he is a shoplifter, you will be prepared, you will follow what he is doing, you will be able to react appropriately. If a woman is contactedapproached by a person with a rapist mark, she will have the opportunity to extricate herself from the situation.

"How would this not contravene Article 5? That would be a wave of discrimination against these people."

"You see, the desire for non-discrimination is as laid down in laws and is inherent in human nature. In essence, nobody wants to be discriminated against. If the danger of acting in a criminal way is being marked and discriminated against because of his choice, there is a good chance he would act differently. Most criminals violate the law in the hope that they will not be caught and recognised. We must give humanity the right to make the correct choices. You do not punish a child by giving them toys. Imagine the following situation. You have two children, one is 6, the other 3 years old. While they are playing, they start fighting over some Lego and the big kid beats up the little one. You interfere and punish both by making them stand and face the wall

Millie's scar

for 10 minutes and neither get to play with the Lego for two days. But the bigger kid starts screaming, hitting and throwing blocks. And you tell him, "If you stand quietly for 5 minutes I'll let you play with the Lego after one day! What do you think, will this kid learn his lesson? You have just reduced his punishment by half after he behaved badly. And what will the two children learn? The older child learns that he can do whatever he wants, and he will be pardoned through good behavior. And the little one, that he gets punished for being a victim. That's what the victims learn. How can this be a fair and equitable situation?"

"What do nanotechnologies offer then?"

"There are many variations, we are still in the early stages. We can temporarily mark criminals by implanting a subcutaneous tracking implant in the form of an initial, showing their offense. For example, the thief may be marked with the letter "T", rapists with "R" and so on. These implants will be embossed and visible, for example, the forehead or cheek so that people notice them. They will be painlessly placed and can be removed when the rehabilitation law allows. They are not designed to be permanent. We believe crime will decline dramatically and the need for marking will not be so big.

"Still, we cannot deny that your proposal will appeal to certain sections of the public."

"Maybe society will accept it, maybe not, so myself and my team are also working on another idea. We are in the process of pushing for legislation that will expand the current sexual offenders register to include anyone convicted of a violent crime. We wish to support the development of a database, that can be accessed by the general public simply by downloading an app. We think the time has come for everyone to have the right to know what kind of people they meet in everyday life. As we take up references for people we want to work with, and do CRB checks, we should be able to check whether people we must deal with on a day to day basis have a criminal record. Our view is that we are trying to help citizens protect themselves and their environment. We need to think about prevention. Let's put our law-abiding citizens first and the convicted criminals second. You must agree that the risk of discriminating against criminals is less important than keeping the innocent secure."

"Thank you for your participation, Professor Johnson. Dear spectators, this was all from "An hour with Peter Dorset".

Liam turned off the TV, leaned his head back, looked up at the ceiling, and said:

"Thank you, God!"

Millie has succeeded!

Thank you for reading Millie's scar.

If this book inspired you, follow me into the social media.

https://twitter.com/MillieScar

https://www.facebook.com/Millies.scar/

https://www.instagram.com/milliesscar/

https://www.milliesscar.wix.com

Sincerely yours

Stela Nova

The stories in this book are artistic fiction. Names, characters, places, events, and incidents are either a product of the author's imagination or are used in a fictitious manner. Any resemblance to actual people or events is accidental. The book is not intended to cause discrimination or aggression against people from different classes of society, against gender or race, institutions, and any kind of units or elements. The book is not intended to incite anyone to act against the law and the human rights.

Printed in Great Britain
by Amazon